Corporate Corner Boyz

Corporate Corner Boyz

a novel by

Anya Nicole

Q-Boro Books
WWW.QBOROBOOKS.COM

An Urban Entertainment Company

Published by Q-Boro Books
Copyright © 2008 by Anya Nicole

ISBN-13: 978-1-933967-51-6
ISBN-10: 1-933967-51-X
LCCN: 2007933868

First Printing August 2008
Printed in the United States of America

10 9 8 7 6 5 4 3 2 1

Cover layout/design by Candace K. Cottrell
Editors: Melissa Forbes, Candace K. Cottrell

Q-BORO BOOKS
Jamaica, Queens NY 11434
WWW.QBOROBOOKS.COM

Dedication

To my mother Jacqueline: Mommy, I love you so much. I know you aren't promised to me for forever, but I can't imagine what I would do without you.

Acknowledgments

First and foremost, I want to thank God for allowing me to see my talent. I always wanted to write a novel but never had the time. It's funny how circumstances make you sit down and do it. I trusted in God to see me through, and without a doubt, my prayers were answered.

I'm so proud of what I've accomplished over the past year; I'm just a little black girl from the hood. I grinded my behind off to get here and it wasn't easy. This book is my baby; it took me through so much pain and even more happiness. I hope you enjoy the read and understand that *Corporate Corner Boyz* is a way of life to me. I hustled, but the legal way, and even though it may not be as lucrative as huggin' the block, it served its purpose of getting me where I needed to go.

To my mother **Jacqueline**—Mom, you have been there for me no matter what. We may not always see eye to eye, but you have supported my dreams from day one. I know you are not perfect, but you sacrificed to care for us, and for that I am truly grateful. You taught me the meaning of hard work. I love you and thank you for being not only my mother, but my father too.

To my husband **Termayne**—We've been through so much together. I remember when our car was in the shop every other week and we would be hustling to pay the rent. We may not have much, but we ride out for each other. I knew you were the one when I saw how crazy your grind was. We made it work when others thought we were going to fail. You are my heart, and you have been a part of my family since the first day I met you. Even though we graduated from squattas, we'll never forget where we came from. You already know what it is, so let's get this money and do what we do best ☺.

To my nieces, **Amissa, Jamiyah, Journee**, and my nephew **Jaden**—you all are so special to me. I hope what I'm doing will make you realize that you can all be great. Dream big and never let anyone tell you, you can't do something.

To my sisters **Josette** and **Angel**—I love you both with all my heart. I will always be there for you no matter how much I fuss and cuss.

To my second mother **Mrs. Gloria**—I wouldn't dare call you my mother-in-law, because you are so much more than that to me. You are one of my closest friends, and I enjoy our Saturday nights together and let's not forget our many shopping trips.

To **Rueben, Ross, Ant**, and **all the other "REAL DUDES"**—thank you for teaching me everything I know about the game. You schooled a sista too well. **Reuben and Ant**, I consider you both to be my brothers. We have known each other for over ten years, and when I needed to cry or vent ya'll let me. Thanks for that.

To my best friend **Iris**—I met my best friend at Temple, and that was you. We were just two little girls from the ghetto trying to get through school to make something out of ourselves. Look at you now, making all that nursing loot. Love ya!

To **Terry Lewis Photography**—Terry, you take some beautiful pictures, and I will always support you. Thanks for making sure my pictures are up to par.

To **Mona,** the best make-up artist known to women—Mona, 2008 is going to be a big year for us. You are so talented that I know it's only a matter of time before I won't be able to book you at all. Thanks for everything, momma.

To the original Corporate Corner Boy—**STY.LIST**—Big bro, you will always be the original Corporate Corner Boy, and no one can take that away from you.

To my mentor, **Wavey**—Thanks for all the resume help and career advice. You really helped me prepare myself for life after college. Without you, I would have never been able to find such great jobs.

To my closest friend **Stefan**—I know we haven't known each other long, but you have become such a good friend. Thank you for lending a listening ear when I needed it. I know I drove you crazy with my nonsense.

To **Celeste**—I remember talking to you every morning on the phone about doing this book thing. I made it, and every time I think about it, I smile. People doubted us but guess what? They're eating their words. Thanks for being a wonderful part of my life.

To **LaKeisha Thorpe**—you were my first editor, and you believed in my project when I was ready to give up on it. Thanks for your help and your honesty.

To **Barbara, Shantel, Vernicka**, and **Lamont**—thank you for being my first fans! When I was at work writing my way out of that hell hole, you all gave me the feedback I needed to make *Corporate Corner Boyz* a success. I can't tell you how grateful I am.

To **Karen E. Quinones Miller**—if it wasn't for your self-publishing seminar, I would have never made it. Thank you for being honest about my work and making me go back and make changes; it really made a difference in the long run.

To **Shalena**, **Shannon**, and the entire **BIG-Graduates group**—thanks for sharing my hopes and dreams. I really enjoy being around so many positive people.

To **Nakea S. Murray**—From the first day I met you, you were advocating on my behalf. You have become one of my closest friends, and that means more to me than anything. Thank you for accepting me as not only a client, but a friend.

To **Anna J.**—Girl, you have been so supportive of me. All the phone conversations and encouragement means so much. Thank you for being there for me. Thank you for accepting me also. You have such a beautiful spirit, and I'm honored to be signed to the same publishing house as you.

To **As the Page Turns Book Club**—Thanks for accepting me; I love being a part of a group of such beautiful, talented Black women.

To **E.M.P.I.R.E Books**—Thanks for supporting me since day one! It means a great deal to me.

To **Mark**—When you called me on the phone to offer me the deal, I had just received a rejection letter from an agent. My heart was crushed and I asked God what was I going to do? The phone rang and it was you. Thank you for allowing me the share my talent with the world; I appreciate it from the bottom of my heart. Thank you for your advice, and I pray that you continue to allow me to share my voice.

To **Sabine**—I remember the first email I received from you asking me to forward you the rest of my manuscript. I also remember you reading it and telling me that you loved it and you were pulling for me to make the schedule, but there was no room at Q-Boro. I could tell by your words that you were indeed in my corner, and I am so grateful that you continued to look out for me.

To **Candace**—I know I wore you out with choosing a cover. Thanks for seeing my vision and being patient with me. I am thankful for everything you have done for my project. Thanks for allowing me to bother you on the weekends with my editing questions.

To the **rest of my family and friends**—Some of you

thought I was crazy when I talked about writing a book. I charge it to your head and not your heart. Thank you all for being an intricate part of my life. You have all fueled my fire to succeed in one way or another.

Finally, **to the readers**—Thanks for the love and support. I hope you enjoy the read, and please continue to look out for me. I love this writing thing. It makes me feel alive, and I'm doing something I love. I promise to do my best to bring you the best.

Anya Nicole

Prologue

"**H**ello," Brandon said as he sipped his apple juice.

"B, meet me at the office," Chris said. "It's important."

"Right now?" Brandon asked.

"Yeah, nigga!" Chris said and hung up the phone.

Chris paced back and forth as he waited patiently for Brandon to arrive. He slammed his fist on the desk, allowing his anger to get the best of him. Chris knew for a fact that Brandon was going to get defensive when he asked him about the money that was missing from the safe; he just wanted to know what the hell was going on.

Brandon rushed over to the office. Chris was sitting on the couch in the lobby with his hands folded when Brandon arrived.

"What's up?" Brandon asked. "This couldn't have waited until tomorrow?"

Chris paused for a moment.

"Naw, man, this couldn't wait. Money is missing from the safe." Chris looked at Brandon, waiting to see what his response would be. "B, there's about nine or ten grand missing."

"Yeah, man, I used it to pay for the party," Brandon replied. He could see the anger building in Chris's face.

"Why didn't you tell me?" His voice was rising. Chris's face reddened.

"Since when did I have to clear anything through you?" Brandon snapped back.

They stared each other down. Chris got up from the couch and stepped to Brandon like was just another nigga off the street.

"I put all my money into this business, and from now on, I want shit to be cleared with me."

Brandon flagged him. He had had enough. This whole partnership thing was starting to be more drama than he had ever imagined. He knew opening a business with Chris was a bad idea from the gate, but he insisted on doing it anyway.

"Whatever, man. I've been handling shit since we started this, and I do believe I am your partner. Now all of a sudden you ready to get ya feet wet and do some work. Fuck you."

Brandon reached for the handle of the door and Chris snuck him, punching him in his jaw. Brandon turned around and they began tussling around the office. Chris swung Brandon over the receptionist's desk, sending papers flying everywhere. Brandon jumped back on his feet and charged Chris with all his might.

Neither could manage to get the best of the other, so Brandon finally let go of Chris and fixed his clothes.

"I'm outta here," Brandon said.

As Chris tried to catch his breath, Brandon slammed the door and drove back to his place. He was fuming. How dare Chris come at him like that? Brandon worked his ass off to make the label successful. They would have never opened the other office in New York if it wasn't for him. All of a sudden Chris cared about the label? There had been times that he didn't come to work for weeks, and Brandon had covered for him.

Brandon looked in the rearview mirror and noticed that his bottom lip was bleeding. Things had never got ten out of hand with them before.

Chris looked at the mess they had just made; Brandon had broken the receptionist's desk with his fall. He had the nerve to think he was running shit; he didn't put a penny toward the label, but when it came time to get paid, he was always the first person in line.

Several important files lay splattered across the lobby area. He bent down and began cleaning up the mess. In that moment, Chris knew that their friendship would never be the same.

Chapter 1

Only the Baddest Chicks . . .

Brandon Brunson was no everyday brother. When he stepped into clubs chicks knew who he was, and they immediately wanted to fuck him. He had that kind of effect on females. His tall, dark-skinned body resembled an African warrior. His chiseled chest protruded through his Burberry suit as he strolled up to the bar and ordered a glass of Seagram's gin. Brandon always ordered gin. He liked his alcohol dry and his pussy wet.

The crowd inside the Red Sky Lounge in Philly was kind of thin for a Saturday night. He scanned the room, searching for Chris. This dude was always late. It was already midnight, and there was still no sign of him. Brandon ordered his third glass of gin and sipped slowly while he scanned the crowd a tenth time and finally spotted Chris sitting in a booth with two fine-ass chicks.

Brandon threw back the rest of his drink and headed toward the table. Chris smiled while standing and shook Brandon's hand.

"What took you so long? The ladies and I been watching you over there downing drinks for a half-hour now,"

Chris said and grinned. "You looked like you were enjoying yourself, so we didn't want to bother you." Chris smirked as Brandon took a seat next to him.

"Ladies, forgive Chris for being so rude. My name is Brandon Brunson." He extended his hand to greet them.

"Hey, man, I'll take care of all the introductions once we hit the road. We outta here." Chris winked at Brandon before turning to the women. "Ladies, you ready?"

Chris was always planning a last minute trip. It was a quality Brandon hated at times because he was always the one who was unprepared.

Chris got up from the table and signaled for the two women to follow. Brandon was irritated.

"Chris, can I see you for a minute?" he asked.

Excusing himself, Chris swaggered over to Brandon.

"What the fuck is up with you, man? You trying to blow this good ass? I pulled a lot of strings to get these broads here," Chris mumbled.

Brandon was about to blast Chris, but thinking about potential pussy changed his mind. Brandon looked at Chris with a grin on his face.

"How did you hook this up?" Brandon asked. "That's all I wanna know."

Chris smiled back and led Brandon to the door where the two chicks were talking amongst themselves.

"Ladies, forgive us," Chris said. "I hope you two are feeling lucky tonight, because there's a crap table with my name on it." With that the two couples headed outside to begin their night.

The valet pulled up in front of the club and handed Brandon the keys to his black on black Lexus LX 470. Chris jumped in the backseat before the women were able to make their way to the car.

"Chris, man, sometimes I forget you're my partner and not some punk-ass nigga off the street. Where the hell are your manners?" Brandon opened the car door for the two women. "So are you two gonna tell me your names? I mean you gettin' into my car, and I still have no idea who you are. You two may be murderers or something."

Brandon knew exactly who the two chicks were. In fact, he had wanted to set up this meeting for several months now.

They laughed and then formally introduced themselves.

"I'm Sam." The curvy, brown-skinned sista smiled and shook his hand. Sam was the VP of The Precision Group, a leading PR firm for major artists and models. Sam continued smiling and then introduced her friend. "This is Mia." Brandon reached for the hand of the tall, light-skinned woman and helped her into the car.

Mia's long, slender legs glistened as her black Gucci dress flared up from the soft breeze.

"I've heard a lot about you, Mr. Brunson, and I'm glad to finally make your acquaintance." She smiled and kissed him lightly on the cheek.

Mia was one sexy chick. She had a body that would make any dude wish he was her man. She had short, wavy hair, high cheekbones, and almond-shaped eyes. Her full lips shimmered with MAC lip gloss. Her hourglass figure complemented her phat, round ass. Brandon was getting hard just thinking about her lips wrapping around his dick.

"What did you hear? Good things, I hope." Brandon shot Mia a smile that he hoped conveyed exactly what he was thinking.

Chris peeped out of the back window.

"Man, get in the car. I'm ready to hit the tables, and we got at least an hour drive ahead of us." Brandon jumped in the car next to Mia and pulled off.

* * *

Since it was late, the expressway was moving smoothly. By the time they arrived in Atlantic City it was about three in the morning. Jill Scott sang softly in the background, and Brandon moved his head to the mellow beat. He was so into the mellow groove that he didn't even notice Mia had been staring at him for the last half hour.

Chris and Sam slept in the backseat during the ride, and by the time Brandon parked the car, they were lazily awaking. After gathering themselves, they left Brandon and Mia alone and went to gamble in the casino. Brandon took a moment to stare into Mia's hazel eyes.

"So, what exactly did you hear about me, Miss Mia?"

"The only thing that I needed to hear about you, Mr. Brunson, is that you are available. I've had my eye on you for a while now." Mia grabbed his hand and massaged it. Leaning closer, she whispered in his ear. "I can't wait to see what's under that suit." She kissed him hard on the mouth, and then began kissing his face, leaving traces of her MAC lip gloss on his cheek until she ended up at his ear again. "Mr. Brunson, I want to finish this tonight."

Brandon leaned in to kiss her again and slipped his hand under her dress, only to find out that she wasn't wearing any panties.

"Please, call me Brandon. Mr. Brunson is my father's name."

Brandon's dick was beginning to rise. He was trying to keep his cool, but Mia had his blood boiling.

Ever since Brandon and Chris announced the opening of their recording company, Indigo Records, last fall, pussy had been falling at his feet. Mia was indeed the best to date. She was a runway model and had worked for top designers such as Marc Jacobs and Dolce & Gabbana. She had graced the covers of *Vibe*, *Essence*, and *Vogue*. Her career was definitely on the rise, and he needed to be with someone who could take him to the next level.

Brandon admired Mia's straight-up attitude. She wanted to fuck and had no problem telling him that. He wasn't concerned that his shot wouldn't be good, because he knew he would leave her begging for more. His only fear was keeping her around for the long haul.

He too had done his research on Miss Mia. She liked her men well hung and able to pamper her with the finer things in life. Brandon thought he might be out of his league since Mia usually dealt with professional basketball players or well-established dudes. Although he was definitely on his way up, Brandon's paper was not as long as what Mia was used to seeing. He knew Mia would keep a dude on speed dial and fuck him until she got bored or found another nigga of interest. Brandon wanted to make sure that she never lost interest in him.

While Chris and Sam were starting the night off in the casino, Brandon had one thing on his mind, and gambling had nothing to do with it. Brandon and Mia skipped the casino and headed straight to their hotel room.

Chris had booked two identical luxury suites at the Sands overlooking the fountains. As Brandon opened the door Mia gasped in surprise. She was instantly stunned by the expensive pieces of art that adorned the walls. She kicked off her heels and allowed her feet to sink into the plush carpet, and then she headed straight to the balcony. The casino lights cascaded beautifully over the fountains. She took one last look over the balcony and came back inside. Brandon watched as she explored the suite.

She entered the bedroom next. The bed was draped in red silk sheets. *This had to be specially ordered,* she thought. The Sands was a pretty fancy hotel, but silk sheets were well beyond their sophistication. She looked over to the nightstand and there were two vases of fresh yellow roses. She was impressed. Brandon had definitely done his research. She loved a man who knew how to please her both inside and outside the bedroom.

"How did you know yellow roses were my favorite?" Mia began picking off petal after petal and dropping them onto the bed.

"I know more than what you think I know," Brandon said while pulling Mia close to his chest. "I know that I'm not the type of dude you usually holla at."

As he began to passionately kiss her on the lips, Mia's breasts began to swell and ache with desire.

"I've been watching you, Brandon, and I like what I see."

Brandon and Mia stood face to face. His long eyelashes complemented his big, dark brown eyes. She grabbed his face with both hands and kissed him seductively. Brandon smiled and continued to press his lips against hers. She rubbed her hand through his curly, short hair.

Brandon began to undress her. He pinched the hard tips of her nipples as they began to explore each other's body. After dropping her dress around her waist, he caressed her breasts and suckled each nipple as he squeezed her round ass with his large hands.

Mia unzipped Brandon's pants and released his dick, which was already at full erection. Brandon was well hung, and that made Mia excited. Rumor had it that his shot was so good bitches would be on the verge of stalking him afterward.

She quickly pulled down his pants around his ankles and ran her hands along his well-sculpted thighs that matched the rest of his muscular frame. She enjoyed caressing him. Simply touching his smooth, chocolate skin triggered a lingering sensation throughout Mia's body. She was ready to give everything she had and take everything Brandon was going to offer her.

Brandon prided himself on looking good. He wanted

to look his best to attract the best. He worked out on a regular basis and always made sure that his diet was on point. His hair was cut once a week, and he always looked neat and sexy. Mia liked her men well groomed and black as hell. Luckily for Brandon, he fit the whole bill. She could see that he was going to be a keeper. He had all the qualities she liked in her men except for fat pockets, but that would come easy once he started being seen with her. Dudes were known to become A-list members once she blessed them with the ass.

Brandon laid Mia on the bed as they continued to kiss each other's bodies. He placed the yellow rose petals all over her chest and stomach. By the time he got down between her inner thighs she was already wet, but he still dove right in. He slid his face between her legs and began thrusting his tongue back and forth in circular motions. Mia moaned and squirmed for mercy as she exploded into what would be the first of many orgasms she would experience that night. She had never had a man treat her so passionately before. She pulled him up from between her quivering legs and kissed him on the mouth.

He reached for his pants beside the bed and grabbed the condom out of his back pocket. Brandon unwrapped the condom, placed it on his full erection, and guided himself slowly, inch by inch, inside her.

Mia gasped for air as he swayed up and down on top of her.

"Harder, baby, harder," she said breathlessly.

He positioned her legs toward the ceiling and started banging his body against hers. Brandon was moaning right along with her.

"Damn, baby, you feel so good." Brandon could feel himself coming to a climax as she whimpered his name over and over again. He convulsed in a chain of spasms as he collapsed in her arms.

All he could think about was how crazy the night had been. He had one of the baddest chicks in the city lying right next to him. He never expected Chris to pull off setting them up, and he never thought he would get the ass this soon. Usually Chris fucked up when it came to women, but he really came through with the right connect this time.

Brandon pulled Mia on top of him and kissed her on the forehead. The scent of her Chanel perfume filled his nose as he kissed her sweetly on the neck. She ran her hands through his hair and smiled. She looked deeply into his eyes and rested her head on his chest. Brandon knew in that moment that he had found his meal ticket to the top. He knew that it was gonna cost him to keep up with Mia and her extravagant lifestyle, but he was willing to put all he had into it to stay on her arm. It was all a part of his plan.

When Brandon and Mia woke up to Chris and Sam banging on the door, it was two in the afternoon.

"Yo, man, come on. We got a meeting with that new artist, Bré, at five!" Chris yelled through the door. "We need to leave now!"

Brandon and Mia scrambled to find their clothes, which were thrown all over the room. Mia stopped to glance at Brandon while he pulled on his Calvin Klein boxer briefs. There was something about him that made her aroused. He was a pretty black man with a heavenly body and the biggest dick she had ever seen. Mia grabbed him from behind and kissed the middle of his back.

"I want you, Brandon," Mia whined.

Brandon turned around and grabbed her waist. "You had me last night and I enjoyed every bit of it."

He smiled and leaned in to kiss her while Chris continued to bang on the door.

"What the fuck are y'all doing in there?" Chris yelled impatiently.

"Let's go, baby, before Chris breaks down the door," Brandon said.

Mia grabbed her purse.

"By the way, thank you for last night, Mr. Brunson."

"It was truly a pleasure, Ms. Mia, a pleasure I hope to have again."

It was well past four when the foursome arrived back in Philly. Brandon stopped by the office and dropped off Chris. The car was silent as he approached his next stop. Sam felt extremely awkward. Even she could feel the sexual tension between Mia and Brandon.

Brandon pulled up to the curb of Mia's condo building in Rittenhouse Square. He hurried to the other side of the car and opened the door for Sam. When he got around to opening the door for Mia she slipped him a card. Sam's face lit up in surprise the minute Mia pulled out the card from her pocketbook. Mia had never given any nigga the key to her crib, not even her ex-boyfriend to whom she was previously engaged. Mia was getting soft after just one night with this dude. *He must have been damn good in bed,* Sam thought as she hurried off into the building to give them their space.

"What is this?" Brandon asked.

"The key card to my condo, which I expect you to use tonight," Mia cooed.

Brandon had accomplished in one night what would have taken other dudes years. He had pulled an industry bitch. He smiled and kissed her on the neck. Mia headed into the building after Sam, and Brandon pulled off to meet up with Chris at the office. By the time Brandon got there, Chris had already sealed the deal. Bré was officially signed to Indigo Records, and Chris and Bré were already talking about the production of her album.

Chris not only knew music and talent, but he also knew the streets. In the boardroom he was Christopher Black, but on the streets he was known as Chief. Thanks to running the streets, Chris's money was long. He was a street millionaire, and he had invested almost all his cash in Indigo Records. He trusted Brandon because he was, after all, his nigga.

They had come up together in Blumberg Projects. Chris ran the Blum and lived across the hall from Brandon. When Brandon's mother died from cancer, he spent the rest of his teenage years with Chris and his family. Brandon was a hustler in his own right. He was what you called a corporate corner boy—a nigga from around the way with an Ivy League degree. He hustled, but the legal way. Brandon handled the logistics of the projects. He determined the contents of the contracts and met with other businesses to promote the label.

Although Chris and Brandon usually worked well together, they were like night and day. Brandon handled all his business before the sun went down, and Chris usually did nothing until late at night. Brandon and Chris's friendship was simple. They always looked out for each other. They never really had any arguments, and small disagreements were handled before they got out of hand. Chris watched Brandon's back on the streets, and Brandon watched Chris's back in the boardroom. Chris knew he could count on Brandon to have his money right. He wouldn't trust anyone else with the job.

Now with another new artist signed, everything seemed to be falling into place. Brandon had met the baddest bitch in the city and signed a new artist all in the matter of a weekend.

As Brandon sat at his desk with his hands folded, Chris wrapped up the meeting with Bré. After showing her to the door, he hurried back upstairs to talk shit with Brandon.

"You hangin' tonight?" Chris asked while glancing at his watch. "We can meet up downtown to celebrate closing this deal, just like I know you closed that deal with Mia last night."

Chris sat on the desk quietly waiting to hear the details. Brandon rocked back in his chair with a stupid smirk on his face. He began reminiscing about how good the sex had been.

"Man, that ass was so good that I'm getting hard just thinking about it." Chris laughed.

"You fuckin' pervert. I don't want to hear about ya dick. I want to hear about that ass. Was she really that good?"

"Damn good," Brandon confirmed. Mia's Chanel perfume was still lingering in his nose. He grinned at the thought of her beautiful, tanned, naked body.

"I should have kept her for myself. Sam was average pussy. I could live wit it or without it. I thought the ass was going to be off the hook because her head game was crazy! I thought she was going to bite off my dick. That chick was deep throatin' my shit for like an hour, but her shot was shitty. When I crapped out at the casino and lost a grand, I just kept thinkin' that at least I was gonna get some good ass, but that was fucked up too." Brandon chuckled at Chris's bad luck. "Anyway, man, are you hangin' or what?" Chris asked again.

Truthfully, Brandon was still tired from driving back, and besides, he was supposed to meet up with Mia later that night. He still needed to get dressed and make sure he could grab a small gift for her. Brandon knew that would keep her interested.

"I'm tired. I'ma head home. I'll holla at you tomorrow."

"Nigga, I know you going to see Mia and tear that ass up

again. You think I'm stupid, huh?" They both burst into laughter. "I know you too good for that shit. I'll get wit you tomorrow. I gotta go check up on my money anyway. I heard them young bulls out there fuckin' up."

Chris walked toward the door and stopped to pull something out of his pocket. He threw three condoms on the desk.

"Use all of these for me." He smiled and left.

Brandon gathered his briefcase, locked the office, and followed behind Chris.

Brandon drove to the King of Prussia Mall and purchased a Louis Vuitton overnight bag for Mia's soon-to-be sleepovers at his house. He had it all planned out. He would give her the monogrammed Vuitton bag now, and then a key to his crib in a couple months. By then she would think she was the only chick he was dealing with, period.

In order to make his plan come together, he knew he had to put some work in and spend big cash on Mia. He maxed out his platinum card on just this one purchase, but she was worth it. She was worth whatever he needed to do to get ahead in his career. He figured he would pay the price now and live lavishly later. He headed home to get dressed.

It was just about ten PM, and Mia would be expecting him soon. Brandon didn't live that far from Mia's place, so it would not take him long to get there. He lived in the Pennsylvania House, about five or six blocks from her condo. Chris would always joke about him selling out because he moved out of "da hood." Brandon never liked the projects, and he left as soon as he was able to stand on his own two feet.

His condo was quite small. It was a one-bedroom with a view of the Art Museum. Even though it was a tiny apartment, he filled it with expensive pieces from artist William Tolliver and furniture from Bob Mackie. His bed alone was worth almost five grand. It was a hardwood, leather sleigh bed with a nutmeg finish and side tables to match. There was just enough room for Brandon in his apartment, and he enjoyed living there.

Brandon finished up a hot shower and decided to throw on a pair of dark denim Evisu jeans, and a plain white T. He slipped on a pair of Prada sneakers and covered himself in Issey Miyake cologne. As he walked past the answering machine he noticed the light was blinking with three new messages. He decided that all business would resume tomorrow morning when the work week began.

Once he arrived at Mia's condo he slid the card through the front door and called out to her. He looked around the place, and was in awe. Mia was very well off, and her condo represented that fact. He ran his hand across the back of her cream leather couch. The smooth feel led him to believe it was Italian and probably cost her at least ten thousand dollars. From the couch alone, Brandon confirmed that she had good taste. But then there were the handmade Persian rugs that graced the hardwood floors.

Brandon was further impressed with Mia's class and style when he saw her collection of paintings and sculptures. There were all types of handmade sculptures throughout the living area, and paintings from Africa and Asia graced her walls. But when Brandon noticed the crystal chandelier in her dining area, he fell in love. He could tell by the design that the chandelier alone had to be worth over twenty grand. Brandon prided himself on being the type of dude that usually kept up with the finer things in life, and he knew he hadn't seen anything like that chandelier in his travels, not even in the five-star hotels he visited. He stood and admired it for ten minutes before making his way through the rest of her crib.

Brandon left Mia's gift in the living room to enhance the surprise. Making his way to the bedroom, he found Mia barely clothed, wearing only four-inch heels and a pink see-through bra and panty set. He looked at her perky breasts, which were so full that they were protruding from the confines of her bra, and prayed he could keep to his plan.

Brandon had no intention of doing Mia tonight. It was time to start phase two of his plan, and that was to develop this casual fuck into a full-time relationship. He pecked her on the mouth and she frowned.

"What was that?" she asked. She sat on the side of the bed and patted the space next to her for him to sit. Brandon stepped up on the platform that held her bed and a forty-two-inch flat screen TV, and took a seat next to her. Mia looked at the handsome man before her. "Brandon, I'm leaving for Milan in the morning and I won't be back until next week. I have a photo shoot out there and a couple publicity events."

This was the perfect time to give her the gift that he had bought her.

"I have a going-away present for you."

Brandon walked out into the living room and returned with the finely wrapped gift. Mia's eyes lit up and she gasped like a little girl on Christmas morning when she saw the LV logo print on the package. She opened it and pulled the overnight bag out of the box. Mia immediately pushed him down on the bed and started to undo his belt.

Brandon leaned up from the bed and stared into space.

"What's wrong with you?" Mia asked as she sat up. "I love the gift."

Brandon folded his hands. "Last night was amazing, and I don't want to mess that up," he said, turning toward her and placing her hand in his. "I hope this was not just sex for you, because I am looking for so much more."

Mia became furious. "Do you think that I would have wasted my time giving you the key to my apartment if I was just going to fuck you? If that was the case, I would have left in the middle of the night."

Brandon was amused by her little tantrum. Now that he knew she was digging him, he could relax a little. Without a word Brandon got off the bed and began to take off his clothes as Mia watched. She loved the sight of him naked. There was something about this man that made Mia want to settle down. She was already practicing his last name with hers over and over again in her head. She grabbed his throbbing hard-on and wrapped her moist lips around it.

Brandon moaned breathlessly as she massaged his balls with her hands. His mind was racing a mile a minute. If he smashed again she would have nothing to look forward to once she got back home. He ripped her thongs off and started to massage her. He wanted to sex her badly, but he had to control himself. That was the only way he was going to stay focused.

"You want me to go down there again, don't you?" He continued to massage her and she became even wetter than before.

She groaned while saying, "Eat it, baby." Mia was vulnerable at this point. She wanted him to taste her, and she wanted it now. Brandon flipped her on her stomach and began to bite her from behind. Mia clenched the sheets as pleasure escaped her body.

Brandon was still trying to keep his cool, but he wanted her. Her coochie was so wet and warm that he couldn't resist. He ran his hands from the nape of her neck to the bottom of her ass. He eased himself in and began rocking inside her over and over again. Her ass smacking back and forth turned him on even more. He loved fucking doggy-style. As he climaxed he pulled out and covered her ass with cum.

Brandon collapsed on the bed as Mia went to wash up. He lay with his hands behind his neck and stared at the ceiling. Turning toward the clock, he saw that it was already two-thirty AM. When Mia returned from the shower Brandon was fully dressed.

He couldn't remember ever being this turned on by a woman. Brandon's dick was beginning to harden all over again as he watched Mia. Her soft, curvy flesh threw him into an erotic high. As she began drying the dripping water from her naked body, she asked, "Aren't you going to spend the night?"

"Damn, girl, every time I see you naked I can't control myself."

He grabbed her around the waist and kissed her. His tongue slipped in and out of her mouth more forcefully than before.

"I know you have an early flight, and I have a long day ahead of me tomorrow. If I stay here, neither one of us will get any sleep tonight."

She walked him toward the door and kissed him one more time.

"I will call you as soon as I land. Get some sleep."

Brandon handed her the key card. "Will you be needing this back?" he asked.

Mia pushed the card back in his hand.

"I'll let you know when you need to give it back." She smiled and closed the door.

When he got in the door, it was close to three in the morning. His answering machine was still blinking and he had a shit-load of voice messages on his cell, but he was too tired to care. Brandon knew he was not going to make it to the office on time. He undressed and lay on the couch to catch a glimpse of the late night news while nodding in and out of sleep. He woke when he heard loud screaming on his answering machine.

"Brandon, where are you? This is Mom. Chris got shot! We have been trying to call you all night. Please call me back!"

She was crying hysterically. Through Ms. Ruth's heavy sobs Brandon was able to catch the hospital and room number before she hung up.

Brandon was scared. Chris was the only brother he knew. He reached for the phone and dropped it right back on the cradle. Deciding against calling back Ms. Ruth, he thought it would be best if he went down there to meet her. He quickly threw on some sweatpants and a thermal shirt and headed for the hospital, where he met Ms. Ruth in the lobby.

Chapter 2

Business Before Pleasure

Brandon kissed her on the cheek as she cried in his chest.

"Is he OK, Mom?" Brandon's body quivered at the thought of Chris dying. "Where is he? What happened?" Ms. Ruth finally pulled away from Brandon's embrace.

"In surgery right now."

She tugged a tissue out of her pocketbook and started to blow her nose. Her eyes were red and she looked tired. Ms. Ruth worked two jobs, and she was no young lady. Chris had bought her a huge home with a porch in the Northeast part of Philadelphia. When they were living in the projects she always dreamed of having a home with a porch so she could sit, read her books, and enjoy beautiful summer nights. As soon as Chris had enough money he bought her the house of her dreams. Chris had offered to pay all her bills, but she refused because he had already done so much. So she worked her fingers to the bone, and every time Chris gave her money she would put it in the bank for his son, instead of using it for herself.

"He was shot in the projects, and the bullet is lodged in

his right shoulder blade," she said and began sobbing all over again. "They say he should be OK, but I just can't get it together. He is my only child, and if he dies, I don't know what I will do." She stared into Brandon's eyes. "I told him to stay from around them projects. He just won't listen, and now look what happened."

Brandon hugged her again. "Everything will be fine, Mom." They took a seat and he tried to change the subject to take her mind off the situation. "We just signed a new artist yesterday."

Chris's mom smiled.

"Congratulations. I am so proud of you and Christopher. Your mother would be very proud too, Brandon. You have turned out to be a good man." She grabbed his hand. "Next weekend is Mother's Day, and I would like you and Christopher to join me in church."

Brandon put his right hand on top of hers.

"I will be there, and if I have anything to do with it, so will Chris."

The doctor greeted them in the lobby a few minutes later.

"Ms. Black, the surgery went well, and Christopher should be able to come home by the end of next week." She collapsed with relief. "Thank you, doctor. Thank you, Lord!" Ms. Ruth yelled. Brandon shook the doctor's hand.

"Mom, let me take you home to get some rest and I will keep an eye on Chris."

Brandon dropped off Ms. Ruth and made his way back to the hospital. By the time Brandon made it back to Chris's room, he was out of surgery and conscious enough to have visitors. Brandon walked in the room and there was Tracy, Chris's baby's mama and their son, little Chris. Tracy was sitting by the bed holding little Chris on her lap.

"What's up, Tracy?" Brandon kissed her on the cheek. He could tell that she had an attitude.

"Where the fuck was you last night? We were trying to call you to let you know what happened, and you was nowhere to be found."

Who the fuck did she think she was asking him where he was last night? He loved Chris like a brother, but he was not his keeper.

Brandon had told Chris on several occasions to leave that hustling shit alone, but he would not listen. Chris loved the streets. It was like a family relationship for him. The streets fed him and his family when nobody else would, and he was truly loyal.

Brandon stayed calm and focused all of his attention toward Chris.

"How you feelin', man?" he asked.

Chris was drained. He could barely talk. The drugs from the surgery had taken over his body.

"I got caught up in some shit. One of my young bulls robbed this dude, Mike, and he came back blastin'."

Brandon was mad at himself for not checking the answering machine before he went out last night, and for ignoring his cell's voice mail notification. He felt like he had let his nigga down. He was also pissed with Chris because he told him to stop fucking with those project dudes and start focusing all of his energy into the business.

Chris positioned the hospital bed so he could sit up.

"Yo, take Tracy and little man home for me." He kissed his son good-bye. Tracy leaned over to kiss him and walked toward the door.

Tracy had never liked Brandon. She thought he was a bitch. Every time some drama went down, he was nowhere to be found. When she mentioned this to Chris, he always took Brandon's side. Now she had to ride home with the nigga. Tracy rolled her eyes at him as she walked out of the hospital room.

Brandon shook his head. If she only knew that the only

reason Chris stayed with her was because they had a baby together, she would shit her pants. Chris smashed other chicks on the daily and came home when he felt like it. Tracy never questioned him because he took good care of her and their son. Truth be told, Brandon didn't want to be around her, but for Chris he'd put up with her.

"You need anything else before I leave?" Brandon asked.

"Just take care of business, man. I'll be straight. I should be outta here soon."

"Aight, man." Brandon shook his hand. "I'ma hold shit down. You try to get some rest." Brandon closed the door and walked to the lobby to find Tracy and Little Chris.

Brandon drove Tracy home as fast as he could with minimal conversation. She was his man's baby's mama, but he hated her just as much as she hated him. When Tracy and Chris first met, she had tried to fuck Brandon behind Chris's back. He never told Chris because at that time he was really feeling her. She was truly a ho who only saw an opportunity to get with a nigga who was getting paper. When she got pregnant, it was all she wrote.

After he dropped them off he made his way to the office. Half of the day was already gone. He checked the messages, made a couple phone calls, and decided to call it a night. As he drove home he could not help but wonder what Mia was doing. He dialed her cell phone and left a message.

"Hey, baby, I was thinking about you. Call me when you get a chance."

Brandon didn't like leaving messages, especially in a situation like this. He waited several hours for Mia to return his call, but she never did. It was eleven PM when he decided to try calling again. He started dialing and hung up before the line connected. Brandon could not understand why she didn't call. He didn't want to sweat her, so he decided that until she called him, there would be no thoughts of Ms. Mia or the weekend that had just passed.

Mother's Day arrived and Brandon found himself staying true to his promise of attending church with Ms. Ruth. Chris was still in the hospital, and she needed someone to be there for her like she had always been there for them.

Brandon had stopped believing in God when he took away his mother. Besides, he had not seen the inside of a church since he was about fourteen. After service, Brandon and Ms. Ruth visited Brandon's mother's grave as he did every Mother's Day to leave daffodils, his mother's favorite flower. Ms. Ruth waited in the car while he walked swiftly through the cemetery to his mother's tombstone. Brandon kneeled down and laid the bouquet of flowers in front of her grave. Mother's Day was always hard for him. Brandon's mother had been his last living relative. He didn't count his father because he had left them when Brandon was three, and hadn't shown his face since.

After dropping off Ms. Ruth, Brandon headed toward the bar for a quick drink. Things had been hectic since Chris got shot, and he needed a break. He ordered his usual and sat at the bar watching the game. When his phone started to ring, he looked down to see who it was. The screen said it was Mia, so Brandon didn't answer. It had been over a week since they had last spoke. After he left her a message, she had never returned his call. He never had a woman treat him like that before, and he admired her for being the first. He knew that she liked him, but there was no way he was going to let her get the upper hand.

Brandon decided to shake shit up and give Mia a taste of her own medicine. He guessed that she was back from Milan, since she was calling him. He knew when she was in town she always attended the 32 Degrees lounge on Sunday nights, so he decided to go there and bring some eye candy along.

Brandon rushed home and called the best looking chick in his phone book. Vikki was just as fine as Mia, but she was too loose of a woman to keep Brandon's attention. Originally from Harlem, Vikki had moved to the Philadelphia area about six months ago. Brandon met her at a club in Manhattan where she was hosting an event for her agency. She owned an upscale escort service that catered to high-end clients like rappers and CEOs. Vikki was gorgeous, classy, and well groomed, so niggas paid good cash to tap that ass.

Brandon pressed his best Armani shirt and shined his Gucci loafers. It was time to play hardball, and he knew he would win this round.

When Brandon picked up Vikki about ten PM, he immediately knew he was going home with her tonight. Vikki walked in the door of 32 Degrees and every nigga in the spot turned their attention to her. Her long, straight hair flowed down the middle of her back. She wore a short, red, Christian Dior dress with black, four-inch Manolo Blahnik pumps. Her lips were smothered in Bobbi Brown's Cinnamon Spice lipstick. She was a bad-ass chick, and a white girl at that.

Vikki waited inside by the front door while Brandon parked the car. Dudes were already flocking to buy her drinks. Brandon came through the door and escorted her to the table next to where Mia and her girlfriends were sitting. He pulled out the chair for Vikki and then took a seat across from her with his back turned toward Mia. He grabbed Vikki's right hand from across the table and stared into her eyes as if she was the only woman on earth. She smiled and put her left hand on top of his. He waved the waitress down and ordered a Mimosa for Vikki, and a gin for himself. The dimmed lights and the candlelit tables made their date look even more intimate than he could have hoped.

Brandon began talking loudly over the soft music, anxious to gain Mia's attention. The waitress returned, put their drinks in front of them, and disappeared again.

At first Mia didn't notice him, but she kept hearing a familiar voice, and when the waitress said gin she was forced to turn around.

It couldn't be, she thought. Mia dropped her fork on the floor next to Brandon and waited for him to pick it up. She wanted to make sure she wasn't trippin'. He ignored the piece of silverware and continued to talk loudly across the table to Vikki.

"Excuse me," Mia said.

Brandon turned around in his seat and smiled deviously. Her heart instantly dropped.

"Yes," he replied.

"Could you please hand me that?" She pointed to the fork beside his left foot. He picked it up and handed it to her. She snatched it out of his hand and quickly turned back around.

"You're welcome," he said sarcastically and continued his conversation with Vikki.

Mia's face couldn't help but turn bright red. This nigga had the nerve to bring a bitch to the bar he knew she and her girls went to every weekend. She was furious. Mia waited for the chance to confront him. Her foot was tapping the floor in such a violent manner that even Brandon could hear it.

He knew he was getting the best of Mia, so he decided to take it a little further. Brandon kissed Vikki on the cheek before excusing himself from her company and walking to the bathroom. Before he could reach the door, Mia grabbed his hand.

"What the fuck is this about?" she asked, folding her arms in front of her. Mia was trying to suppress the tears of anger that were starting to form in the corners of her eyes.

Brandon smiled and acted as if he had no idea what she was talking about.

"I'm just enjoying a night out with a friend. Nothing different than what you're doing here." Brandon politely stepped around Mia to use the bathroom. To his delight, when he came out she was standing there waiting for him.

"So who the hell is she, Brandon?" Mia folded her arms in front of her chest. "How dare you bring a bitch to my spot?"

Brandon could see that Mia was truly hurt. He didn't care at this point, though. After all, this was all part of his plan. He had to teach her a lesson and regain control over the situation. Still, he didn't want to take it too far, because Vikki was clingy. He knew if he showed off too much, it might really take Mia over the top, and besides, Vikki was just bait. He still wanted Mia, but he wanted all of her attention, and not just some of it.

Mia stormed past Brandon and straight out the door of the club. It was definitely time to take Vikki home. He needed to tend to Mia before she decided that she could do without him all together.

After dropping off Vikki, Brandon quickly drove to Mia's place. He slid the key card through the door, and slowly walked into Mia's apartment. He could hear the shower running as he quietly shut the door behind him. There were clothes all over the place. Her once clean apartment looked like a war zone. The living room was so crowded that Brandon had to step over shoes and skimpy cocktail dresses just to get to the bedroom. Her suitcase was lying on the bed as if she had just arrived back in town.

Brandon cleared the bed, undressed himself, and was under the covers by the time she finished in the bathroom. She was happy to see him there, but pissed off at the same time because of the stunt he had just pulled at the club.

"Mr. Brunson, I would appreciate it if you would put your clothes on and leave." Mia stood in the middle of the bedroom, clasping the towel around her chest.

Brandon wanted to grab her, pull her down on the bed, and fuck the shit out of her sexy ass.

"Why should I leave?" he asked.

"Because I asked you to, and I don't want to fuck with you."

"I called you and you didn't even return my call. What the fuck was that about?" Brandon started putting on his clothes. "Fuck it, man. I'm outta here." He threw the key card on the bed and walked toward the door.

"Brandon, wait!" He folded his arms and stood to hear what she had to say. "Look, I'm not used to checking in with a man. Every time I dialed your number I hung up before the phone rang."

Brandon sighed inside. He was relieved that this shit with Mia might still work out. He unwrapped her towel and admired her naked body.

"Look, baby, that chick in the club was just a friend." Brandon was massaging her shoulders. He was starting to get aroused. "I just wanted your attention," he said.

Mia wrapped her arms around his neck.

"Well, you have my attention now. Did you miss me?" she asked.

"You damn right. I missed you and all that good lovin' you was giving me, too."

"We both missed you, too."

"So now what?" Brandon grabbed her ass and pulled her close.

She tugged at his pants.

"Go get washed," she said.

"Only if you come with me."

Before they could even get to the bathroom Mia was ripping off his clothes. She had spent her whole trip craving his sex. She didn't call him because she didn't want to sweat him either. Little did Brandon know, Mia had a motive of her own.

Mia turned on the shower and they got in. The water splashed down on his ebony skin and they began kissing furiously. Brandon's tongue darted repeatedly inside her mouth. Mia wrapped her soft, long legs around his waist, and he began bouncing her up and down as she screamed loudly.

"Oh, I missed you, baby!"

Water poured down Mia's face as she climaxed. Brandon released her legs and gently pushed her down to her knees. He pressed his straining erection against her mouth and began guiding her head back and forth.

"Damn, girl, I missed you, too."

After he released in her mouth they showered together, and then they made their way back to the bedroom. He dried off her damp body as she lay in the bed exhausted from their sexual escapade.

Brandon awoke the next morning to the sound of his cell phone ringing. It was Chris.

"Hello," Brandon answered.

"Man, where you at? Come get me. I'm ready to get the fuck out this hospital." Chris was anxious to get back to the streets. He had some business to handle.

"I'm on my way." Brandon jumped out of bed and began scrambling for his clothes.

"Where are you going?" Mia sat up and watched him dress.

"I'll be back later." He pulled on his last shoe and left.

Chris was waiting by the hospital doors when he arrived. His right arm was in a sling, but other than that he was ready for action.

"Did you pick up my shit up?" Chris asked.

"Naw, I forgot. I'll drive past ya crib right now." Brandon quickly made his way through the streets and pulled over to the corner of Ridge and Master. He parked and waited for Chris to return. Chris came out with a black duffel bag and a navy blue hoodie.

"Ride me past the projects. I gotta get something."

Brandon hated driving his car to the projects. Niggas were always gritting on him when they saw his wheels, but he couldn't refuse Chris when he had just gotten out of the hospital. Parking across the street from Blumberg, Brandon turned off the car and prepared to wait.

Without taking much care for his shoulder, Chris put on the hoodie, grabbed the bag, and pulled out a .45.

"Yo, B, I gotta handle my business with this nigga, Mike."

"Damn, Chris, what the fuck are you doing? You ain't been out the hospital for a fuckin' day yet," Brandon said.

"I'm gonna go handle this nigga and then I'm gonna roll a blunt and get some ass." Chris was beginning to believe Tracy about Brandon being a bitch. He could see the fear in his eyes. Chris jumped out the car, tucked the gun in his pants, and made his way to the fifth floor.

When Mike opened the door he never expected to see Chris on the other side. Before he could even close the door in his face Chris let off three to his chest and headed for the steps. The stairwell reeked of urine. He took two steps at a time until he reached the bottom floor. He walked quickly to the car and slammed the door.

"Drive, nigga, drive!" Chris yelled.

Brandon sped off as fast as he could. He pulled over once they got to Twenty-ninth Street.

"What the fuck were you thinking? My fuckin' plate was showing." Brandon was paranoid. All his plans could be ruined by Chris's revenge.

Chris pulled out his weed and started to roll a blunt.

"Nigga, stop bitchin'. He had that shit coming." Chris lit up, took a puff, and passed the blunt to Brandon. Brandon pushed his hand away.

"You fuckin' crazy?!" Brandon was mad as hell. "You gonna fuck everything up with this street shit."

Chris took another puff off his blunt and began to cough.

"Man, I ain't gonna let no nigga fire me up and not hit that dude up when I get home. I got a reputation in the streets, and I ain't 'bout to let no nut-ass bull come between me and my money."

Chris's shoulder began to ache from all the action, so he dug down into his bag and pulled out a bottle of painkillers. He popped a Percocet and continued to smoke.

Brandon knew the shit with Chris and that dude Mike was not over. He knew he should have dropped that nigga home. Chris was smoking his second blunt at two-thirty in the afternoon.

"You high as shit, man, and we need to get some work done," Brandon said.

"Nigga, I'm straight." Chris wasn't sure if it was the blunt, the painkiller, or the fact that he had just protected his rep, but he was feeling better as each minute passed. "Call that jump-off broad you know. What's her name? Natalie. I want some ass." Chris laughed. "I ain't doing no work until I get some ass."

Brandon picked up his cell and dialed as he drove to the office.

"Hello," Natalie answered. Her voice was light yet seductive.

"Yo, Nat, it's B. My nigga Chief wanna holla. What up?"

"Where?" she asked.

"The office."

"I'll be there in about an hour. You game, too?" she asked.

"I don't know. I'll answer when I see how phat the ass looks in that thong." Brandon hung up the phone.

As soon as they arrived Chris went into his office and started checking his messages. An hour later Natalie buzzed the office from downstairs. Brandon went down to greet her. He wrapped his muscular arms around her curvy body and grabbed her ass tightly as they embraced. It had been almost a year since Brandon had seen Natalie. She had been out in Hollywood trying to establish her acting career since they left school, and he was doing the music thing.

He always knew he could count on Natalie if he couldn't rely on any other chick. Brandon and Natalie had been sexing since college. She was a straight-up jump-off. She was ready whenever you called, and had no problem being a freak. She loved being the center of attention, and she loved sharing her body with others—male and female.

Brandon led Natalie into Chris's office. Standing behind her, he unbuttoned her trench coat to reveal that she was butt ass naked underneath. Her pubic hairs were cut neatly to resemble a heart, and both of her nipples were pierced with two little, red barbells. Grabbing her coochie from behind, Brandon massaged it slowly. She moaned lightly and threw her head back from the heightened pleasure.

After watching the little show, Chris hung up the phone without even finishing his conversation. Brandon left the office, making his way to his own office, and leaving Chris and Natalie alone. Chris turned his attention to the beautiful chick standing before him, hoping she could satisfy all his needs.

Chapter 3

What you don't know...

Chris pulled off his sling and pushed everything off his desk and onto the floor. Then he grabbed Natalie and placed her on the desk. He dropped his pants to the ground, climbed on top of her, and stuck his firm flesh into her mouth. She began to suck fiercely until he was at full erection. Chris pulled his hard rod out of her mouth and unwrapped a condom. He fell into her deep, hot body and began banging her back out.

Natalie was a fine-ass Rican chick with the biggest titties he had ever seen. Chris grabbed her breasts so hard that he left red imprints of his hands on them. He was never the type of dude to make love to a chick. He did what he had to do, and when he came the action was over. He never cared if a woman enjoyed herself. Chris was out for his, and nothing else mattered.

Natalie squirmed and screamed from pleasure.

"Damn, poppi!" she yelled.

Chris pulled her up from the desk, ignoring the pain in his shoulder, and positioned her between him and the wall. She wrapped her legs around him, and before she could get into the position change, he came inside her. Chris dropped her legs and put her back down on the ground. She stood there and watched as he grabbed his clothes and began to put them back on.

"Get dressed," Chris said as he zipped his pants.

"Chief, I didn't cum yet. Make me cum," Natalie begged him. She rubbed her hands around the barbells on her nipples and licked her lips. "Make me cum, poppi," she said again as she tugged at his pants. Chris pushed her away, and she hit the wall with a loud thump.

"Put ya shit on and roll," he said while glaring at her. Natalie could see that Chris was becoming aggressive, so she gathered her trench coat and left without saying another word.

Chris sat on the desk and looked around at all the papers that were scattered on the floor. She was just a quick fuck for him. He still wanted some, and he knew just who could satisfy him the way that he wanted. Chris walked out and grabbed the keys to Brandon's car.

"B, I'll be right back. I need to make a quick run."

"Don't fuck up my ride, man," Brandon yelled from the next room.

"Nigga, you must have forgot that I bought that shit for ya nut ass."

With that Chris left the office and walked toward the car. His cell phone was ringing and he knew it was Tracy, but she was the last chick he wanted to be bothered with right then. He rolled another blunt and headed for West Philly.

Chris parked in front of the Monte Vista Apartments on Sixty-third Street, smoked his blunt, popped a painkiller, and buzzed Kane. When he got upstairs, Kane was playing Xbox and drinking a Corona in his boxers and a wife-beater. Chris plopped onto the couch next to him and watched as he played the game.

"When did you get out the hospital?" Kane asked when he finished playing the game. "I tried to call your room, but I couldn't get through."

Kane walked into the kitchen, grabbed two more Coronas, and handed one to Chris. After Kane sat back on the couch, Chris pulled out a bag of weed and started to roll.

Kane glanced over at Chris as he started to play the video game again. Chris was just too sexy. He had that thug appeal Kane liked in his niggas. He watched Chris lick the blunt to seal it, and he could feel himself harden. He knew Chris could tell. Kane was in love with Chris's lips. They were nice and full, and they were always soft. He leaned over and kissed Chris on the mouth before he could even light the blunt. Chris pulled Kane on top of him and pulled down his boxers. He began slowly grinding against Chris until he reached a full erection.

"Jerk off for me," Chris ordered as he unzipped his own pants and removed his sling.

Kane stood in front of him, massaging and stroking himself until he came. Chris pulled him down to his knees. Kane took his cue and began sucking Chris off with the force of a vacuum. Chris loved for a dude to give him head because their jaws were so much stronger than a woman's and they knew exactly what to do to make him cum.

Chris watched as Kane's mouth slid up and down. He lit his blunt and spaced out until he felt himself about to release. Kane swallowed as Chris came in his mouth. Chris then put Kane down on all fours in the middle of the living room and began to eat Kane from behind.

"Fuck me," Kane begged.

"Tell daddy how much you want it." Chris smacked him on the ass.

"I want it. I want it now," he pleaded.

Chris opened a condom, put it on, and smacked Kane's ass again. He slowly shoved himself into Kane, and then quickly gyrated his body back and forth until he could feel himself about to cum a second time. The feeling was so good that Chris forgot about everything—the shooting, the business, and the fact that he was fucking a dude.

Kane's body was shivering from every stroke. Chris wanted to bust, but managed to hold it until Kane came first, and then Chris allowed himself to cum shortly after. They then both fell to the floor.

"You staying the night?" Kane asked while gently rubbing Chris's injured shoulder.

"Naw. I gotta go home and check up on Tracy and little man," Chris said, rolling over to his back. "I needed to see you first. I haven't even been home yet."

Kane rested his head on Chris's chest. "We been fuckin' around for two years and you always tellin' me you gonna leave that bitch, so when is it gonna happen?"

Chris's eyes grew dark. "Look, I told you what the deal was. You know I'm just there for my son." He kissed Kane on the mouth and got up to take a shower.

Kane was jealous of Tracy. He wanted to have Chris around all the time, and not just when he felt like coming through to smash. Chris had told Kane that he would leave Tracy once the baby was born, but he never did. Yet Kane continued to wait. He had never messed with a light-skinned nigga before, and the one that he did decide to fuck with had him caught up.

"I'll be back later, aight?" Chris lazily kissed Kane on the forehead and left.

But Chris had no intention of coming back later. He was tired of Kane pressuring him to leave Tracy and Little

Chris. He liked fucking with Kane, but there was no way he could leave his family for another man.

Chris returned to the office to meet up with Brandon. When he pulled up Brandon was waiting at the door and came right out. He jumped in the car and Chris drove off.

"Did you fuck up my wheels?" Brandon asked, looking around his car.

He was always uptight about this nut-ass car. Chris was tired of Brandon acting like a bitch.

"Nigga, shut up. Ain't shit messed up," Chris said as he glanced over at Brandon.

Brandon looked good, and Chris had a thing for Brandon, ever since high school when Chris was introduced to the life. It was hard for Chris to keep his feelings suppressed, and he had found himself slipping on several occasions. Chris just thought that fucking with niggas was a phase, though. He didn't think of himself as a cake boy, because he was always the one doing the fucking, and he never sucked dick.

"I'ma crash at ya crib tonight," Chris said. "I don't feel like fuckin' with Tracy's naggin' ass right now."

Brandon just nodded in agreement. Chris stayed over Brandon's house when he didn't want anyone to know where he was. He slept on the couch and stayed for as long as he wanted. After all, he did help him pay for that, too.

It was the middle of the night and Chris's phone kept ringing. If it wasn't Tracy's crazy ass, it was Kane hitting him up every five minutes. Chris finally answered after his voice mail kept beeping from being full.

"What the fuck do you want, man?" Chris asked when Kane called again.

"I thought you were coming back."

"I changed my mind."

"I'm not ya bitch, Chris, and I don't have to put up with ya shit."

"You're right. You ain't my bitch, but you startin' to get on my nerves just like her dumb ass, so stop fuckin' callin' me." Chris hung up his cell and turned it off just as Brandon stumbled into the living room in his boxer briefs to see what was going on.

"Is that Tracy calling like that?" Brandon asked, suppressing a yawn.

"Some other bitch that keep sweatin' me. I told her to stop fuckin' calling me."

And with that Chris rolled over and acted as if he was going back to sleep. As soon as Brandon went back to the bedroom Chris dialed Kane.

"Look, I'll be over tomorrow," Chris said, leaving a message when Kane didn't pick up. He hung up and gazed at the ceiling. Chris knew that he was going to have to stop dealing with Kane. It was getting out of hand, and Kane was demanding too much of his time. Kane was starting to want more than Chris could possibly offer him. A relationship with a faggot was out of the question, because Chris was not a homo. He liked women. He just craved the touch of a man from time to time.

Someone banged on the door of Brandon's apartment. It was seven-thirty in the morning, and Chris and Brandon were both still asleep.

"Brandon, Chris, open this damn door!" It was Tracy. She yelled like she was about to break down the door if someone didn't answer. Little Chris stood by her side and began to cry. She just knew she had caught Chris this time. He was in there with a bitch, and she was ready to fight. She started pounding her fist harder against the door.

"I know you're in there with a bitch, and I'm going to fuck her up!" she screamed.

Chris jolted to the door before Brandon heard her. He opened the door and she smacked him in the face.

"Where is she?" Tracy asked as she searched the apartment. She shoved the magazines and picture frames off the coffee table, shattering them. As she continued to search the apartment, knocking over any and everything she could find, Brandon dragged himself into the living room still half asleep.

"What is going on in here?" he asked as he looked around the room and saw his personal things broken and lying all over the floor. The African sculpture he bought on his trip to Ghana was broken in two, and the picture of his mother that he kept on the table was lying face down on the floor. There was glass embedded in his Persian rug.

Brandon looked at Tracy, and then down at Little Chris, who was still crying violently from all the commotion. He picked up Little Chris and took him to the bedroom to lie down. When he returned to the living room he stared Tracy down as if he wanted to strangle her.

"Get out!" Brandon said. "Get the hell out of my house." He picked up his broken sculpture and chucked it into the kitchen trash.

Chris was speechless. He had never seen Brandon this mad. Chris had never seen a man as black as Brandon turn red in the face. He grabbed Tracy and pushed her into the hallway. By this time Tracy was hysterical and started hitting Chris in his arm. Chris was so shocked he almost didn't feel the pain screaming through his right shoulder. He grabbed Tracy's hands and tried to get her under control.

"Where is she?" she asked. "Where is that bitch you're cheating on me with?"

Tracy leaned against the wall and slid down toward the floor. She knew that Chris had been seeing someone, but she never knew who it was. Tracy was tired of being number two in his life. He took good care of her and Little Chris, but waking up to an empty bed was growing hard on her. She tried to overlook his staying out all night, and his cell phone ringing at four in the morning when he did decide to come home.

"I'm tired of ya shit, Chris. I'm tired of you not coming home for days at a time," she said. "I'm tired of being alone. We're supposed to be a family."

He picked her up from the floor and wiped her face.

"There is no one else," he said. "You know that when I'm not home I'm out here gettin' this money. How are we supposed to live and afford all that designer shit you used to wearing?"

"I don't need all of that anymore. I just want you to come home and be a family for me and ya son," she said. "I just want us to be a family."

He kissed her on the lips and rubbed her back to soothe her pain. He knew that Tracy had had enough of his playing around. It was time to give the hustling up and focus on his record company.

"Promise me," she begged. "Promise me we will be a family again."

Tears flowed from her eyes as she searched his face for an answer. He grabbed her close to him. Chris always knew that the time would come when he had to change, or else he was going lose Tracy, Little Chris, and everything that meant anything to him. There was one major problem that he had to take care of, and that was breaking it off with Kane. Chris took Tracy down to the car and went back up to change and grab Little Chris.

"You aight, man?" Brandon asked.

"I'm cool," was all Chris could say. He was in too much pain—mentally and physically.

Chris quickly changed and went into Brandon's bedroom to get his son. He awkwardly picked up Little Chris and stared at him. Little Chris had striking features—dark brown eyes and reddish brown hair—a spitting image of Chris when he was a child. That was when it occurred to him that he had a gorgeous little boy he barely saw because of his life on the streets.

"I'm gonna drop them off at the house and I'll meet you at the office around eleven," Chris said as he walked out of the apartment.

On their way to the house, Chris's cell phone went off and he looked to see who it was. It was Kane, and he was not ready to face him just yet, so he didn't answer, and Tracy noticed.

When they pulled onto their street there were police cars and fire trucks everywhere. Someone had set the house on fire. Smoke covered the sky above the house. The flames were so high that the firemen were unable to contain the fire. It had already spread to the house next door. They watched from afar as the blaze grew bigger.

Chris noticed a white, tinted out E-Class parked on the opposite side of the street. It was Mike's right-hand man Shake's car. It didn't take long before Mike's homies found out about what happened. He needed to lay low for a while until shit blew over. Chris figured the cops were going to be looking for him, so he hooked a U-turn and headed toward his mother's home in the Northeast. Tracy turned around in her seat and watched the flames as they drove off.

Chris drove up Broad Street and jumped on Roosevelt Boulevard. Tracy was frantic and crying. They had lost everything.

"What are we going to do?" Tracy sobbed. "All of our stuff is gone."

He grabbed her hand. For once in his life Chris was actually worried. Mike had just as much clout as Chris did in the streets.

Ms. Ruth was sitting on the porch reading her Bible when Chris pulled into the driveway. Tracy grabbed the baby and headed into the house. Chris sat on the porch with his mother as he always did when he was in trouble and needed advice. He folded his hands and continued to search his mind for an answer.

"They already been here looking for you," she said as she closed her Bible and took off her glasses.

"Who?" he asked. His heart started to beat faster as he waited for her reply.

"The police," she answered. "I don't know what you did this time, but I just hope and pray that nothing bad happens to you. I can't take too much more of this. Christopher, I worry about you. I worry that one day I'm going to get a call from some strange man telling me that my son is dead or in jail. I thought you were gonna do right when you and Brandon started that record business?"

She turned toward him and looked in his eyes. She could see the fear in his face. Ms. Ruth knew that her son had gotten himself into something that he might not be able to get out of. He was a man and had to handle his life himself. Yet he was her only child. She felt the need to say something.

"Son, I love you and I don't want to see anything happen to you or your family. The detective left a card for you to call him. I left it on the kitchen table." With that, she opened her Bible back up to where she had left off and continued to read.

Chris walked inside the house and grabbed the card from the kitchen table. He slid it into his back pocket and walked out the door toward the car. After driving around for several hours, and thinking about what he was going to do, he realized that he had to turn himself in. He called Brandon and asked him to meet him at the Franklin Mills Mall. The last place someone would look for him was at a shopping mall. Brandon arrived at the mall in about forty-five minutes. They met at the back entrance near the movie theatre. Brandon and Chris shook hands and got right down to business.

"Some detective came past the office looking for you," Brandon said.

"What did he want?" he asked.

"He just asked me if I had seen you today. What the fuck is going on, man?" Brandon asked.

"That nigga Mike, well his homies burned down my crib. I need to go turn myself in before somebody tries to hurt my family."

"What about the business?"

"That's the last thing on my mind right now. I need to make sure my family is safe. Just hold shit down until I can figure things out." Chris paced as they continued to talk.

"So when are you going to turn yourself in?" Brandon asked, trying to learn as much as he could.

"Tomorrow," Chris answered, staring off in the distance.

"Chris, what if they try to shut down the business?"

"Call the lawyer when you get back to the office and tell him what's going on. I'll holla at you tomorrow before I turn myself in."

They shook hands and walked toward their cars. Chris pulled off and honked his horn as he passed Brandon. Before Brandon could even get to the car he was already on the phone with the lawyer. There was no way he was going to let Chris fuck up all the hard work he had done. Brandon asked the lawyer to draw up papers allowing him to become the sole owner of the company. It would be in the best interest of the business, and it would only be temporary until Chris handled his legal issues.

Chris was still upset about what had happened. He was so deep in thought that before he realized it, he was sitting in front of Kane's apartment building. He turned off the car and sat there. He needed the comfort that only Kane could provide. But he had promised himself that he would not fuck with him anymore. He turned the ignition back on and drove off. Kane watched him from his bedroom window.

It was all over the news. There was nothing left from his house but ashes and soot. Chris's phone was ringing every five minutes. People were calling to see if he and his family were OK, and if he was going to retaliate. Chris told his homies to chill and let him handle things.

When Chris got back to his mom's house she was asleep in the recliner. He took the throw off the couch, covered her, and went upstairs to check on his son, who was also sleeping soundly. He tiptoed down the hall to his room and quietly eased himself into the bed next to Tracy.

Chris was nervous about turning himself in. He didn't know if the cops knew he shot Mike or if they had him on some other charges. He lay in bed for about an hour until he finally fell asleep. It was the longest night of his life. He kept dozing in and out of sleep, and when he finally began to rest, it was time to get up. He could smell freshly made blueberry muffins baking in the kitchen. His mother knew they were his favorite. He got out of bed and sat at the kitchen table with his mother. She got up and fixed him a plate.

"Brandon called," she said. "He said to meet him at the office around eleven."

Chris glanced at the clock, and it was already ten-thirty.

He wolfed down his food, threw on some clothes, and headed to the office.

When he arrived Brandon was sitting at his desk reading through some papers.

"Wassup, man?" Chris asked as they shook hands. Chris took a seat across from Brandon.

"I talked to the lawyer yesterday and he sent over these papers this morning," Brandon said.

"Did you look over them?" Chris asked.

"Yeah," he replied.

"What do they say?" Chris asked. Brandon took a deep breath.

"They just say that everything will go into my name until you get your legal issues handled. All we have to do is sign and send them back."

"Aight, cool."

With that, Chris took the papers and signed them. He trusted that Brandon would take care of shit for him, so he had no reason to read through the legal mumbo jumbo. And besides, there were more important things on his mind right now.

"I'll send them right back to the lawyer and everything will be taken care of," Brandon said. "Once everything is smoothed over, we will change it back."

"Did the detective come past here?" Chris asked, changing the subject.

"No," he said. "But Kane came by here to see you. Who is that?"

"Some nigga I used to run ball wit. What he say?" Chris asked. He became fidgety as he waited for a response, but Brandon barely noticed.

"He just said to tell you he stopped by," he said.

"If that nigga come back, tell him that you ain't seen me around, aight? Listen, I gotta go, man."

Chris left the office and drove to the police station. He parked the car and sat there for about thirty minutes trying to rehearse what he would say to the detective. Chris felt sick. Tracy's CLK Coupe was too small, and he felt like he was suffocating. Jumping out of the car, he took two deep breaths as he reached in his back pocket to retrieve the card the detective had left with his mother.

"Detective Gary Sims," he read out loud. He crumbled the card up in his hand and threw it on the ground. Chris lit a Newport, took a few puffs, and paced in front of the police station. He used the bottom of his shoe to put the cigarette out, and placed it behind his right ear.

Entering the station, Chris stopped at the front desk and asked to speak to Detective Sims. A tall, female cop escorted him down a long hallway to a holding room. He couldn't help staring at her round ass as he followed closely behind her.

Chris took a seat on a cold metal chair. He sat there with his hands folded, praying to God that if he got through this one he would leave hustling alone and focus on having a family and doing things the right way. If there was one day that he needed a blunt, this was it. Someone had snitched and usually he would be thinking about revenge, but after losing everything he owned he was grateful to still have his family. Chris rested his head in the palms of his hands. He prayed and thought of his family. He jumped when the door slammed. In trudged two plainclothes cops.

"Which one of you is Detective Sims?" he asked.

"Neither one of us is Detective Sims, you punk-ass nigga," the tall, dark-skinned cop said as he eyed Chris up and down. "He ain't here. So you gotta deal with us." He slapped Chris in the back of his head with his nightstick. Chris started bleeding and instantly became angry.

"What the fuck is your problem?" Chris yelled and jumped up from the table.

"Sit," he said. He pushed Chris back in the seat, causing him to hit his still healing shoulder. Chris was holding his head and blood was dripping down the back of his shirt.

"I know you had something to do with that shooting in the projects," the white cop said as he lit a cigarette and blew the smoke in his face. Chris coughed.

"Fuck you, man. I don't know what you're talking 'bout." Not only was his shoulder killing him, but the back of his head was throbbing.

"You know exactly what I'm talking about. Your boy Reds already tipped us off," he said.

Chris started to get nervous. He was trying to remain calm and keep his cool, so he gave a slight smile.

"Man, I don't know what you talking about," he said again and folded his hands on the table.

The white cop slapped Chris in the face. "Boy, don't play games with me. We know you shot Michael Johnson." His breath smelled of stale coffee.

"Fuck you!" Chris yelled. He started to lose himself for a minute before calming down. "Like I said, I don't know what you talking about."

When Chris next looked up at the clock on the wall it was already a little past two AM. He had been in the holding room for well over twelve hours. They were still trying to break him, but he managed to keep his cool. His hair was matted with dried blood, his face was swollen, and his shoulder ached.

The officers paced in front of Chris. They knew that they would have to let him go. They had no real evidence against him. There were only rumors of who was involved in the shooting, and in the projects snitching meant risking your own life or the lives of your family, so no one would speak up. The black cop threw a cup of warm coffee in Chris's face and walked out of the room. The white

cop leaned on the table and stared Chris in the eyes as if
he could kill him at that very moment.

"You better watch yourself because when you slip up,
I'm going to haul your black ass off to prison. And I know
you will. You niggers are all the same. You like killing your
own people." The white cop stood up straight and before
he turned to walk out of the room he said, "Oh, yeah,
you're free to go."

A feeling of relief swept over Chris. He wiped his face
with the sleeve of his shirt. By the time he left the police
station it was just about three in the morning. He was hun-
gry and needed a place to wash up and get dressed. His
shirt was sticking to his body from the dried up blood. He
didn't want to go to his mom's house because if he came
through the door looking the way he did, it would just
worry her. He drove over to Brandon's house and buzzed
his apartment from the lobby. When he answered you
could tell that he was still asleep.

"Hello," he said, yawning into the phone.

"Yo, man, let me in."

"Aight."

When Chris got up to the apartment he could see that
Brandon had company. There was a pair of black lace
panties on the couch. He picked them up, smelled the
crotch, and then flung them on the floor. Taking off his
shirt, which was covered in blood, he turned on the TV.
His cell phone rang and he picked it up without looking
to see who it was.

"Hello," Chris said. He continued to flick through the
channels.

"Why haven't you called me?" Kane whined. "I saw the
news."

Chris was startled when he heard Kane's voice. He
missed Kane and wanted to see him, but he had promised

himself that he would do right by Tracy, so he acted like he didn't care.

"I was busy, nigga. Stop questioning me. And who told you to come past the office? I told you to never, ever come past there."

"I was worried about you."

"Look, it's over. Don't fuckin' call me no more!" Chris said.

"What you mean it's over? I gave you two years and you telling me it's over!" Kane was yelling at the top of his lungs. "Fuck you, Chris. I thought we were going to be together!"

"Well it's over, and I don't know why you thought we was going to be together. You's a fuckin' man, and I'm a man." Chris tried to keep his voice low so that he would not wake Brandon. "Look, don't call me no more. I'm staying with Tracy." And then Chris hung up the phone and went into the bathroom to take a shower.

Chapter 4

Baby Momma Drama

Brandon was sitting on the couch watching TV by the time Chris returned from his shower. Chris felt like a new man. Besides the fact that his shoulder was still healing and his face was a little fucked up, he felt good. He knew the cops were going to be watching him, but he wasn't worried about that. As long as he kept his nose clean, he would be cool. Chris had work to do. In order to leave hustling alone he needed to beef up his artist intake at the label. So he decided that it was time to go head hunting.

"B, get dressed. We need to find new heads for the label."

Brandon rolled his eyes. He wasn't feeling about business right now. It was still early and he was tired from staying out last night with Mia. She was still asleep, and he planned on going back into the bedroom and joining her.

"Man, I'm tired. Why don't you go, and I'ma meet up with you later?"

"Aight. I'll let you know what the deal is tonight. We need to hit the club and celebrate."

"Celebrate what?" Brandon asked.

"Celebrate my exit from the game," he replied with a straight face.

At that comment Brandon doubled over with laughter. Chris's face started to become flushed.

"Nigga, I'm serious. I'm out the game," he said.

"Just like you were last year and the year before that? Every time the streets get hot, ya ass always talking that shit," he said.

Even though Brandon was clowning Chris a little, he saw that Chris was truly serious this time. Chris had gotten into shit with the law before, but never to this degree. He was now homeless, and the main suspect for an attempted murder wrap. Brandon wiped the smile off his face and became serious himself.

"Hey, Chris, look, man, I believe you. I'm glad you finally see things the way I have for years. You're twenty-five years old, and it's time to leave that shit alone and get serious about life."

"Look, man, keep that preaching shit to ya self. I got work to do."

Chris grabbed his car keys and left. He got off the elevator and walked toward the parking lot. As he approached the car, he noticed someone standing beside it smoking a cigarette. Chris patted his back pocket for his .45. He had left it under the passenger's seat. He slowly walked up to the car and there was Kane looking as if he had been out there waiting for him all night. He had cold in his eyes, and his lips were chapped. He was surprised Kane remembered where Brandon lived. He'd only taken him there once before, and that was to pick up mail while Brandon was out of town on business. Chris sat on the hood of the car and waited for Kane to start talking.

"What do you mean it's over?" Kane began as he lit another cigarette, his hand trembling from nerves. "You just gonna throw two years out like that?"

"I told you it's over. I'm staying with Tracy, and that's it. Now get off my fuckin' car!" Chris jumped off the hood and opened the driver's door. Before he could get in the car Kane shattered the window with a brick. Chris pushed Kane to the ground before walking back toward the building.

Chris was already thinking about what he was going to tell Tracy about her car. He knew this was going to start some drama between the two of them once she found out her window was busted.

"Fuck you, Chris!" Kane yelled while he jumped up from the ground and started kicking the car.

Chris never looked back. He couldn't help thinking that he had made a big mistake. Kane had become the most important person in his life until now. He wanted Kane, but he wanted his family more. Brandon was in the hall wearing only boxers and a pair of slippers when Chris stepped off the elevator.

"I need your car," Chris said.

"What happened out there?" Brandon asked, trying to read the expression on Chris's face.

"The car is fucked up," he answered, looking down at the floor. "So I need to use yours. I'll be back in enough time for us to hit the club."

"What happened?" Brandon asked while opening his apartment door to grab the keys off the kitchen counter. "One of the neighbors said someone busted the window of the car."

"Yeah, some crazy-ass bitch I just cut off," Chris said uneasily.

"You need me to walk with you downstairs?" Brandon asked as he handed Chris the keys to his car.

"NAW . . . NAW . . . I'm cool," Chris quickly responded.

Grabbing the keys, Chris made his way back to the elevator. The last thing he needed was for Brandon to find

Kane outside having a faggot tantrum. Chris managed to leave the parking lot this time without any sign of Kane. This whole thing had fucked up his day. He couldn't think straight because he never knew when Kane might show up. If anybody found out that he was fucking with a nigga, his street rep would be done.

Chris drove around for what seemed like hours. Kane kept calling his phone and leaving messages. Chris finally got tired of hearing his phone ring, so he chucked the phone out the car window. He hurried to the Radio Shack at Progress Plaza and grabbed another phone with a new number. He was finally able to breathe knowing that Kane no longer had his number and had no way to reach him.

Chris called Tracy and let her know someone had tried to break in her car and had busted the window. She was upset at first, but Chris was so reassuring that everything was going to be OK, she soon calmed down.

The day was wasted. The sun had fallen and a warm day gave way to a breeze that cooled the city. It was nearly summer and the streets were packed. There were niggas hanging on every corner of North Philly shooting dice and grinding. The young bulls were so busy chasing ass that money was being neglected. They were too busy pulling half-ass naked bitches looking for a good time.

Chris rode past Blumberg to holla at his young bull about this rapper named Potts that he kept hearing about. This dude was said to be raw on the mic and that was just what he needed. He got the word that the nigga Potts could be found at the King Center, so he rolled over to Cecil B. Moore and parked on the corner.

He could see a crowd of people standing around on the basketball courts. He walked through the playground until he reached the courts. There were two niggas battling in the middle of the circle. After Chris stood there for a good twenty minutes, he knew which nigga was Potts. The bull had a swagger about him. His style was edgy and he had the attitude to go right along with it. Chris definitely needed Potts added to his roster.

After the battle was over Chris strolled up to the bull Potts and introduced himself. They shook hands and walked out of the playground toward the Chinese store. The streetlights flickered on as they stood on the corner. Chris rolled a blunt, lit it, and took a few puffs before passing it to Potts.

"I like ya style," Chris said. "I might want to add you to my roster."

Potts held the Philly between his lips while he dug in his right pocket for his demo.

"This is my latest shit," he said, handing the demo to Chris as he continued to puff on the blunt, which was just about a stub now.

"So is this where I can find you?" Chris asked. He slid the demo in his back pocket as he did with almost everything that was important to him.

"Yeah. I'm out here battlin' niggas every day. This is what I do." Potts laughed. "I make niggas run home to mommy."

Chris looked Potts up and down. He was straight hood. He had on a fresh pair of Air Forces and a white T. A NY fitted hat covered his eyes, and a diamond Jesus piece dangled from his platinum chain. He was everything Chris had decided to leave alone in the game.

"So why they call you Potts?" Chris asked.

"Because I smoke and sell more pot than any other nigga in the streets," he answered with a smirk. "I used to run with these white boys out Fishtown and they gave me the name. It just stuck, know what I mean?"

Chris laughed dryly.

"Well, we will see. I'ma get at you in a week," Chris said as he walked off. He dialed Brandon to see if they were still hitting the club.

"Hello," Brandon answered, panting heavily.

"B, you still comin' out tonight?" Chris asked. He could hear rumbling in the background.

"Naw, man, I'm kind of into something."

"You takin' that bitch Mia serious, huh?"

Chris was feeling jealous. He knew Mia was a freak. Brandon had never been into any bitch like that before. It was kind of sickening. He had lost his playa card and they hadn't even been seeing each other long. Chris could only imagine how good the pussy was for Brandon to be all caught up.

"Yo, I'll catch up with you tomorrow. Oh, and Tracy called the office for you."

"Aight, man. I'll bring your car back later." Chris hung up and made his way to his mother's house. Tracy and Ms. Ruth were sitting on the porch talking when he walked up.

"We were wondering when you were coming home," Ms. Ruth said.

"Everything is fine," he responded and walked in the house to check on the baby. He was sleeping on the couch.

Chris walked upstairs to his bedroom and turned on the light. His mother insisted that he keep a room at her house. He was always going to be her little boy, and when he needed a place to stay, his room would always be there. Chris's room was decorated just like it was when he was a child. There were pictures of his favorite rappers all over the room. He had Jay-Z, Nas, and Fifty on one wall, and Jadakiss, and the whole State Property crew on the other wall.

He walked over to his dresser, took off his Rolex, and picked up the *XXL* magazine lying on the dresser. He sat down on the loveseat beside his bed and began flipping through the pages. Suddenly he stopped flipping the pages in shock. There was a picture of Mia and Brandon standing with their featured artist, Bré. He was confused. Brandon hadn't told him about this article. He skimmed the page and then threw the book at the wall.

Chris was fuming. He had found Bré and signed her. Brandon didn't know shit about talent. The article had the nerve to mention Brandon and Mia as the hottest couple to be watched in the industry.

Brandon was supposed to be Chris's nigga. Maybe Brandon just forgot to mention the article, and those magazines always exaggerated their stories. Chris calmed down and convinced himself that he was overreacting, and Brandon was just handling business for the label.

A little while later Tracy walked in the room and began taking off her clothes. Chris watched her as she peeled off her Seven jeans to reveal her Vicky's. He loved her in boy shorts. She put a robe around her petite body and went to the kitchen to get a glass of water.

Tracy looked just as fine as she did when they met. Her body was perfect. Her full hips and thighs complemented her small frame. At a B cup she had the perfect size chest. Chris liked his women well proportioned, except in the ass area. He liked their asses big and their waists small. Chris would stab anything moving, but when he looked for a chick he was going to fuck with like that, they needed to be within the guidelines.

Chris could never pinpoint what made him stray from Tracy. She was a beautiful, black woman with flawless skin, a ghetto booty, and a face that was full of innocence. She looked as if she had just turned twenty-one and she was just about twenty-five now. Her lips were small, but full, and her eyes wide and bright. Tracy never wore makeup, because she didn't need it.

When Tracy returned to the bedroom, Chris followed her every movement as she moved about the room. She was fine and he knew that like him, she could have anyone she wanted. She was indeed a ghetto princess, and she rode out for Chris when he needed her. Tracy had held guns for him and had even made runs out of town to pick up packages with him and his niggas.

"Come here," he said.

She came over and stood in front of him. He pulled her down on the bed and climbed on top of her. He kissed her sweetly on the lips and uncovered her chocolate brown body. She was excited by every touch. It had been almost a year since they had sex. Tracy was always mad, and he was too engrossed in his own wants and needs to notice.

"I've missed you," she spoke softly into his ear. They began groping each other all over. Tracy ran her hands up and down his back, taking care not to touch his shoulder. He stopped to take off his clothes. Tracy was lying on the bed with her legs spread wide open, slowly massaging herself. He climbed back on top of her and stared at the tears streaming down her face. She was finally happy. She knew he had decided to be with her, and no one else. He kissed her again.

"I love you, baby," he said.

Chris grabbed her hips and pulled her body toward the end of the bed so that her ass was hanging off. He opened her legs and began to taste her. Tracy was in heaven. He hadn't touched her in so long that she forgot what it felt like. She squirmed around as he bit her over and over again. She grabbed his head and pushed it deeper into the swollen opening between her legs. Sweat poured off her body as she had orgasm after orgasm. Chris turned her over and began eating her all over again. Then he began sucking her toes. She muffled her moaning with a pillow so his mother wouldn't hear.

Tracy pushed Chris back on the bed and started to ride him. He bounced her up and down on top of him, and Chris felt himself about to cum. He held it until Tracy released, and then followed shortly after. This was it. He knew that he had treated her wrong over the last two years, and he had to make it up to her. They fell asleep in each other's arms.

Tracy and Chris spent the whole summer rekindling their relationship. Chris had signed the bull Potts and spent days at a time in the studio with him while he was recording. His album hit the shelves two months later. Chris was finally eating the legal way. After he proposed to Tracy, things had been different. They did family things together, and every time they had an argument Tracy would look down at the four-carat platinum engagement ring and remind herself that she had finally won.

Chris no longer thought about Kane. He was lost memory, a skeleton in his closet that he no longer cared about. He rented a small two-bedroom apartment for the three of them on Seventeenth and Girard. Chris and Tracy spent many happy nights in that apartment together laughing, talking, watching their son grow, and making love.

Chris's family life wasn't the only thing on the positive swing. Potts's record was tearing up the charts. Niggas from all over was feeling him. In a matter of months Indigo Records had a name for itself on the streets and in the industry. Chris and Brandon were now working out of New York as well as Philly. Brandon handled most of the projects coming out of New York, and Chris held down the Philly office.

Chris and Brandon were driving back from a long week in Manhattan after a meeting with Epic Records to talk about merging Indigo with that company. Chris wasn't feeling the idea, but Brandon was convinced that it would be in their best interest. Chris still felt that it was a bad plan, but he went along for the meeting anyway to see what they were talking about. The meeting ended with Chris walking out and Brandon apologizing for his partner's actions. Brandon was annoyed, but Chris didn't care. They wanted to take almost seventy percent of their earnings, and he wasn't about to line another nigga's pockets with that type of cash.

"You ain't have to walk out like that," Brandon said. "That was unprofessional."

"Fuck being professional. That nigga ain't getting no seventy percent from me."

"You not thinking, man. We could make major money with Epic, Chris."

"I ain't gonna let them tell me when to eat and shit. We made this business, and I ain't givin' them that type of control or that type of money."

"Man, you just cost us a lot of money," Brandon said as he pulled up to Chris's apartment.

"We makin' good money now," Chris said. "We don't need some big label telling us what to do."

When Chris got out of the car he noticed four big boxes by the curb with what looked like his clothes inside. He walked over to the boxes and peeped inside. They were his clothes. He could tell from the yellow Polo boxers that lay at the top of the pile. Chris was clueless. He had no idea why Tracy would pull this type of stunt. Things had been good for months now. They had even set a date for the wedding, and would be sending invitations out by the end of the year.

Brandon waited a moment before lowering the passenger side window and yelling out to Chris.

"Yo, man, you want me to wait?" It wouldn't have been the first time Chris and Tracy went through a breakup. Brandon figured that meant he'd have a roommate for a while.

Chris almost did ask him to hang around, but he had a strange feeling that he might regret that later.

"Naw, man, it's cool. I'ma go talk to her. I'll just get at you lata." With that, Brandon pulled off.

Chris pulled out his key to let himself in the apartment, but it didn't work. She had changed the locks. He rang the bell and Tracy appeared in the doorway. She took one step forward and closed the door behind her. Her eyes were red from crying. He tried to touch her and she pulled away.

"What's wrong wit you?" he asked. "Why did you change the locks and why is my shit on the curb?" Tracy opened the door without answering.

Chris walked into the apartment and stopped in his tracks. Kane was sitting on the living room couch with his hands in his lap. Chris gave Kane a look that told Kane he would most likely soon be a dead man. He quickly looked away from Chris.

"I know everything!" Tracy yelled. "I can't believe that you was cheatin' on me all this time with a nigga!"

"Baby, wait. . . ." Chris felt ashamed. He didn't know what to say, but he knew he couldn't lose Tracy.

"No, Chris, you been fuckin' a nigga behind my back for two years. You a faggot!"

Chris smacked her in the face. It was an instant reaction to her harsh yet truthful words. She ran into their bedroom and took his .45 from under the mattress.

"Baby, I'm sorry," he said. "I didn't mean to hit you." As Chris started toward her, Tracy pulled the gun from behind her back and aimed it at his forehead.

"Tracy, baby, put down the gun," he said calmly.

"Fuck you, Chris!" she shouted.

"Baby, please, I love you. I never meant to hurt you. I left him alone months ago," he said. "I want us to be a family. I still want you to be my wife."

The gun fell to the floor and she collapsed in his arms. Tracy's fairytale life seemed to be coming to a quick close.

"How could you, Chris? How could you?" she asked as she cried into his chest.

Kane stood up and began easing his way toward the door. Chris pushed Tracy away, picked up the gun, and aimed it at Kane.

"Why did you come here?" he asked. "Why are you trying to break up my family?"

"I need you, too," Kane pleaded. "I need you in my life."

Chris cocked the gun and started moving toward Kane. "Get the fuck outta here!" he said. "If I ever see you near here again, I swear I'm gonna fuckin' kill you."

Kane hurried to the door and took one last look at Chris. His expression was hollow. He could tell that Chris meant business.

Tracy had run into the bedroom to pack her clothes. Chris stood in the doorway and watched as she stuffed her and the baby's clothes into three big trash bags.

"Where are you going?" he asked.

"I'm leaving," she said, her face still streaked from crying.

"Baby, please don't leave," Chris begged. "I know I fucked up."

"I've taken so much shit from you over the last two years, and I can't take anymore, especially this." She finished stuffing the bags and stood face to face with Chris, who was blocking the door. He would not move. He couldn't move. Losing Tracy meant losing his life.

"You can't leave me," he said. His eyes started to water and his voice was cracking. "I love you . . . and my son . . . our family," he begged.

"Please move. You are only making this harder. I just need some time to think things over."

"Where are you going?" he asked.

"To my sister's house. Little Chris is already there," she said flatly as she passed by him.

Once Tracy reached the front door, she threw the keys in Chris's face, slammed the door to the apartment, quickly loaded the car, and drove off. Chris took a look around the apartment. There was no Tracy, no Little Chris, and no family.

As Chris stood in the middle of the silent living room, he looked at the picture of his family on the mantle. They had taken family portraits this summer for the first time. Chris was so excited when he saw how good they came out that he kept a picture on him at all times. This was his family and he loved them.

Plopping down on the couch, he blankly stared at the TV, which was turned off. He was out of ideas. He grabbed Little Chris's Teddy bear off the couch next to him and held it in his lap.

Kane had fucked up everything. Chris needed to focus. He had never been in a situation like this before. He was usually the one who had the upper hand. Now Tracy had the opportunity to string him along like a puppy, and he couldn't do anything about it, except deal with it. He didn't have Kane or Tracy. Chris had never been alone before. He always had someone to lean on.

He dialed Brandon and asked him to drop him off at his mother's house. At least he wouldn't be alone there.

Chapter 5

Gettin' Back to Business...

Brandon was at the gas station when Chris called him for a ride. He was still pissed off about Chris fucking up the deal with Epic. Chris could be stupid at times, and that had been one of them.

When Brandon pulled up to the apartment building Chris was sitting on the steps. Brandon got out of his SUV and helped Chris load his clothes into the back. They both jumped in and Brandon pulled off. Brandon could sense that something was terribly wrong, but he didn't feel like asking what was going on. Chris sat silently during the whole ride staring out the window. He seemed to be in another world, which was fine by Brandon. As soon as Brandon dropped off Chris, he dialed Mia.

"Hello," she answered.

"Hey, baby, wassup? I'm on my way over."

"I'll see you when you get here," she said and hung up the phone.

He stopped by the bar and bought a bottle of Merlot. Mia had become a serious bill and Brandon was running low on cash. He barely made his mortgage payment the previous month. That deal with Epic would have paid a hefty advance, and he needed that money. Although being with Mia was starting to pay off, it was still putting a strangle on his cash flow. The expensive jewelry and the shopping trips to Bloomies had left his bank account bare. He had been living off of credit cards for over four months now. It was time for him to flip the script and have her spend some cash on him. Brandon knew just what to do to put a lock on her and her pocketbook.

The terrace door was cracked when he walked into her apartment. Mia was standing outside smoking a cigarette and sipping a glass of red wine. She had on a pair of skin-tight True Religion jeans, a white tank top, and a pair of three-inch Prada sandals. Her hair was pulled up in a soft ponytail. She was beautiful. Brandon put the bottle of Merlot in the fridge and joined Mia on the balcony. He could smell her perfume as he kissed her on the cheek.

"I didn't even hear you come in," she said as she continued to sip her drink.

"The door was already open. I have something for you, baby."

Brandon pulled her into the apartment, took the glass out of her hand, and placed it on the kitchen counter. He slowly began taking off her clothes until she was in only her bra and panties. Picking her up, he placed her on the counter and pulled her panties down around her ankles, letting them fall to the floor. Brandon was at full erection.

He pulled Mia's hair out from her ponytail, and it fell to frame the shape of her face. She had let her hair grow out since they first met, and it suited her well. Unfastening her bra, he stepped back to look at her. She was perfect. Mia was the one. He needed her in so many ways.

Mia began playing with herself while Brandon undressed. She was driving him mad the way she kept stroking her pussy and moaning from self pleasure. Brandon watched as she made herself cum. He grabbed her naked body from the counter and bent her over the arm of the couch. Entering her from behind, Mia began to squirm from pleasure. They moved together back and forth, moaning and enjoying each other's bodies. Mia came and Brandon quickly followed her with an orgasm of his own.

When Mia got up to take a shower, Brandon made his way to the bedroom and turned on the radio. Kanye West's "Slow Jamz" was playing. He loved that song, and he admired Kanye for the type of hustler he was. Brandon made moves like Kanye did. They were both from the ghetto, and like Kanye, Brandon had also made it out. Brandon knew he was destined to be great. He had made Indigo Records grow financially. They were getting offers from big labels on the regular. That Epic deal was worth four million. That was enough for him to pay off all his bills and live lavishly.

There was just one thing in the way of his success. Chris was becoming a problem. He was a talent scout, and that was it. He didn't know anything about real business. Brandon was the one who graduated summa cum laude from an Ivy League college, and because of that Chris had always trusted him when it came to the financial side of the business. But ever since Chris left the streets alone, he had become more active in the business, and it was driving Brandon crazy.

After Mia finished her shower, she got in the bed next to Brandon and lay on his chest.

"So where is my surprise?" she asked, her eyes filled with excitement.

"Oh, I almost forgot." Brandon went into the living room and returned with a small gift-wrapped box with cascading ribbons. She opened the box carefully, and inside lay set of keys. Her eyes widened.

"I wanted you to be able to be with me whenever you

wanted." He kissed her on the cheek and lay back down. Mia was happy. They had been messing around for six months now, and even though they had agreed to be exclusive, the keys really meant that they were officially a couple. She jumped on top of him and kissed him sweetly on the lips.

"I love you," she blurted out.

Mia was embarrassed. She had never told any dude that. She looked deeply into his eyes, searching for a response. Brandon was stunned. He didn't know what to say. He did know that if he said the wrong thing, it would fuck up everything. He didn't love Mia, but he did like her a lot. Brandon looked her in the eyes and delivered the response that she wanted.

He spoke softly in her ear. "I love you, too, baby."

He figured that if he told her what she wanted to hear, it would make shit flow easy. Mia tried to fight back her tears. She was truly happy that she had met Brandon. She was tired of messing with this one and that one. The last six months had been a dream for her. He was everything she ever wanted—sexy, smart, and a true gentleman.

Brandon felt somewhat guilty inside. He knew that he could love Mia, but right now that was the last thing on his mind. She was a business venture for him. He needed her, and so he decided he would do whatever he needed to make and keep her happy, and right now her falling asleep in his arms did the trick.

Early the next morning Brandon was awakened by the smell of freshly made pancakes. He dragged himself to the kitchen and took a seat on the stool next to Mia. She had prepared breakfast for him, something she had never done before. She cooked one hell of a meal. He had bacon, eggs, grits, pancakes, a side of home fries, and to top it all off, a tall glass of orange juice.

"Thank you for the meal." He kissed her and headed for the shower. Mia cleared the table and took out the trash. She had ordered the meal from a takeout joint. Truth was that Mia couldn't cook. She burned everything she tried to make. She came back from the incinerator and washed her hands. She didn't want Brandon to know that she didn't know her way around the kitchen. A man always wanted a girl who could cook, and a freak in the bedroom.

Mia sat on the bed and waited for Brandon to finish his shower. Brandon returned to the room naked with water dripping off him. She handed him a towel to dry off.

"So what are we doing today?" she asked.

"Well I need to head over to the office and handle some paperwork." He pulled up his pants and fastened them. "I'll meet you at Zanzibar for lunch around one."

After finishing getting dressed, Brandon grabbed his keys, kissed Mia good-bye, and headed for his car.

When Brandon reached the office parking lot his cell went off. It was a text message from Vikki saying to meet at her house in a half hour. Brandon hadn't seen her in several months, ever since he took her to the club to make Mia jealous. They talked on the phone a lot, but that was it. He pulled out of the parking lot and got to Vikki's house in forty minutes.

Her kids were at school, so she had time to play. Brandon wanted to make this short and quick. He looked under the passenger seat for his emergency condom stash. He packed three in his jacket pocket and started toward the house.

Vikki had a nice crib. She lived in Ardmore, a suburb not far from the city, so it was easy to get to, plus since she was located in the outskirts of Philly, he never had issues with running into her while he was with other females. He walked around the back of the house and Vikki was lying poolside in a gold Dior bathing suit with matching sandals. Her hair was wisped back in a loose French braid. Vikki had an indoor pool. She didn't care what time of year it was, she always liked to have on the least amount of clothes possible. She looked at Brandon from across the pool, untied her bikini top, dropped it to the ground, and slowly submerged into the water.

"Do you want to go for a swim?" she asked while holding up the bottoms to her suit and throwing them on the side of the pool.

She was naked and Brandon was ready. There was nothing like getting your dick sucked underwater. He stripped down as fast as he could and jumped in, splashing Vikki in the face. He kissed her as if she was the only girl in the world. Vikki disappeared under the water and began sucking his dick. Brandon could not hold it in. He quickly busted in her mouth.

Jumping out of the pool, he grabbed a condom out of his jacket pocket. Vikki lay waiting patiently on the marble floor. He pulled her legs up as high as he could and entered her wet pussy. Brandon stroked her until she came. When he was finished he got up to use the bathroom, and noticed that it was already one-thirty. He took a quick shower, gathered his clothes, and began to get dressed. He needed to meet Mia for lunch, and he would have to hurry if he was going to be on time.

Vikki lay naked on the lounge chair drinking a glass of wine.

"Leaving already?" she asked, sipping slowly.

"I've got a meeting with a new artist, and I'm late," he said while looking at his watch. "I'll call you later." Hurrying out the door, Brandon jumped in his car and headed toward Center City. He was trying to gather himself. He didn't want Mia to get suspicious and he wanted to make sure he always kept Vikki happy. He needed Vikki and him to be cool, because when he needed cash, Vikki always came through and blessed him with a couple dollars. She had paid his mortgage last month without asking any questions.

Brandon was stuck in traffic.

"Shit," he said. "What the fuck was I thinking messing around with Vikki?" He was talking to himself. Brandon knew that something just as small as being late for lunch could hurt his chances with Mia. He dialed her cell phone.

"Hey, baby," she said. "Where are you?"

"I got caught up with a potential artist, but I'm on my way." Brandon was weaving in and out of traffic, trying to get to the restaurant as quickly as possible.

"I'll see you when you get here," she said. "I have some good news."

It was almost two by the time Brandon made it to the restaurant. He could see the disappointment in her eyes, but she acted as if nothing was wrong. Brandon sat down across from her as she continued to eat her salad.

"Sorry I'm late," he said. "I lost track of time."

Mia stared at Brandon. Her smile quickly turned to a look of disgust.

"What is that on your shirt?" she asked.

Brandon looked down and there was a smudge of red lipstick on his shirt. He didn't know where it had come from, and he started to panic.

"I have no idea," he said calmly, hiding his panic.

Mia pulled out a fifty-dollar bill and left it on the table. She got up and walked out of the restaurant. Brandon followed right behind her. Mia walked as fast as she could. She couldn't believe this was happening. How could he do this to her? Brandon grabbed her shoulder and she pulled away.

"Don't touch me. I can't believe you," she hissed as she continued to walk in front of him.

"I didn't do anything. I promise," he said. "Why would I try to hurt you like that?" He grabbed her arm and pulled her toward him. "I am telling you the truth. I don't know how it got there." His heart was beating fast. How could he have fucked up like this? He replayed the session with Vikki over and over in his mind, searching for an answer. She must have set him up. There was no way he would have let something like this ever happen.

"Leave me alone," Mia said as she pushed him away.

Mia began walking swiftly down Walnut Street until she reached her building. Brandon lost sight of her in the crowd.

He walked toward the nearest bar and ordered a double shot of gin. The piano bar was quite crowded for a Wednesday afternoon. He took a seat in the corner of the room and sipped his drink. He dialed Mia on his cell to see if she would pick up. There was no answer. Brandon was fucked. He was out of ideas. He called back and left a message.

He decided just to go home. When Brandon opened the door to his apartment he noticed the light in his bedroom was on. He came in, dumped his jacket on the couch, and grabbed a bottle of Heineken from the fridge. When he turned around Mia was standing in front of him.

"Who is it going to be, huh? Me or her?" Mia folded her arms in front of her chest.

"I swear there is no one else." He got down on his knees and looked up at Mia. Her eyes were glassy.

"I know you can have any bitch you want," she said. Mia was a little insecure about being with him. She knew that pussy came easy to him, and especially now that the record label had gained major recognition.

"Mia, I'm on my knees. I want you," Brandon said as he

got up from the floor and brushed off his pants. "You are going to have to trust me. Why would I give you the key to my house if I was fucking with someone else?"

Mia stared at him as if she could read his soul. Brandon did have a point. Why would he give her the key if he was messing around? She wanted to trust him. She wanted to be with him, but she wanted to be the only one. Mia excused herself from his company and went to the bathroom. She looked at her appearance in the mirror. She had to get it together. This was the second time he had tested her. First it was with that white bitch at the club, and now this. Mia decided that she was going to give him a run for his money this time. She smiled at her reflection and rejoined him in the living room.

Taking a deep breath, Mia opened her purse and handed him the keys to his apartment. Brandon was stunned. He didn't know what to say. She let herself out of his apartment and waited in the lobby for a cab.

The following weeks were a blur for Brandon. He didn't talk to Mia for almost a month. He got word through Sam that Mia went out of the country on business. It seemed like everything in his life was falling apart. He and Chris had been clashing on a daily basis since Brandon had asked him to reconsider the offer from Epic. Chris would not budge, and Brandon felt like Chris was starting to overstep his bounds, and trying to control everything.

The two friends hadn't hung out in a long time. Chris was always out chillin' with Potts, and Brandon was flying solo. Ever since Tracy left, Chris spent almost all of his time at work. He was there before Brandon the majority of the time, and he had the nerve to try to leave Brandon a "to do" list. Brandon was sick of his shit. He had promised himself that once the contracts were up with the current artists, he was going to leave. He was tired of being partners with Chris.

Finally one day Sam called Brandon to let him know that Mia was back in town. She had been gone for over two months and had spent Christmas in the Dominican Republic. He called ahead to the doorman to see if she had arrived, and he was told she wasn't yet back to the apartment. Mia might have given back the key to his apartment, but he still had hers. The last few months had been hell for him. He hated to admit it, but he really did miss her.

Brandon hurried over to her apartment and arranged the five-dozen long-stemmed, yellow roses he had ordered. He bought two bottles of Moet and made arrangements at the Metropolitan, the most expensive restaurant in the city. It was, after all, New Year's Eve. He was wearing his most expensive black Prada suit with a dark red shirt and a black tie. He pulled two glasses out of the cabinet and placed them on the counter. Looking around the kitchen, he began to reminisce about all the good sex they had shared there.

"What are you doing here?" Mia asked a few minutes later as she dragged her luggage through the door.

Brandon was startled. He didn't hear her come in. Looking her over, he noticed that she was about three shades darker than before. Mia had on a Juicy sweat suit that hugged her in all the right places, and a pair of Pumas. He wanted to grab her, throw her on the bed, and fuck her brains out.

"We need to talk," he said. "I want things to be like they were before." Brandon walked over to her and brushed the hair out of her face. She had missed him too. He hugged her tightly.

Mia searched Brandon's eyes as to question his motives;

she could tell that he truly did want her back. Plus she wanted him more than he knew right now.

"So, I take it we are OK now?" he asked. "Because I really missed you."

"I missed you, too."

Brandon loosened his tie and sighed with relief.

Mia was acting like nothing had happened. Brandon was a bit confused, but he decided to let sleeping dogs lie. He took another glance at Mia. She looked like she might have picked up a few pounds, but it looked good on her. He hugged her again and grabbed the suitcases to carry them into the bedroom. She followed behind him and closed the bedroom door. Brandon almost let the dinner reservations slip his mind.

"Baby, get dressed. I made dinner reservations for us" he said. "Wear that sexy black dress. You know, the one you wore the first night we met."

"Are you sure you want me to wear that?" she asked. "Last time I wore that dress you had trouble keeping your pants on." She smiled, pulled the dress out the closet, and held it up to her body. Brandon grinned.

"You better not tease me because we may not make it to dinner," he said. "Hurry up and get dressed. The reservation is for seven-thirty."

Mia laid her outfit on the bed and took a shower. She put on her little black Gucci dress and sprayed herself with perfume. Brandon watched as she applied her makeup. Brandon always told Mia that she didn't need any makeup, but she insisted on wearing it.

Once Mia was dressed, they hurried down to the lobby where they were met by a valet. Brandon had rented a 1969 Corvette Stingray for the evening. It was a burgundy two-seater with black leather interior and the cleanest finish you ever saw. Brandon opened the door for Mia, tipped the valet, and headed toward the restaurant. He had booked the best table in the whole joint. They were seated riverside overlooking Penn's Landing. It was a beautiful winter night and they couldn't stop looking at each other. Brandon stared across the table at Mia as she sipped on a glass of red wine.

"You look beautiful tonight," he said. Mia started to blush.

"Thank you," she said. "You don't look half bad yourself."

He laughed. He was caught up in the moment. Brandon was losing focus of his goal. He was really starting to have deep feelings for Mia. She had it all— beauty, brains, and not to mention a phat-ass bank account.

He was trying to focus. Just this evening alone had set him back a good ten grand. He borrowed the money from the escrow account at the label. He figured he could put it back before Chris would notice. Besides, there was no reason for him to check on the account, because Brandon took care of all the books.

Leave it to Mia to order the most expensive meal on the menu. *Who the hell really eats smoked duck,* Brandon wondered. He had one good credit card left. He was up to his eyeballs in debt, and creditors were beginning to call the office. He tried to concentrate on the task at hand. Dinner was nearly over, and the night was still young.

"Dinner was delicious," Mia said, patting her mouth with her napkin. The waiter poured her another glass of wine. She took a sip, pulled out a cigarette, and lit it. Brandon hated that Mia smoked, or any female in general. He gave her a disgusted look, and she immediately put it out.

"Let's go," he said. "We have somewhere else to be."

Mia gathered her fur coat and purse. They were on their way to New York to the 40/40 Club. Brandon was flying down the New Jersey turnpike, swerving in and out of traffic.

"This car really handles well," Mia said. "Let's see how fast it can go." She squeezed Brandon's hand while he put the pedal to the floor. He had to be doing well over a hundred. Mia loved the forcefulness of his driving. She started to become aroused.

"I have a surprise for you, too," she said. Mia unzipped his pants as he continued to drive, and began sucking his dick. Brandon pressed as hard as he could on the pedal. He was the luckiest man on earth. He had one of the hottest models on the scene giving him head in a two-seater. Mia swallowed as he climaxed.

Brandon slowed down as they approached the Manhattan Bridge, and Mia reapplied her MAC lip gloss and fixed her hair. They pulled up to the 40/40 Club around eleven-thirty PM. The crowd was huge, but they walked straight to the Cognac Room. Brandon had rented the room to host a party for the label. All of the artists were there, not to mention Chris. They took a seat on the plush leather couch next to Chris and Potts. Brandon shook Chris's hand.

"I didn't think you two were going to make it," Chris said.

"We left dinner a little late, but I managed to get here before midnight," Brandon said.

"I need to holla at you a little later about some business, aight, man?" Chris asked. "I'm gonna get back wit you. Me and Potts going to mingle with some of these fine-ass broads," Chris said as he watched this thick shorty walk past.

"Aight, I'll catch up with you before the night is over," Brandon said as he shook Chris's hand again. Chris got up and joined Potts at the bar.

Everybody who was anybody was at this party. Most importantly, the media was there. Brandon was psyched. He was finally getting the exposure he wanted. There were major players from all the major magazines. Indigo Records was officially on the map, and everyone knew who he was.

Mia excused herself and walked to the ladies room. Brandon walked over to order another drink when someone tapped him on the shoulder. He turned around and his face went blank. Vikki smiled and kissed him on the cheek. Brandon was beginning to sweat. If Mia caught him talking to Vikki, everything he worked hard for would go up in smoke. He pulled Vikki to the side.

"What are you doing here?" he asked.

"I came to surprise you," she answered. "I wanted to congratulate you on your artist going platinum. Plus it's New Year's Eve."

Brandon looked around, searching the crowd for Mia. He spotted her talking with the reporter of *Complex* magazine. He was playing it too close. Brandon knew that if he told Vikki he was here with someone else, she would make a scene and possibly start a fight. There was too much on the line at this point. He had a room full of media and his main chick was less than ten feet away from his fuck jon. His career was at stake. He had to think fast.

"Let's get out of here," he said. "Go out the back door and meet me out front."

Vikki smiled deviously.

"OK, daddy. Meet out there in ten minutes."

She walked off, and Brandon quickly found the head of security and ordered that Vikki not be admitted back into the bar. He hurried to the bathroom and checked his clothes. Vicki had left red lipstick on his cheek. He wet some tissue and proceeded to wipe it off. Taking one final look at himself, he washed his hands and went to look for Mia. When he found her she was still talking with the reporter.

"Sorry, I'm going to have to steal her from you," he said

to the reporter. He pulled Mia away before she could end the conversation.

It was five minutes till midnight, and Brandon and Mia were getting ready to celebrate their first New Year's Eve together. Brandon gazed at Mia as they started the countdown. They kissed when the clock struck twelve. Confetti dropped from the ceiling, and everyone held their glasses up to toast the new year. After the toast Brandon pulled Mia toward the back exit where the valet was waiting with the car. They pulled around front and there was Vikki standing in the cold with a miniskirt and four-inch heels. She spotted Brandon and Mia at the light and began ranting and raving at the car. Luckily for Brandon, the windows were up.

"Who is that poor girl out here in zero degrees weather with no coat on?" Mia asked. "She keeps screaming at us." The woman looked somewhat familiar to Mia, but Mia couldn't quite place her.

Maybe we have the same hair stylist or something, Mia thought.

Brandon stared straight ahead. He didn't want to make any eye contact with Vikki.

"She seems to be a little crazy," he said.

He sped off as soon as the light changed green and headed back to Philly. He had planned the grand finale of the evening at his place. Brandon had one last surprise for Mia. He had the surprise flown in from L.A. When they reached the apartment door he turned around and gave Mia the key.

"Open the door," he said. "Someone wants to meet you on the other side."

Mia was anxious to see what was waiting on the other side of the door. It had been one of the best nights she had in a long time, so she figured it could only get better. She unlocked the door and handed the keys back to Brandon. She turned around in time for a tiny Yorkie pup to run up to her feet. She picked him up and held him tightly. She was so excited. She had always wanted a dog, but could never have one because she had agreed to no pets in her lease.

"Oh, I love him!" she said.

"He can stay here," Brandon said. He held out the keys to his apartment and handed them to Mia. She grabbed them and went to put them in her purse. Everything was set. He had blown a lot of money trying to make things right after that incident with Vikki. Now all he had to do was make sure it never happened again. Mia lay on the floor beneath the foot of the bed and played with the pup until the wee hours of the morning.

Brandon got up early the next morning and drove to his mother's grave. He visited her two times a year— Mother's Day and New Year's Day. He laid a bouquet of flowers beside her grave and hurried back to the car. It was freezing outside. Brandon pulled his Armani Exchange scully out of his pocket and put it on.

Mia had breakfast on the table when he returned home. He had finally learned that she wasn't much of a cook, but that was one thing Brandon was willing to sacrifice. The eggs were runny and the turkey bacon was burnt.

Oh hell, he thought, *at least she didn't burn the toast.* He was finishing up his breakfast when Mia handed him the phone.

"Hello," Brandon said as he sipped his apple juice.

"B, meet me at the office," Chris said. "It's important."

"Right now?" Brandon asked.

"Yeah, nigga!" Chris said and hung up the phone.

Brandon rushed over to the office. Chris was sitting in the lobby with his hands folded when Brandon arrived.

"What's up?" Brandon asked. "This couldn't have waited until tomorrow?" Chris paused for a moment.

"Naw, man, this couldn't wait. Money is missing from the safe." Chris looked at Brandon, waiting to see what his response would be. "B, there's about nine or ten grand missing."

"Yeah, man, I used it to pay for the party," Brandon replied. He could see the anger building in Chris's face.

"Why didn't you tell me?" His voice was rising.

"Since when did I have to clear everything through you?" Brandon snapped back. They stared each other down.

"I put all my money into this business, and from now on, I want shit to be cleared with me."

Brandon flagged him. He had had enough.

"Whatever, man. I've been handling shit since we started this, and I do believe I am your partner. Now all of a sudden you ready to get ya feet wet and do some work. Fuck you." Brandon reached for the handle of the door and Chris snuck him, punching him in his jaw. Brandon turned around and they began tussling around the office. Papers flew everywhere.

Neither could manage to get the best of the other, so Brandon finally let go of Chris and fixed his clothes.

"I'm outta here," Brandon said.

As Chris tried to catch his breath, Brandon slammed the door and drove back to his place. He was fuming. How dare Chris come at him like that? Brandon worked his ass off to make the label successful. They would have never opened the other office in New York if it wasn't for him. All of a sudden Chris cared about the label? There had been times that he didn't come to work for weeks, and Brandon had covered for him.

Brandon looked in the rearview mirror and noticed that his lip was bleeding. Things had never gotten out of hand with them before. Brandon drove right past his house and headed for the first bar he saw for a drink to calm his nerves.

Chapter 6

Here We Go Again

The pub was bare inside. Besides the barmaid, there was no one else in sight. It was New Year's Day and he was already starting off the year on a bad note. He took a seat near the door and ordered his usual.

"Give me a glass of Seagrams," he said to the barmaid. Brandon took off his hat and placed it on the stool next to him, running his fingers through his curly, dark fade. It was still early in the day and he was already worn out. His body was aching from tussling around, and his lip was slightly busted. Brandon couldn't wait to have the taste of gin rolling around in his mouth.

"Did you hear me? I said give me a glass of Seagrams," he said again, his tone a bit more demanding than before.

She turned around slowly and instantly became startled by how sexy this man was. His dark brown eyes turned her on. She smiled deviously.

"What's your name?" she asked as she topped off his drink.

"Keith," he said. There was no way he was giving another bitch his real name. She didn't know who he was, and he wanted to keep it that way.

The glass slipped from her hand and fell to the floor. She bent over to clean it up, and Brandon stood up from his chair to peep over the bar and admire the view. Her skirt was so short that he could see her ass.

"I'm sorry," she said as she picked up the broken glass and tossed it in the trashcan. "Let me pour you another one."

She leaned over the bar so he could see down her blouse, and she didn't have a bra on. She placed the glass in front of him on a coaster. She continued washing out glasses and putting them on the shelves. Brandon tossed down his gin in one gulp and ordered another. She stopped what she was doing and filled his glass up again.

He was the only customer in the entire bar, and the barmaid kept giving him the eye, so he decided to try his luck.

"So what's a fine woman like you doing working on a holiday?" he asked.

"I need to make some money to pay for college," she said.

"If you had a man like me, you wouldn't have to worry about that."

She blushed. She was really pretty, a natural beauty. Her hair was dyed a bright golden red. She wore a wild, curly afro and big hoop earrings. Her soft pink lipstick complimented her honey brown complexion.

"So what's your name?" he asked.

"Lynn."

"That's pretty," he said. "How old are you?"

"I'm twenty-one, and you?"

"Twenty-five"—he paused for a minute—"twenty-five and a half." He smiled as he lifted the glass to his lips and took a drink. Lynn laughed.

"What's a fine man like you doing in a bar on New Year's Day?" she asked as she looked him over again. His beautiful, black skin made her body tremble. She loved a man with a pretty face and sexy lips.

"I came out to get a drink to celebrate being single," he said.

This caught her interest.

Lynn noticed his jaw. It was slightly swollen and he had a small cut on his lip. She filled a sandwich bag full of ice and gave it to him. He placed the bag on his jaw as Lynn walked around the counter and placed the OUT TO LUNCH sign on the door. After pouring Brandon another glass of gin, she sat on the stool next to him while he nursed his glass.

"So tell me again, what would you do if I was your girl?"

She unbuttoned her shirt and revealed her double-D-sized chest. He was practically drooling. Brandon wanted some of that young, sweet ass. He sat still while she caressed her nipples. Jumping off the bar stool, she grabbed his hand and led him to the back. He followed her through the area marked employees only and stood by the door to look around. There was an old, dingy pullout couch and a floor model TV. She stripped down in front of him, and the sight of her body made him harden immediately. He was ready to beat the pussy up.

She lay on the couch and he ran to the men's bathroom in search of a condom dispenser.

"Yes!" he said aloud. He put in seventy-five cents and pulled the lever.

On his way back to the room he stopped at the bar and grabbed a bucket of ice. Lynn was lying on the couch with her legs wide open when he returned. He took a piece of ice and sucked it as she began playing with her breasts. He took another piece of ice and massaged it against her pussy. She screamed in excitement. The cold sensation made her body quake from pleasure.

Lynn had her clit pierced, and the sight of the barbell drove Brandon practically insane. Brandon backed off and sat on the chair across from the couch. He watched as she played with herself.

"Come here and give daddy some of that young pussy," he said, stroking his dick up and down.

She smiled, got up from the couch, and joined him across the room. Brandon put on the condom and Lynn jumped on his dick and began to ride him hard. The chair was rocking back and forth as he bounced her tight ass up and down on his lap. As they continued to fuck, Brandon learned that Lynn was a stone cold freak. She liked ass shots.

"Put it in my ass, daddy," she moaned. They changed positions and Lynn kneeled in the chair while Brandon put his dick in her ass. The pain from him thrusting back and forth had her on an erotic high. Lynn loved it. She moaned and groaned at the top of her lungs.

"Oh, yeah, baby, I love the way you're fuckin' me."

Brandon was even more turned on than before. It had been so long since he had some young ass that he forgot how nasty it could be. She played with her pussy while he beat it up from the back. Brandon pulled out before he came, took off the condom, and squirted in her mouth. Lynn swallowed and proceeded to suck his dick right after. Brandon knew that she was a keeper. He needed a young chick on his roster, and she was definitely a team player. Lynn was a freak and cute as hell.

When they were finished, Brandon got up, fixed his pants, and walked over to the bar. He wrote his number on a napkin and left.

Since early that morning Mia had been calling him like

crazy. He didn't want to go back home with his face swollen because Mia would just start talking shit about Chris. She didn't really care too much for Chris. She thought he was ignorant and he was too hood for her taste. Mia believed that Brandon would be better off by himself. Chris was just holding him back.

Brandon went straight to the bathroom when he got back to his apartment. He was trying to avoid Mia. She walked in while he was taking his shower and sat on the toilet seat. The shower curtain was clear so she could see the water hit his body as he lathered up.

"Chris called here about five times since you left," she said. "He kept talking about how sorry he was." Mia looked down at her finely manicured hands.

Brandon shook his head and continued to let the warm water trickle down his body.

"Fuck him," Brandon said.

Mia was surprised by his anger. She had never heard him talk bad about Chris, at least not around her.

"What happened?" she questioned, clearly more interested.

Brandon turned off the shower and emerged from behind the curtain. Mia gasped at the site of his swollen jaw.

"We got into a little something at the office," he said and walked out of the bathroom and into the bedroom with Mia on his heels.

"Why were you fighting?" Mia touched his jaw gently, and Brandon pushed her hand away just as gently.

"I'm fine and I'd rather not talk about it."

She decided to change the subject.

"Pack your bags. You need a vacation."

"Are you serious?" Brandon asked as he spread lotion on his legs.

"Our flight leaves in the morning. My treat," she almost

sang and kissed him on the lips. "I'm going home. Meet me there when you're finished packing."

As Mia left Brandon began thinking. He was in no mood to vacation. He had to figure out what he was going to do about the label, and most importantly Chris. Chris was the only family Brandon had, and this whole thing was becoming a disaster. Brandon threw a couple things in his bag. He heard the door open and figured it was Mia. When he looked up it was Chris. He stopped at the doorway of the bedroom and stared at Brandon, who was sitting at the foot of the bed with his hands folded.

"I was out of line," Chris began. "We've been too cool for too long for some shit like this to happen. It's just that I've being going through some shit ever since Tracy left." Brandon could smell the liquor on Chris's breath and his speech was slurred. He was semi-drunk.

"B, you like my brother, man," Chris continued. "I fucked up." Brandon saw tears in Chris's eyes, so he stood and shook Chris's hand.

"Let's just forget about this," Brandon said. "We're family, and family don't do each other like that."

The two embraced and then headed toward the living room. Chris was relieved. He had lost Tracy and Kane, and he didn't want to lose Brandon, too.

"I'm going away for a couple days," Brandon said. "I need time to get my shit right too."

"I'm going to crash here," Chris said. "I don't think I can make it home, and Moms be trippin' when I come there drunk." He plopped down on the sofa and put his feet up on the coffee table.

Brandon took his bag and moved toward the door. He turned around and took one last look at Chris.

"Man, you right, I should have cleared those expenses through you. I'll make sure it never happens again."

Chris only nodded in affirmation and leaned back on the couch to relax.

Brandon hurried to Mia's condo. Mia wasn't there when he arrived, but her brother was sitting in front of the TV eating a huge bowl of cereal and watching *The Real World.* Brandon walked right past him without speaking. He made himself comfortable in the bedroom, looking at all the pictures of Mia on the wall. There was a picture of her first photo shoot for *French Vogue.* Brandon loved that picture of Mia. She had on a skintight black dress and platform sandals. Her hair was wild like Lynn's, and her eyes were soft and vulnerable.

Suddenly he became distracted by a bank statement sitting on the night stand. He had a strong surge of curiosity. Eager to find out how much she was really worth, he rolled over to her side of the bed and decided to take a peek.

As he read the number listed on her bank statement his mouth dropped open from shock. Mia was worth well over three million. He knew she was getting paper, but not to that extent. She lived pretty simply for a chick with that amount of cash flow. She only had one condo and hardly ever spent her own cash. She was used to spending other people's money.

Brandon decided at that moment that he was going to milk the shit out of Mia. With that type of cash, he would never have to work again. He could live life and let her pay for everything.

Brandon's heart began to thump when he heard the front door open. He scrambled to put everything back the way he found it, and he almost tipped over the crystal vase where she kept her fresh yellow roses. Brandon made it back to the bed in just enough time not to get caught. Mia walked in with several bags from the mall.

"I'm sorry, baby, but I had to run out. The mall was having a New Year's sale and I just could not miss that," she said. "Look at the bikini I bought for our trip." She held out a gold Gucci two piece and a matching sarong. She was packing it into her bag when her Blackberry went off. She read the e-mail and frowned.

"We're going to have to postpone the trip," she said. "My manager needs me to come to New York tonight. Apparently my name was mentioned for a role in a film. I hope you're not mad," she said.

"I know you're a busy woman," Brandon said as he kissed her on the cheek. "I'll see you when you get back."

"He's sending a car for me in about an hour. I should be back by tomorrow night."

"Well, I'll see you later. I'll go home and keep the puppy company," he said with a laugh.

He grabbed his bag and took one last look at Mia. Her skin was glowing. She was indeed a beautiful woman, although she had gained a few pounds recently. Brandon wondered what her agent was going to say about the couple of pounds she had put on. She usually stayed on a strict diet, but she had been eating a lot of junk food lately.

Truth be told, Brandon was glad that something had come up. He didn't want to go on that trip anyway. His mind was on Lynn and how much of a solider she was. She took it in the ass and loved it. He had tried it once with Mia and she wouldn't even let him put the tip of his dick in before she started complaining about how much it hurt.

Brandon didn't want to have any more incidents that would mess shit up with Mia, so he decided that he needed to cut off Vikki and every other broad he was messing with. Lynn wasn't really a threat at this point; she didn't even know his real name. Brandon knew at some point he was going to have to cut her, but he wasn't ready to let that

young pussy go just yet. Vikki, on the other hand had a
habit of popping up places. Mia was worth way too much
money to have another episode with Vikki jump off. He
needed to call Vikki on the phone. There was no way he
was going to her house, not after what happened last
night. He decided to call her from the phone booth in the
lobby of his condo building. He was going to change his
cell phone number so he wouldn't have to worry about
her playing on his phone, and he would just go past the
bar where Lynn worked and give her the new number.

"Hello," Vikki answered.

"Hey, it's me," Brandon said flatly.

Her voice automatically jumped ten decibels.

"Why the fuck you leave me outside the club? And then
you told them not to let me back in. Are you crazy? I almost froze to death!" she managed to say in almost one
breath.

"I'm not fucking with you no more," he said.

Her voice started coming back to normal when she
heard that. "What are you trying to say?" she asked. Brandon could hear the begging in her voice. "I'm sorry for
yelling at you. I was just so upset about what happened."

"I can't keep fuckin' with you," he said. "You cause too
many problems. I'll catch you around." He hung up the
phone and headed for the elevators.

Before Brandon even made it all the way in the door he
could hear Chris snoring on the couch. He looked down
and saw that the dog had pissed on his Persian rug. After
trying to clean up the mess, Brandon scooped the dog up
in his hands and locked him in the bathroom for the rest
of the night.

He lay down on his bed and thought about Lynn. He
had promised himself that he would not get caught up
with any other bitches, but he couldn't help himself. She
had the body of a porn star and brains to go along with it.

Lynn was a college girl. He had to trap her ass and keep her under his wing before one of those football or basketball niggas at her school grabbed her up.

The next morning Brandon rushed to the cell phone store to buy a brand new Blackberry. He had always wanted one, but never got around to buying it. He left a message on Mia's cell with the new number. The bar where Lynn worked was about two blocks away. He walked swiftly down Chestnut Street until he reached Twenty-first and walked up one block to Sampson. There were a few people inside when he walked in. Lynn wasn't there. He walked over to the bar and ordered a drink. The barmaid sat a glass in front of him.

"Is Lynn working today?" he asked.

"She's off today," the barmaid replied, "but she did say that she may stop by."

Brandon took the napkin from under his drink and wrote his new number on it. He stopped himself before he wrote his real name.

"Can you give her this and tell her Keith stopped by?" He then folded the napkin in half and handed it to barmaid. He hoped Lynn did stop by, because he was anxious to meet back up with her.

The barmaid grabbed the napkin and put it in the pocket of her apron

"I'll make sure she gets it."

Brandon finished his drink and headed to the office. He had business to handle. He needed to fix up the documentation from the party to make it look like he had spent ten grand. He created several receipts on his computer for the file. That way Chris would have the receipts and he didn't have to worry about this ever coming up again. He printed them out, filed them, and finished checking his messages. Now that the majority of their business was handled in New York, the office in Philly was quiet. He cleaned up the mess they made yesterday and was getting ready to leave when Tracy came by looking for Chris. She had lost weight since the last time Brandon had seen her. Her cheeks were sunken in and she had dark circles around her eyes. Her hair, which was always done, looked dry and dull.

"Is Chris around?" she asked.

"No, he didn't come in today." Brandon was not about to tell her where he was. He didn't want to be a part of the dumb shit Tracy was capable of putting niggas through.

"Can you tell him I stopped by?" she asked. "And let him know that I need to talk to him."

"I'll let him know when I see him."

Tracy pulled a picture of Little Chris out of her Dior bag.

"Give him this." It was a picture of Little Chris with Santa Claus. She pulled the door open and left without another word.

Brandon felt kind of bad for Tracy. She seemed to be out of it. He never did find out why those two stopped dealing with each other. He just figured it finally came to an end. She was sick of Chris staying out all night and being with other girls, and Chris was sick of her nagging and spying on him all the time.

Brandon's thoughts were interrupted by his cell phone chirping. A text message from Lynn told him to meet her at her apartment in fifteen minutes. She left her address and he sent her a text back, locked up the office, and drove over to her spot.

Lynn lived on Twentieth and Girard, which was right near the office. Brandon wondered why he never saw her in passing before. He also realized that he needed to be careful about her finding out where he worked. If she knew that piece of information, then she would be lingering around all the time, and trying to pop up unannounced.

He didn't need any more incidents, especially at this stage in his relationship with Mia.

Lynn opened the door as Brandon pulled up. It was already dusk, and the air was much colder than earlier. Goosebumps formed on Lynn's exposed arms. She had on a tank top and a pair of sweat shorts that had Temple painted across the ass. He walked up the front steps and gave her a hug. She invited him in and shut the door. As he followed her up the tall staircase to her apartment, Brandon watched the word Temple sway back and forth. Lynn's roommate Corinne passed them on the steps on her way out. She and Brandon exchanged glances as they brushed shoulders. She flashed Lynn a thumb's up, and they smiled at each other as Corinne continued out the door.

"Who was that?" Brandon asked.

"That's Corinne, my roommate."

Lynn led Brandon into her bedroom, which was at the back of the apartment. He looked around as he walked slowly behind her. He was impressed with how nice their apartment was kept. The living room looked like a floor sample straight out of Ikea. Everything matched. Her black couch was complemented by black and white pillows and curtains to match. She had an eat-in kitchen with marble counters and wooden bar stools. It wasn't half bad for a college apartment. Brandon could see himself getting used to hanging out here. Pictures of Lynn and Corinne on vacation, and a few other black art pieces, lined the hallway walls.

Brandon took off his jacket and made himself at home, sitting on the beanbag chair she had beside her bed. Lynn kicked off her sneakers and took a seat next to Brandon. She leaned across Brandon's lap to grab the remote. Her perfume lit up Brandon's nose with the smell of wildflowers.

"What is that scent?" he asked.

"What scent? Do I stink?" she checked her armpits for perspiration. "I did just come from the gym."

Brandon chuckled.

"No, silly, your perfume. It smells so good." He took another whiff and closed his eyes. "Damn, that smells good. Tell me what it is. Is it Addict or Happy?"

"Sorry to disappoint you, but this is Perfect Calm by Healing Gardens. I can't afford those other labels, and even if I could, I would not spend that type of money on perfume." The room fell silent.

"I'm sorry if I offended you," Brandon said as he turned to the right and kissed her. She returned the gesture. Lynn was a good kisser for a young buck. Brandon loved every minute of her tongue sliding in and out of his mouth. Grabbing her hair and pulling her on top of him, he continued kissing her as he loosened her shorts.

"Wait," she said. "I don't have any condoms here." She got up and started to fix her pants, but Brandon grabbed her hands before she could tie the drawstring on her shorts.

"So we won't have sex," he said and kissed her softly. "But I still want you." They stood in the middle of the room as he continued to unclothe her. Her young, perky breasts stood at attention. She had the most stunning features. Her eyes were big and beautiful, and her lips were small yet full. Brandon wanted to play for keeps with this girl, but he knew that she didn't have the type of cash that he needed. There was no way they could both be broke. He sat down on the bed and pulled her toward him. Kissing her stomach while she stood in front of him, he played with her belly ring. Lynn rubbed her hands through his curly hair. She could feel the stubble from his face brush up against her bare skin.

Lynn pushed Brandon onto the bed and pulled off his pants and shirt. Caressing his muscular arms, she licked his chest. Brandon grabbed her by the waist, positioned her pussy on top of his face, and began licking her softly. She started playing with her nipples as he licked swiftly around her clit ring until she came.

She lay beside him and smiled as their eyes met. She was impressed with him. She didn't have a condom, but he didn't try to fuck her raw like all the college dudes she usually fucked with. He had class. She jerked him off until he was satisfied.

When Brandon woke up the next morning there was a breakfast tray set up beside the bed with a note that said LET YOURSELF OUT. Lynn had to work, but she had still managed to cook Brandon a four-course breakfast. He looked at the husky plate of food in front of him. He tasted the veggie omelet first, and then the turkey bacon and grits. He was kind of skeptical about her cooking since Mia was such a bad cook, but after he tasted the pancakes all doubts were gone. Lynn was a bad-ass bitch in the bedroom and in the kitchen.

After Brandon cleaned his plate, he was so full that he lay back down and fell asleep. He woke to the ringing of his phone. He looked at the screen and saw that it was Mia.

"Hello," he answered.

"Where are you?" she demanded.

"Whoa," he said. Brandon didn't like her tone of voice.

"Where are you?" she asked again. "I called your house and Chris said you didn't come home last night."

"He's half drunk and has no idea what he's talking about. He was asleep when I got in and when I left this afternoon."

"It looks like I'll be out here all week," she said, her voice softening at Brandon's explanation. "I miss you already."

Brandon rolled his eyes. Mia was having mood swings lately, and it was starting to bother him.

"Look, baby, I'm on my way to the gym. I'll give you a call later. I love you," he said.

"I love you, too, baby," she said and hung up the phone.

Brandon threw the phone on the bed and continued to lay there and watch TV. He just couldn't get up from the bed. He lay there until Lynn got back from work. As he looked at her outfit, instant jealously flooded his face. Lynn was wearing a short blue jean skirt with thick black tights and stiletto boots. She kicked them off as soon as she closed the bedroom door.

"Hey, how was your day?" she asked as she took off her jacket and placed it in the closet. As soon as the jacket was hung, she turned around and ran right into Brandon's chest.

"What do you have on?" he asked as he looked her up and down. "If you're gonna be my woman, you can't be out here walking around half naked."

She walked around him and sat on the side of the bed. Brandon's face grew hot with rage.

"Did you hear me?" he asked. Brandon liked his woman to look sophisticated and even though Mia wore short dresses, she wore them with class. Lynn was walking around looking like a whore with half her ass out.

"I was wearing this same skirt when we met. I don't see what the problem is." She pulled a magazine out of her bag and started flipping through it casually. He was aggravated. She wasn't taking him seriously.

"If you're going to be with me, you can't be out here wearing that type of shit." He tugged at the bottom of her skirt. It barely reached mid thigh.

"Who said I was going to be ya girl?" she asked as she kept flipping through the magazine without looking at him.

Brandon was speechless. He took the magazine out of her hands and held them.

"I thought it was already confirmed when we fucked in the bar," he said.

"If you want to be my man, that's fine. Just don't think that you can change me, because I'm comfortable just the way I am."

"You're right, baby. I'm sorry," he said. "Let me make it up to you." He kissed her delicately on the lips. "Grab your coat. We're going shopping."

Lynn put her boots back on and grabbed her coat.

Brandon drove over the Ben Franklin Bridge to the Cherry Hill Mall. He had one good credit card left, and he wanted Lynn to have the best too. She was, after all, his girl. He took her to Nordstroms and bought her a pair of Seven jeans. Her round, fat ass filled out those jeans so well that he wanted to take her to the mall bathroom and fuck her.

Brandon felt so comfortable around Lynn. She was funny, smart, and down to earth. She didn't really care about designer clothes. She shopped mostly in thrift stores looking for pieces that she could bring back to life. Lynn was her own woman and didn't care what anyone thought about her.

He had already decided that he was not going home that night. He called Chris on the phone and told him to tell Mia he was in the shower if she called, and to text him so he could call her back.

How can this be happening? he wondered. He liked Mia a lot, but Lynn was young and too sexy. He couldn't resist her. And she had a bright future in front of her. She was in school to become a journalist. Mia had the looks, the body, and the cash, but she was missing the brains. Mia was smart, but not like Lynn.

Plus Lynn and Brandon had more in common than Brandon and Mia. Lynn, like Brandon, had lost her mother at a young age. Lynn's father raised her on his own, so she had to grow up fast and become street savvy. Lynn and Mia had totally different pasts. Mia grew up in Lower Merion Township, and both of her parents were still alive and well. Mia went to school with white people and had no idea what it meant to struggle. She was clueless about the streets. She came from money and always had enough at her disposal to do anything she wanted.

As Brandon and Lynn headed back to Lynn's apartment, Brandon stared at Lynn and felt bad. Here he was starting to really like her, and she didn't even know his real name. If he told her now she would never trust him again. He didn't know how, but this was going to work between him and Lynn. As they walked into Lynn's apartment Brandon knew he couldn't give her up, and yet he didn't know how he could afford to keep her.

Brandon watched while Lynn sat on the bed and painted her toes a bubblegum pink. He took the bottle out of her hand, propped her foot on his thigh, and continued to paint where she had left off. She bit her lip as she watched him paint her toes.

Lynn kissed him as he finished her pinky toe. She thought he was sweet and generous, and of course fine as hell. The only thing that bothered her was how he tried to tell her what to wear. She promised herself that she would not pass judgment so quickly, though. After all, Keith was an older man and he may not be used to his woman dressing like that. She thought she would tone it down a bit with the short skirts, but there was no way she was going to give up her halter tops and deep cut shirts.

It was eight in the morning when Brandon finally left Lynn's apartment. He hadn't been home in two days, and he had no idea what he was coming home to with Chris staying there. Chris was lying on the sofa butt ass naked when Brandon got home. As Brandon made his way to the bathroom he saw Chris's pants hanging on the shower rod, and his boxers lying on the bathroom floor. Brandon gathered Chris's stuff, placed it in a duffel bag, and handed it to Chris.

"Did anybody call?" Brandon asked.

"Mia left a message on the machine this morning," Chris said.

Brandon noticed the spilled milk and cereal on his coffee table and tried to control his temper. Rushing to the kitchen, he wet a dishrag and cleaned up the mess. Chris was a pig. *No wonder Tracy left him,* Brandon thought.

"Tracy stopped past the office looking for you." Brandon cupped the crumbs in his hand and walked them over to the trash. Chris jumped up from the couch and followed him into the kitchen.

"What did she say?" Chris was serious.

"Man, put on some clothes. I'm not trying to look at no other nigga's dick but my own." Brandon laughed. He could see that Chris wanted to hear what he had to say. "She gave me this." Brandon took the picture out of his wallet and handed it to Chris.

Chris smiled at the sight of his little man sitting on Santa's lap. He had missed Christmas with his family. Tracy wouldn't even tell him where she was staying. He kissed the picture and put it in his duffel bag as he took clothes out to get dressed.

"She told me that she wanted to talk to you, man." Brandon leaned on the counter while Chris gathered the rest of his clothes and shoved them in the bag with the rest of his stuff. He put on his boxers and a pair of sweatpants.

"I gotta go," he said. "I'ma try to catch up with Tracy, and then I have a meeting with Potts." They shook hands and Chris left.

Brandon opened the fridge and grabbed a cold one. Brandon never drank beer in bars because he thought it made him look poor, so he only drank it in the privacy of his home. He took another swig of his Heineken and sat back on the couch. Turning the TV to ESPN *Sportscenter*, he started to watch the college basketball highlights from the night before, but he couldn't keep his mind off Lynn.

Damn, he thought. Why couldn't she have cash? It was going to be hard to fuck with both her and Mia. Both of them seemed to be demanding about spending time together, and he was only one person. Brandon was not going to give up Lynn. He liked that young, sweet ass and her vibrant pussy. She was young and full of energy. They could fuck all night and she could still get up and go to work the next morning.

But Mia had that change. She was wealthy and sexy— the best of both worlds. He had already made up his mind. He was keeping both of them, and that was that.

Chapter 7

When It All Falls Down

Chris dialed Tracy's cell phone as he drove up Roose-velt Boulevard to his mother's house.

"Hello," she said, her voice almost a whisper.

"Hey, how you doin'?" he asked calmly as he weaved in and out of traffic.

Tracy cut straight to the point when she recognized Chris's voice.

"We need to talk."

"I'm on my way to my mom's crib. Can you meet me there?"

"I'll be there," she said.

"And Tracy"—he paused—"Can you bring little man?"

"Yeah, I'll bring him," she responded and quickly hung up the phone.

Chris hadn't seen his son in over four months. He missed playing with him and carrying him to bed when he fell asleep in the car. He hoped Tracy was ready to forgive him so they could continue where they left off. Chris figured she had a lot of time to think things through, and he was ready to become a family again. He knew Tracy was probably mad, but she had caught him cheating with other girls before and had gotten over it. So he felt that she should be able to get over this little affair, too.

He pulled into the driveway of his mother's house and parked the car. He could tell by the curtains being closed that she was not home from work yet. He opened the front door and dropped his duffel bag on the couch. Before he could sit down and turn on the TV the doorbell rang. He opened the door and there stood Tracy and Little Chris holding hands. He grabbed his son from the ground and hugged him tight. Tracy walked past him and took a seat in the chair by the fireplace. Chris was overwhelmed with happiness. He hadn't realized how much he had missed his family until he held Little Chris in his arms.

After putting Little Chris down on the couch, Chris sat in the chair across from Tracy. He folded his hands and waited patiently for her to talk.

Tracy stared at Chris and tears welled up in her eyes. She loved this man. She loved everything about him. She stared into his hazel eyes and reminisced about the first time they met. She was in the Palmer Social Club. He saw her and bought her a drink, and then they went home together. She couldn't understand why he would want or need another woman to satisfy him, let alone a man. He could have almost any woman he wanted, so why choose to be with a man? Chris was not the sexiest nigga, but he had a thug appeal that made bitches crazy. He was a light-skinned hood nigga with reddish-brown braids that extended towards the middle of his back who loved to throw cash around, and he took care of his family.

Chris watched as tears flooded down Tracy's face. She looked down at her diamond engagement ring one last time, and then took it off. Chris started to get nervous.

"Please don't do this," he pleaded.

Tracy handed him the ring and sat back in the chair.

"I can't be with you. I took your cheatin' and lyin' for four years, Chris." Tears started to flow heavier as she continued speaking. "I love you, but I can't accept the fact that you cheated on me again, and this time . . . with a man."

"Baby, I know we can work it out," he said, gazing into her eyes. He could see her hurt and regret, but he was looking for her love. "I told you I was sorry and that it will never happen again."

"I can't, Chris, I just can't." She got up from the chair, picked up Little Chris, and walked toward the door.

"Tracy, please, let's start over," he begged. "I love you . . . I miss you . . . I miss us, my family."

She backed out of the door, shaking her head and grasping the baby tightly.

"I'll make sure that Little Chris is here every other weekend to visit you and your mom. I gotta go," she said as she turned around and walked down the front steps. After strapping Little Chris into his car seat, she got in the car and drove off.

Chris stood in the doorway watching as her car disappeared down the street. Once he could no longer see the car, he walked back in the house, shut the front door, and leaned against it, throwing up his hands in defeat. It was finally over. Tracy was gone and he was officially a weekend baby's daddy.

Chris sunk into the couch and played the scenario over and over in his head. He could not believe that she gave the ring back. He held up the ring and looked at it. He had spent a lot of money on that ring. He placed the ring on his pinky finger, since that was the only finger it would fit. Chris felt like shit.

Glancing at his Movado watch, Chris saw that it was almost five in the evening. He put his feelings on hold for a moment while his mind turned to business. He was supposed to meet with Potts to discuss signing him to another deal. Chris had only signed Potts for one album. He didn't know if Potts was going to blow up, so he didn't want to give him a two album deal in case his record went nickel instead of gold. But now that his album was platinum, it was time to make sure that Potts was going to stay with Indigo Records and put out another hit.

Chris needed to gather himself and focus. He went into the bathroom, wet a washrag, and wiped his face. Taking a quick look in the mirror at himself, he confirmed that he was a handsome man. Tracy would realize that she had made a mistake by getting rid of him, and then beg for his forgiveness. Things would eventually be the same. Chris was just going to play along with her until she was ready to admit that she couldn't live without him. She was useless without him, without his money.

When he pulled up to the office Potts was leaning against the front entrance toting on a blunt. His eyes were bloodshot red and his Jesus piece was shiny as ever. He looked up at Chris from under the brim of his hat. Potts always wore a hat and never left the crib without his chain. He would get a fresh cut and would still leave the barbershop wearing his fitted cap. Chris shook Potts's hand and unlocked the door to the office. Chris took a seat at his desk and pulled out the folder with Potts's new contract inside. Potts sat on the couch.

"About that contract, dawg," Potts said, "we need to discuss that paper amount."

"You know I'ma take care of you, man." Chris opened the folder and placed the signature page up front.

"Chief, last time we did a contract you practically raped a nigga," Potts said. "You signed me for fifty grand and that

shit ain't even last me up to when the album dropped."
Chris folded his hands on top of the contract.

"So what do you have in mind?"

Potts smiled and clasped his hands together on his lap.

"I need a mil, man." Potts leaned back and put his
hands behind his head.

Chris was in shock. *How dare he demand that type of
money?* Chris was the one who put him on the map. Potts
was a small-time hustler turned rapper when they met,
and in a matter of months Chris had turned him into an
overnight celebrity. Potts was getting superstar pussy, and
he was getting a larger percentage from his album sales
than any other artist they had ever signed. Chris swiveled
around in his chair to face Potts.

"I can't offer you that type of money, man," Chris said.
"But I can offer you this." He handed the contract to
Potts.

Potts looked down and it was a deal for 250 grand. He
looked up at Chris and looked back down at the figure on
the page. After crumpling the contract, he threw it in the
wastebasket.

"You gotta come betta than that," Potts said.

"Nigga, what you mean?" Chris asked. "It's more than
what I signed you for last time." Chris could see that Potts
had an attitude about the figures, and he knew then that
Potts wasn't going to sign for less than a mil. Indigo Records
didn't have that type of money to give him. Chris was trying to refrain from getting up from his chair and knocking the shit out of Potts for balling up the contract. He
strived to remain cool and level-headed.

"I can promise you that all your expenses will be paid,"
Chris said. "So when you go out on tour it'll be on us."
Potts got up from the couch and headed toward the door.

"I ain't signing that shit, man," he said. "Do you know
who I am?"

Now Chris was about to lose it.

"Nigga, you act like you Jay-Z or somebody. Get the fuck out of my office."

"You ain't gonna never find another nigga like me. Just remember that shit. Oh, and by the way, I already signed with Epic for two mil, so I was givin' ya ass a deal!" Potts flipped the contract folder on the floor and left Chris alone in the office. Chris clenched his chair until he heard the door slam downstairs. He wanted to strangle Potts.

Fuck him, Chris thought. The streets always had undiscovered talent lurking around. He would just do a little scouting and find another nigga to replace Potts.

After turning the light off to the office, Chris locked up. He wanted to hit the clubs and find a bitch to take home, but Brandon was out of town working at their office in New York, so he didn't have anyone to chill with. Instead he stopped past the deli and grabbed a six-pack of Coronas. Back in the car, he popped the top of a Corona and pulled off. By the time he was on his last bottle he found himself sitting in front of Kane's apartment building. He hadn't seen Kane since the day he pulled the gun on him. Chris could see there was a light on in Kane's living room. He finished off his last beer and stumbled over to the bell.

"Who is it?" Kane asked over the intercom.

Chris felt his dick getting hard just at the sound of Kane's voice.

"Let me in," Chris replied.

Kane was surprised. Chris was the last person he expected to be at his door.

"What? Ya bitch throw you out?" he snapped.

"Just let me in." Chris repeated his words, slurring more than the first time. Kane could tell he was drunk.

"Hell no. Go home to that bitch." And Kane hung up. Chris proceeded to bang on the door to the apartment building. He walked away and threw his empty bottle at Kane's window, shattering the glass. He quickly ran back to the car and pulled off before someone called the police. Chris was out of luck. Kane didn't want to fuck with him either.

Even though he had too much to drink, Chris managed to drive himself to Brandon's crib. He would stay there until Brandon got back from New York. He unlocked the door and swung it open. He could hear noise from the TV blaring in the bedroom. Brandon never left on the TV when he left the house. Chris pulled out his gun and held it by his side as he burst through the bedroom door.

Mia was asleep on the bed in her bra and panties. Chris was horny as hell and Mia looked good as shit in her sea blue bikini briefs and matching bra. He placed the gun on the dresser and turned off the TV. The room fell dark. Chris undressed quickly, making sure that he did not make a sound to wake Mia. Sitting on the side of the bed, he pulled down the straps on her bra. Chris's dick was rock hard. He caressed Mia's nipples and moved down to remove her underwear.

Mia awakened from the sensation of Chris's tongue thrusting up and down on her pussy. He sucked harder and harder until she screamed. Mia reached for the lamp and turned it on. She wanted to see Brandon suck her pussy. He was being so aggressive and demanding that she wanted to fuck with the lights on.

"Oh my God!" she yelled and pulled away from Chris. She covered herself with a sheet. "What are you doing!" she screamed as she backed into the corner of the room.

"You was just telling me how good it was," he said. He walked toward her and kissed her on the lips. The smell of liquor reeked from his breath. She smacked him. He pulled her down on the bed and pried open her legs. She began to yell.

"Help me!" she screamed. He covered her mouth with his hand and forced himself into her.

Mia couldn't believe Chris was doing this. Her body fell still as he moved up and down on her. Finally he came to a stop and rolled off her. She was too scared to move. He was drunk, and there was no telling what he was capable of doing. Mia knew that she could never tell Brandon about this. He would think that she provoked Chris to have sex with her. She lay still and cried silently as Chris began to snore.

Mia turned to the bedside table and looked at the clock. It was six AM and the sun was just coming up. Easing out of the bed, she walked toward the bedroom door. She noticed the gun on the dresser as she walked past. She grabbed it, jumped on the bed, and pointed the gun at Chris's head.

"Get up!" she hollered. "Get up, you asshole!"

Chris's head was spinning. He opened his eyes and Mia was standing over him. He had no clue about what was going on. He pushed her hand and the gun went off. The bullet flew through the wall. She dropped the gun, ran into the bathroom, and locked the door.

"You raped me!" she shouted at the top of the lungs.

Chris was still trying to get his focus back. He had no idea how he got over to Brandon's apartment. He was terrified. If Mia was telling the truth, he was in some deep shit. If she went to the cops, he knew that he would be done. He was going to jail for sure. He paced in front of the door, trying to figure out what to do.

"I couldn't have did no shit like that, you lying-ass bitch!" She must have come on to him. He would never push up on her other wise.

"Just get out, Chris, before I call the cops." Mia sobbed.

He found his boxers and put them on as fast as he could. Grabbing his jeans and shirt, he ran down the hall to the elevators. He dressed in the elevator and hurried out to the parking lot to his car. How was he going to explain this to Brandon? Even worse, how was he going to explain all this to the cops?

"Fuck!" he yelled.

He banged his hands against the steering wheel. He had to come up with an alibi, just in case anyone asked where he was. How could he have been so stupid?

Chris drove out of the parking lot and rushed to his mother's house. It was seven AM, and if he could get there before she woke up she would figure he was there all night, and he could use her to vouch for his whereabouts.

He parked the car at the corner of her block instead of in the driveway. He figured the sound of the car might wake her up and his cover would be blown. Walking swiftly around to the back of the house, he used the back door to get inside. His mom's room was right above the front door, and she would wake up if she heard the door open. He quietly closed the door behind him, took off his shoes, and carried them up the steps carefully enough not to make a sound. He heard the toilet flush as he hit the top of the steps.

"Shit," he mumbled.

Chris lay on the steps while his mother walked down to the other end of the hall to her room and closed the door behind her. He jumped up, ran to his room, and pushed the door shut. Undressing quickly, he jumped in the bed and pulled up the covers. He knew his mother would come in and check on him before she went to work—an old habit of hers since he was a child. Chris lay on the bed and closed his eyes.

He knew he had to talk to Mia. He needed to convince her not to talk to anyone about what had happened. And he needed some dirt on her to keep her quiet. Chris knew just what to do. He would call Sam, Mia's friend from the public relations firm. All Chris had to do was fuck her a couple of times and take her to dinner, and then she would tell it all. Sam was starved for attention. That was how he got Sam to introduce Brandon to Mia in the first place. All he had to do now was wait for his mom to poke her head in his room so he would have his alibi.

Chris woke up around noon and opened his closet. He knew that if he was going to get Sam where he wanted her, he was going to have to play his part. That meant pulling out his best pair of Italian loafers and a crisp button-up. He called Sam's cell phone and left a message. She called him back within a matter of minutes.

"Hey, baby, how you been?" she asked in her most seductive voice.

Truth be told, Sam was a sucker for a light-skinned street nigga. Although she had grown up in the suburbs, she preferred her men real hood. There was something about a man with street appeal that made her pussy wet.

"Meet me for dinner," Chris said, cutting straight to the point. "And then, dessert at your place."

"What's for dessert?" she asked playfully. She already knew the answer, but she loved when he was so demanding.

"Me, you, that wet-ass pussy, and my dick," he said. "I'll meet you at your building when you get off."

He hung up the phone and left his mom's house. Chris needed all the dirt he could get about Mia. He knew it wasn't gong to be easy, but Sam would definitely talk if he got her a little tipsy and ate that pussy. Sam always wanted him to eat her out, but he wasn't feeling her like that to give her such a treat. Desperate times called for desperate measures, so he was eating pussy and ass, and sucking toes tonight. Chris would do anything to get what he wanted, and what he wanted was information.

He stopped by Tiffany's bakery and bought her a strawberry shortcake. He also picked up a bottle of Malibu rum. Coconut rum was Sam's favorite liquor. As he was leaving the liquor store he noticed a police car parked behind him. He pulled off and they followed him down the street. Chris made sure he stuck to the speed limit. He didn't want the cops to have any reason to stop him.

What if Mia had already gone to the police? he wondered. The sirens alerted him to pull over. He grasped the steering wheel tightly as he watched through the side mirror as the two officers got out of their squad car.

"Son," the officer said as he stuck his head in the driver's side window.

"Yes, officer," Chris answered.

"You might want to get that tail light fixed," he said. "Just a friendly warning." He patted Chris's car and walked back to the squad car.

Chris was relieved. The police pulled off and turned the corner heading north on Broad Street. He sat there for ten minutes before he was able to move. Finally turning south on Broad Street, he headed for the Robinson Building where Sam worked. Chris had to make sure that no one knew what happened. He was sure that Sam didn't know, because she would not have agreed to meet up with him if Mia had already spoken to her.

Sam was waiting in front of the building when he pulled up. He never took notice to how fine Sam was before. She was a simple girl. She didn't wear any makeup, but she definitely had class. Chris looked at the shape of her thick thighs through her mint green Anne Klein skirt. He knew he was going to wear that ass out after dinner.

Walking around the car, Chris opened the door for her. Sam immediately knew Chris was up to something. He had never opened the door for her before. He was a thug, and after all, real thugs didn't open car doors. She kissed him on the lips and got in the car. He closed the door behind her. She sat her purse in the backseat as he pulled off.

"So where are we going?" she asked.

"I have reservations at Ms. Tootsies on South Street," he replied.

Sam smiled. "So I guess you're staying at my place tonight?" she asked. He glanced at her, then back at the road.

"I guess so."

The restaurant was only ten minutes away from Sam's job, so they arrived there quickly. He parked the car and rushed to open the door for her.

There goes that door thing again, she thought.

"You must be up to something," she said.

"Why you say that?"

"You have never opened the door for me before. And now you've done it two times in one night. Something's up."

Chris smiled, and she could see the chip on his front tooth. It made him look so sexy that she wanted to fuck him right then. Sam was ready to skip dinner and head back to her crib, but she decided that she would be a lady at dinner and a ho during dessert.

They walked into the dimly lit restaurant and waited to be seated. The hostess showed them to their table, which was located in the corner of the restaurant. Chris pulled out Sam's seat and motioned her to sit. After taking her seat, Sam placed the napkin in her lap. She was overwhelmed by Chris's kindness. He was always nice, but not to this extent. She couldn't wait any longer. She wanted him now. She was not going to last until after dinner.

Chris took a seat across from Sam, took her hand in his, and folded them together on the table. Sam smiled. Chris's hazel eyes were mesmerizing, and those lips—that was it. She leaned across the table.

"How about we skip dinner and go straight for dessert?" she whispered.

Chris knew exactly what she was hinting at. He got up from the table, slipped the hostess a twenty, and they left. He drove furiously down Chestnut Street until he reached Delaware Avenue. Pulling into the parking lot of her building, he turned off the car. Sam took off her yellow satin thong and placed it in Chris's lap. He looked down at it and quickly put it in his pocket. Sam got out of the car and walked toward the elevators. He grabbed the rum and the cake from the backseat and proceeded to follow her inside.

Sam couldn't get the keys in her front door before they were all over each other. He kissed her neck and she fumbled with the keys. She finally managed to get the door open, and she closed it behind him. Chris put down the bottle and the cake and turned to pin her body between him and the door. He ripped off her skirt and threw it to the floor. Sam unbuttoned his shirt, popping a few buttons on her way down.

Sam was a thick size twelve with full and curvy thighs and a flat stomach. Her ass was round and firm, and her lips were big and luscious. Before meeting Sam, Chris had never been with a thick chick. He usually liked his women petite enough for him to throw around the bedroom during sex, but Sam was definitely turning him on.

Sam removed his belt and unbuttoned his pants. He pulled his dick through the hole in his boxers and lifted her right up in the air. Damn, she was flexible. Sam had never turned him on like this before. He had fucked her a couple times after the trip to Atlantic City, but the sex was usually so boring that he would not fuck her unless he had called everyone else and they weren't available.

She's stepping up her game tonight, Chris thought as he slid his dick into her warm pussy and hoisted her up against the door with her legs wrapped around his waist.

Sam grabbed his face and kissed him hard on the lips as they moved up and down in unison. Chris was so thrown off by how good her pussy was that he came in a matter of five minutes. He carried her over to the couch with her body still wrapped around him and dumped her on the couch. He almost forgot what he was there for with the ass being so good. He needed to cover his ass with the Mia shit before it was too late.

Getting up from the couch, he grabbed the bottle of rum and opened it. Sam sat up from the couch, grabbed the bottle, and took a long, hard swallow. Chris watched her lips around the top of the bottle as she sucked the liquid down. He took the bottle from her hands, pushed her back down on the couch, and poured the rest of the bottle on her pussy. Sam screamed from excitement. Chris proceeded to suck her clit and put his finger in her ass at the same time. Sam had never had this type of sex with Chris before. It was usually short and sweet. He would cum, and she would use her vibrator after he left to handle her business. He never cared about pleasing her before.

"Baby, bite it harder," she moaned. "Harder!" She pushed his head deeper into her pussy.

Chris hated to eat pussy. It was like a chore to him. He only did it for Tracy when he had to. This was the first time he had ever kissed Sam, and the very first and last time he was going to eat her out. He licked her pussy up and down like a cat in heat. She pulled him up and positioned his body on top of hers so they could do a sixty-nine. Chris shoved his dick in and out of her mouth to the back of her throat. He loved the tingling sensation he received when his tip hit her tonsils. She came and he turned her around, leaned her against the arm of the couch, and entered her from behind. Chris stroked back and forth and in and out of her pussy until he released.

When they were both satisfied he got up from the

couch and walked into the kitchen. He took the damp dishrag from the counter, wiped off his dick, and threw the rag in the sink. He opened the fridge and found another bottle of rum. He popped the top, took a sip, and handed it to Sam. She pushed the bottle away.

"I'm cool," she said. "I've had enough rum for one night."

She got up from the couch and went into her bedroom to lie down. Truth was that she was already a little tipsy from the first bottle, and she had to work in the morning. Chris brought the bottle into the bedroom and sat beside her. He took another sip and handed it to her again.

"Just have a drink," he said and kissed her on the lips, moving slowly to her neck.

She smiled and grabbed the bottle from him. She took the bottle to the head until it was empty. Chris knew that Sam couldn't hold her alcohol. He knew that once it kicked in she would say and do anything he wanted her to do. Sam was gullible. All it took was for a nigga to fuck her right one time and she would give him the world. She lay back down and Chris grabbed her feet and started to massage them. He gently placed her toes in his mouth and began sucking each one slowly. He couldn't believe he was doing this. He had never stooped this low before. He could tell she was getting more relaxed by the minute. The alcohol was taking over her body.

"You like that, huh?" he asked. He began to massage her feet again.

"I do," she answered, her words slightly slurred. He knew it was time to make his move

"Have you talked to Mia lately?" he asked casually.

"Not since last week," she answered. "She's been sort of staying to herself ever since she found out she was pregnant." Chris immediately stopped massaging Sam's foot and dropped her foot on the bed. He turned to face her.

"She's what?" he asked again as if he had heard her wrong.

"She's three months pregnant," she said.

Chris was shocked. He had no idea that Mia and Brandon were in that deep.

"Does Brandon know?" he asked as he began to rub her feet again.

"She hasn't told him yet."

"So when is she going to tell him?"

"I have no idea. If she keeps putting it off, he's going to get an idea sooner or later. Her belly is growing bigger every time I see her."

Chris lay down beside Sam and waited for her to fall asleep. There was no way that he was going to tell Brandon that Mia was pregnant, and this just made his situation worse.

He looked up at the clock and it was midnight. He crept out of the bed, got dressed, and closed the door quietly behind him. He waited for the elevator at the end of the hallway, and when it opened Mia was stepping off as he was stepping on. She glanced quickly at him and hurried down the hall. He stepped back off the elevator and followed her.

Mia became frantic. She was scared that Chris might try to hurt her again. Tears began streaming down her face and she picked up her pace. He grabbed her shoulder and she instantly froze in her tracks.

"We need to talk," he said coldly.

"Please let me go, Chris," she murmured. "Please don't hurt me again."

Chris's heart was beating fast. He slammed her against the wall.

"Did you tell anyone what happened?"

"No," she whispered and looked away. She could not stand to look him in the eyes.

"Let's keep it like that." He stood there in front of her.

She was shaking all over the place. "Please, I won't tell anyone."

Her stomach was beginning to hurt. She rubbed it with her hand. He backed off and walked back toward the elevator. Mia ran to Sam's door and knocked furiously. Chris got on the elevator and took it to the parking lot. He figured that he could scare Mia into being quiet about what happened. As long as she was scared, he had the upper hand. She wouldn't dare tell Brandon because she was too petrified of what Chris would do if he found out.

By the time Chris reached home it was a little past one AM. He went straight to the shower to wash off the sex smell before his mother noticed. She had a keen nose and wasn't happy with the idea of Chris out there making more babies. And Chris didn't want her coming to him with all that Bible talk. It was late and all he wanted to do was go to bed.

Chris got in the bed and turned the radio on low. His cell phone went off and he scrambled to answer it. He looked at the screen to see who it was. Who the hell would call him at this time in the morning? He knew it wasn't Tracy, and he had just left Sam's house. The number was blocked, so he decided not to answer. He fell asleep with the phone in his hand.

Chris woke the next morning to the alert on his phone notifying him of a message. He threw the phone on the floor, rolled over, and went back to sleep. His mother woke him an hour later.

"Chris!" she shouted as she nudged him on the shoulder. "Wake up. Brandon's on the phone, and he says it's important." He jumped up and grabbed the phone. She disappeared into the hallway.

"What's up, man?" Chris mumbled while wiping the sleep out of his eyes.

"Sam left a message at the front desk of my hotel." His voice was unstable. "She said Mia was in the emergency room. I tried to call her, but no one answered. Please, man, can you make sure she's OK? I will try to get home as soon as I can."

Chris's mind was all over the place. He knew Mia was not stupid enough to tell Sam the truth. Chris thought about the baby. He had done a lot of shit in his time, but if he made her lose this baby he definitely had to get his shit together.

"Calm down, man," Chris said. "I'll make sure everything is fine and give you a call to let you know what hospital she's in. Just stay put until you get word from me."

Chris didn't need Brandon coming back in the midst of all this confusion. He had to be sure that Mia was stable enough not to draw any suspicion to what had happened between her and him.

"Aight, man, call me as soon as you get word," Brandon said.

"I'm sure she's fine," Chris reassured him. "I'll call you as soon as I speak to her." He hung up the phone and lay back down. Chris was mad at himself. He had created a big problem, and it was just getting bigger. He looked at his phone lying across the room on the floor. He got up, grabbed the phone, and lay back in bed.

He checked the message on his phone, and it was from Sam. She was with Mia at Jefferson Hospital in Center City. Chris didn't know if he should call or go down there. He didn't want Mia to flip when he walked in the door. That would make Sam think something was up. He dialed Sam's phone and it went to voicemail. He hung up and tried her office. The receptionist said Sam had called out for the day. He was just going to wait it out until this evening and speak to Sam when she came home.

Chapter 8

Straight Slippin'

An hour or so later Chris got tired of waiting for the evening, so he got up from bed, slipped on a pair of ball shorts and a fresh pair of Air Forces, and went down to the hospital. He stopped at the front desk to find out what room Mia was in. The man at the desk had his back turned when Chris walked up.

"Excuse me, can I get some help?"

"I'll be right with you, sir," the man answered. He continued to put the file in a cabinet and swiftly turned around to help Chris. When the man saw Chris he immediately looked as if he had just seen a ghost.

"So when did you start working here?" Chris asked.

"About two months ago," Kane answered with a tone of indifference. He tried to keep his eye contact to a minimum. Chris looked around to see if anyone was watching before he continued the conversation.

"If you would have opened the door for me the other night, I wouldn't be here."

"Look, what you want?" Kane asked. "I don't have time for this shit." His voice was becoming louder.

"I need to know what room Mia is in," Chris said.

"Last name," Kane said impatiently.

"I don't know. Just look it up in ya computer and lose that nasty-ass attitude."

Kane rolled his eyes and started to type on the keyboard. He looked up at Chris, then back at the screen, and up again at Chris.

"Chris, we need to talk," Kane said frantically. He walked over to the other front desk attendant and told her that he was going on a short break. He motioned for Chris to follow him outside the hospital doors.

"What did you do, Chris? That girl is in here for rape." Kane looked him over carefully and waited for a response.

"I, I was drunk, man. I can't remember what happened." He looked down at the ground. Kane lit a cigarette, took a long drag, and passed it to Chris. He inhaled deeply and let the smoke exit from his nose.

"I don't know what came over me," he said. "I was stupid as shit to do something so fucked up." He took another toke from the cigarette. "It happened the night I came over your house and you wouldn't let me in."

"Look, stay away from here and I will give you a call to let you know if she mentioned your name." He took the cigarette back from Chris and finished it off. "If push comes to shove, I'll just tell them you were with me all night."

"Then people will know that . . ." He stopped before he finished his sentence.

"What, Chris? That you're gay? That you like men? Would you rather do a bid for raping a bitch than let people know who you really are?"

Chris was ashamed. He had been hiding this secret since high school. It was never a lifestyle for him. It was more like a craving. He craved a man from time to time and he made good on fulfilling his need.

"Look, just go home and chill. I'll talk to you later," Kane said as he walked back into the building.

As Chris walked back to his car, he dialed Brandon's cell phone. He had to tell him that Mia was OK. Sam had not called him back, and Chris wondered if Sam knew. He didn't know what was worse—being sent up because he raped Mia, or telling people he had cravings for men. He would rather do a bid in jail. At least that way he would still have his dignity. If he went to jail he could fuck with other niggas and nobody would know. Whatever happened when you were locked down stayed there.

"Did you find out anything?" Brandon asked when he answered the phone.

"She's fine," Chris said. "She had food poisoning from eating sushi. She should be home by tomorrow."

"Did you get the number to the room for me so I could call her?"

"N-n-no, no," he stuttered. "She said she would call you when she felt better."

"Aight, thanks for lookin' out, man. You think I need to come home?"

"Naw, everything's gonna be cool. I'll see you next week," Chris said. "By the way, how are things going up there?"

Brandon stalled for a moment in order to get his words together.

"It's good. Business is slow, but I'm meeting with this new artist tonight."

"Good. I'll talk to you later," Chris said and quickly hung up the phone.

He went back to mother's house and got back in bed. All this shit with Mia was making him tired. He needed to lie down for a little while. He fell asleep, but it wasn't long before he was awakened by his mother nudging him in the shoulder again. This time it was Sam calling.

"Hello," Chris said.

"She was raped," Sam started off. "She said someone raped her, but she won't give the police any information."

"What about the baby?" Chris asked.

"There was some hemorrhaging, but the doctors say the baby is fine. She has been trying to get in touch with Brandon all day. Have you talked to him?"

"Naw, but I'll give him a call and let him know that she needs to talk to him." Chris had already told Brandon that she was fine, and now that Sam confirmed it, there was no need to call him back.

"I'm going to stay at the hospital with her tonight," Sam continued. "She should be able to come home tomorrow and I'll let her stay with me until Brandon gets back from New York. When am I going to see you?"

"I have some business to take care of. I'll get wit you tomorrow."

Getting pussy from Sam was out of the question under the circumstances. He wanted to stay as low key as possible. The more she mentioned him to Mia, the better the chance that Mia would talk. Chris hung up the phone and rolled over to lie on his stomach. He thought about how good Kane looked. His braids were fresh and he looked good in a shirt and tie. Damn he wanted to fuck him again. Their sex was so intense that Chris always left his company satisfied. Plus Kane could suck a mean-ass dick. He turned around on his back and jerked himself off until he fell asleep again.

Chris left the house around eleven PM and stopped at the deli to grab a six pack of Steel Reserve. He wanted to make sure he was drunk. It had been one hell of a day. He got back in the house, sat in the living room, and popped open the first beer. His mother was asleep upstairs, so it was cool to drink in the house. She would go crazy if she saw him drinking. She knew he did, but she would not allow alcohol in her home.

He sat for about two hours watching reruns of *Chappelle's Show* when his cell phone went off. It was a text message from Kane asking if Chris wanted some company. Chris had never met with Kane outside of Kane's apartment, but he was too tipsy to drive all the way to West Philly, so he texted Kane back with the address to his mom's crib.

Kane arrived an hour later, just as Chris was finishing his last beer. When Chris opened the door, Kane walked past him and took a seat on the couch. Chris plopped down next to him. Kane focused his attention on the TV while Chris looked at Kane.

Chris grabbed Kane's face and kissed him on the lips. He couldn't resist. Kane caressed Chris's dick through his sweatpants. Chris was becoming overly excited. He hadn't had a man in quite some time. Quickly Chris got on his knees in front of Kane, unzipped Kane's pants, and pulled out his dick. Chris was kind of nervous about giving head to a man, but the alcohol seemed to relax him some.

He had never sucked a nigga's dick before. He was always the one who got his dick sucked, and he fucked niggas in the ass. He wondered if sucking dick would classify him as a real fag. Tonight he was so drunk, and had missed Kane so much, that he didn't care. There was no reason to care. Tracy had made it clear that she didn't want him. He tried to keep telling himself that she would be back, but he knew deep down inside that she was gone.

Chris licked around the tip of Kane's dick. Kane started to moan loudly as Chris wrapped his lips around Kane's dick and began to suck feverishly. Kane's eyes rolled into the back of his head. He guided Chris's head up and down and watched as his moist lips slipped all over his dick. Kane continued to moan loudly.

They were so into the moment that they didn't hear Chris's mother coming downstairs. She stopped at the bottom of the steps, not quite believing her eyes. Her only son was on his knees giving another man a blowjob.

"Get out of my house, the both of you!" she shouted when she finally regained her voice. She grabbed the first thing in sight—a vase off the mantle—and threw it at them as they scrambled to adjust their clothes. The vase that she threw just missed Chris's head.

"Mom, I can explain," Chris said as he walked over to her, but she quickly moved away.

"Get out of my house," she said again. "You can't stay here. Chris, you are a bad man. Lord knows I didn't raise you to be no faggot. I raised you to be a respectable man, a man that could love a woman, not another man!"

"You got some nerve!" Chris snapped back. "It was OK when you walked in on your boyfriend doin' me!" he yelled.

She slapped him in the face.

"Shut your mouth!" She walked over to the steps and held the wall as she started upstairs. "I want you out of my house tonight!"

"I was only seven and you didn't stop him!" Chris yelled back. He turned back around and slowly moved toward the couch with eyes full of pain. "You let him hurt your son." He sat on the couch and cried softly. Kane was confused. He didn't know if he should hold Chris or just leave.

"Just get your stuff," Kane said. "You can stay with me until you find a spot."

Chris went up to his room and began packing his duffel bag. He looked at his room one last time and turned out the lights. His mother was watching through a crack in her bedroom door. She closed the door as Chris walked past. Chris was hurting inside. His own mother didn't want him. He had no one but Kane, who had taken him back. He had forgiven Chris when everyone else had disowned him.

Chris was straight slipping. He had turned his craving for a man into a full time need for companionship. He was confused, too. Did he want to be with a man or a woman? All he knew for sure was that all the women in his life had abandoned him, and it was a man who had accepted him with all his flaws.

Chris locked the door to his mother's house and left the key in the mailbox. He walked down the driveway and turned back to look up at his mother's window. She closed the blinds as soon as they locked eyes. Chris had grinded for two years straight to buy her that big-ass house. She now lived amongst well-to-do people, and she was the only black person on the block. He had paid two hundred fifty grand straight up. All she had to do was pay the bills. Yet despite all that he had done for his mother, she had still thrown him out on the street.

Chris got into Kane's car and they pulled off. Kane snuck a quick look at Chris and then turned his attention back to the road. Kane wanted to be there for Chris. He wanted to be the one Chris came home to every night. He grabbed Chris's hand and was surprised when Chris didn't snatch it back. Maybe there was hope for a relationship after all.

Chris was sick the next morning. He spent the majority of his time with his face hovering over the toilet bowl. Kane brought him a glass of water with an Alka-Seltzer tablet in it to settle his stomach. After Chris drank the medicine, Kane stood there by the sink and looked down at Chris. He looked pathetic. His face was beet red and his lips were dry.

Kane knew Chris would need him to make sure that

Mia didn't talk. He was finally the one with the power to call the shots in the relationship. He didn't want to be just a fuck for Chris anymore. Kane wanted to be Chris's man, but he knew Chris had heavy mood swings. One wrong word could send Chris into a rage, so Kane took a breath and tried to choose his words carefully.

"Are you going to look for an apartment?" he asked.

"Yeah," Chris said. "I can't live here."

Chris's response irritated Kane.

"But last night you said you were going to stay with me."

"Last night I was drunk." Chris bent his head back toward the toilet bowl and expelled more of the alcohol from the night before. Kane waited until he was finished and handed him a towel. Chris wiped his mouth and leaned back against the wall.

"So why can't you stay here with me?" Kane muttered.

"Look, I'll stay here until I find something, aight?" Chris had to remember that he needed Kane. He wouldn't get any information about Mia if he didn't ease up.

"I have to go to work," Kane said. "Do you need a ride to your car?"

Though still weak, Chris scrambled to his feet. His stomach continued to cramp from his overindulgence the previous night.

"Drop me off at the projects," he said.

Kane drove Chris to North Philly and dropped him off in front of the Blum. He hadn't been there since that shit with Mike had jumped off. Everything seemed cool now. But since Chris wasn't selling anymore, his funds were low. He needed to get with his young nigga Tank and borrow some money. He knew he could find Tank over by the Dominican store, so he walked up the block.

There was Tank sitting on a milk crate rolling a blunt. Chris hadn't smoked in a couple days, and he was fiending for some weed. He sat down on the steps next to Tank and waited for the blunt to be passed. Chris wanted to make this short and sweet so he could grab his car and do what he needed to do.

Tank finished rolling and lit it up. He took a few puffs and passed to Chris. Chris took a drag and nearly coughed up a lung. He looked at the blunt, took another hit, and passed it back to Tank.

"That's some good shit, nigga," Chris said.

"Yeah, this that hydro shit. I copped this from that Dominican nigga, Juan. His shit be on point." Tank blew the smoke out of his mouth and took another hit. "So what's up, Chief?"

"Yo, I need to borrow some change." Chris looked at Tank.

"How much we talking?"

"Only two grand," Chris said. "I'm fucked up right now. My money is tied up in this label and I need to cop a crib."

"Say no more, old head. It's done." Tank finished off the blunt, got up from the milk crate, and shook Chris's hand.

"Slide through here in about a couple of hours and I'll have that for you." Tank pulled up his pants and started to walk away. "Oh, yeah, old head, some cop dude was out here askin' questions about you a couple weeks ago."

Chris raised his eyebrow. That was all he needed now—another problem.

"What he want to know?"

"He was just askin' niggas if they knew you or knew where you stayed. Ain't nobody give up no info, though."

"Aight, good lookin' out. I'ma holla at you a little later."

They parted ways and Chris walked six blocks over to the office. He decided he would chill there until he had to pick up the money from Tank. He knew that those cops was still watching him after that shit went down with the nigga Mike. He had seen them on numerous occasions creeping around outside the office. That was the reason why he stopped chilling around the Blum in the first place.

Chris had never been so broke in his life. He still had a couple of dollars stashed, but he would rather borrow from his nigga Tank than to dip into his emergency money. He knew he really didn't have to give the money back to Tank. Chris had practically raised Tank from a young bull. He schooled him to the game and looked out for him and his family. At least there were a few people he could count on.

He looked at the clock on his office wall. He had a couple hours to kill before he was supposed to meet back up with Tank. Maybe he should get his car now. That would save him time in the long run.

Chris took the bus to his mom's house and grabbed his car. By the time he had backed up into the street, she was taking out the trash. Chris stopped the car in hopes that she would come talk to him, but she wouldn't even look in his direction. She dragged the can to the curb and hurried back inside the house. Chris shook his head and drove off.

As he reached the expressway his phone rang. It was Kane. Chris answered after one ring, hoping Kane had some more information on Mia's condition.

"Is she aight?" Chris asked as soon as he answered.

"She is fine," Kane said. "She was released today and she didn't tell anyone about you."

Chris let out a sigh of relief.

"I'll talk to you later," he said quickly.

"Are you coming over?" Kane asked.

Chris hung up the phone without answering. Kane heard the line go dead and he was pissed. Chris had used him to get the information he needed, and now that he got what he wanted he was back to being an asshole.

As Chris hung up the phone he headed over to the projects to pick up the money from Tank. He noticed a squad car parked in front of the Dominican store where they were supposed to meet. He drove past slowly and he saw the cops patting down Tank.

"Shit," Chris said out loud and sped up.

Those were the same cops that questioned him about the shooting. They must have been following him. He needed that money from Tank. He couldn't go back to his mom's crib, so he took a chance and went back to Brandon's place. He knew that Mia was with Sam, so he went back there to chill. As he made his way to Brandon's spot, he kept looking through his rearview mirror to make sure no one was following him. When Chris got to the apartment he opened the door and took a look around, making sure no one was there. After he put his bag by the door, he took a quick shower.

When Chris walked into Brandon's room to get a towel, he noticed the hole in the wall from the bullet. He needed to cover that hole. There was no lie that he could tell that would cover up a bullet being lodged in Brandon's bedroom wall. He took the picture of Brandon's mother that was on the wall in the living room and put it in front of the hole, then he lay down on the couch and closed his eyes.

Chris thought about Tracy and Little Chris. At first all he wanted was to be with them. Now Chris didn't know what he wanted. Things had gotten so crazy, and the only person he had on his side was Brandon, and he was out of town. He knew Brandon would never do anything to hurt him. That was why he felt so bad about Mia. Chris got up and walked into the kitchen to get a beer. He needed a drink every time he thought about what he had done.

* * *

Chris spent the next two weeks lying around Brandon's apartment. Tank got locked up for having three bags of weed on him and a hot gun. He didn't want to stay with Kane, because he would only keep nagging him about having a relationship.

Chris was turning into a drunk. He only left the apartment to get beer, he ordered Chinese takeout every night, and he hadn't answered his cell phone in days. Kane kept calling and leaving messages, but he just wanted to be left alone. Chris was deeply depressed.

He looked at his watch to see what day it was. It was Friday and Brandon was due back in town by Monday. He looked around the apartment. There were Heineken bottles on the coffee table, the kitchen counter, and on the floor beside the couch. He had been drunk for several days at a time. Stumbling into the kitchen, he grabbed a trash bag, cleaned up all the bottles, and then sat back down on the couch. He wondered what Tracy was doing. If they were together, they would probably be lying on the bed watching TV, and Little Chris would be playing on the floor beside them.

Chris could picture Tracy's face. She was smiling and they were happy. He couldn't understand how things had gotten so fucked up between them. He was actually going to marry this girl. Chris remembered the moment he gave her the engagement ring. She was lying on the bed reading a magazine. He had given Little Chris the box to give to her. When she opened it and saw the ring she jumped up and gave Chris the biggest hug. They had some raunchy sex that night. It was the best they had in years.

Wanting to distract himself from his thoughts, Chris grabbed the remote and flipped the channel to BET. He watched a couple videos and then nodded off.

Chris was awakened by the door slamming. Brandon

was home early. He lugged in his two suitcases and then went straight to the bedroom. When he came out he was wearing a fresh pair of Evisu jeans and a Lacoste hoodie.

Good thing that mess was cleaned up, Chris thought. Brandon would have been acting like a bitch about his crib being dirty.

Brandon came back into the living room and pushed Chris's feet off the couch so he could sit down. He grabbed the remote from the coffee table and turned to the news.

"Any word from Mia?" Brandon asked, his attention still glued to the TV.

"Naw, I haven't heard anything since the last time I talked to you," Chris said. "How is business?"

"Everything is good. We may be having another artist on our lineup soon."

"That's good."

"I'm going to go holla at Mia. I'll be back a little later."

Chris was trying not to look so uptight. He didn't want to give Brandon any reason to think that something was wrong, but inside he was shook.

"Oh, yeah, tell her I said what's up. I'm just gonna chill here. I'll see you when you get back."

Chapter 9

Expecting the Unexpected

Brandon left the house and jumped back in the car where Lynn was waiting. He needed to drop her off at her crib and get to Mia. Lynn had taken the train out to New York and spent the last week with Brandon at his hotel, and what a week it was. Brandon hardly did any work during his whole trip, and the little time that he did spend working he was trying to renegotiate that deal with Epic.

Since Chris had lost Potts, the label wasn't making any money. They were starting to owe more than what they were making. He had told Chris that he was in the process of signing a new artist, but that was far from the truth. The truth was that the streets were starting to talk, and they weren't saying anything good. People knew that Indigo Records was going under. Brandon figured the faster they could get out, the better. He was just waiting for the right time to approach Chris about selling again. Chris's money was starting to run low, so Brandon knew that he might be up for the deal this time. With the right deal, they could pay off all their debts and still have some money left over.

Brandon had a lot to handle. Since he left he hadn't talked to Mia, mostly because he and Lynn had become increasingly closer over the last month, and the last week in New York had brought them even closer together. Brandon made her quit her job because no girl of his was going to work in a bar. He knew for sure that if she continued to work there another nigga would try to holla. He clipped all that shit from the gate by making sure her rent was paid and that she had a few dollars in her pockets. Brandon was becoming a slave to her young pussy. He was so possessive of her that he wanted her to call him before she left the house and he wanted to know where she was going and with whom. Lynn loved the attention, so she did as he told her to.

When they reached her apartment she gave him a long kiss and got out of the car. He waited until she got in the house safely and then pulled off.

Brandon tried Mia's cell again, but there was no answer. He had called her several times and she had yet to call him back. He pulled into the parking lot of her building, got on the elevator, and pushed P for the penthouse floor. Once he got to her door he slid his keycard through the lock and walked inside. Sam was sitting at the kitchen counter chopping up vegetables. She rolled her eyes at the sight of him and continued preparing the food.

"Hey, Sam, where's Mia?" he asked as he slid his coat off and laid it on the couch.

Before answering Sam looked at Brandon with indifference.

"She's in the bedroom resting. I left messages at the front desk of your hotel, Brandon, and you never returned my call."

Brandon leaned on the counter and looked Sam in the eye.

"I did call. She wouldn't call me back." He went into the

fridge and grabbed a beer. Cracking open the top, he stood there, waiting for Sam to speak. Sam finished the vegetables and put them in a pot on the stove. She turned back around and took another look at Brandon.

"Brandon, I wouldn't want to talk to you either."

"What the hell is that supposed to mean?" he asked. Brandon was starting to get mad. Sam was sticking her nose in their business and he didn't like it.

"If I was raped and my man didn't come home to make sure I was all right, I wouldn't want to talk to his sorry ass either."

Brandon's beer went crashing to the ground. Did she say what he thought she had just said? She couldn't have. Not Mia, not his Mia. He ran into the bedroom and swung open the door. Sitting on the bed, he pulled her close to him, and she began to whimper. He couldn't help but to shed a few tears himself. Here he was in New York fucking Lynn's brains out and his baby was here being raped by some lowlife street nigga. Brandon tried to control his rage.

"Who did it?" he asked as he rocked her back and forth in his arms. "I'm going to kill him. Tell me who did it!"

The room fell quiet. Mia wouldn't say a word. All she could think about was the fact that her man's best friend had raped her. She had almost lost the baby. She cried even harder than before. Brandon rubbed her hair and kissed her on the forehead. He pulled the covers back and his body went lifeless. Her thighs were black and blue from where the rapist must have pried her legs open. He could see that the bruises were clearing up some, but she was still hurt. He had no idea that this had happened. Chris had said that everything was cool. Brandon started to break down. He looked into her hazel eyes, and he could see that she was crying out for help.

"Baby, I am so sorry. Chris said that everything was fine."

She sobbed even harder. Brandon couldn't understand why Chris would tell him that. He knew he should have come home. He was so caught up with Lynn that he didn't think twice about the situation. Brandon lay on the bed next to her while trying to hold back his emotions. She felt so frail. He could tell that Mia was in bad shape. She hadn't said a word to him since he got there. She just lay there and stared into space.

Brandon fell asleep with her in his arms. He was awakened halfway through the night by violent screams. He looked over and she was sweating and crying in her sleep. Brandon gently rocked her and she calmed down and began to rest easy. Brandon lay awake for the rest of the night. He was shocked. Someone had hurt his girl. He cringed at the thought of someone forcing his dick inside his woman's pussy. All he could think about was what he would do to the nigga who did this.

He was already awake when the sun came up. He eased out of bed and made his way into the kitchen to start making breakfast. Brandon pulled out the vegetables that Sam steamed yesterday so that he could make a vegetable omelet—Mia's favorite.

Once the omelet was complete, he poured her a glass of orange juice and brought the tray of food into the bedroom. She was sitting up watching Jerry Springer when he put the tray in front of her. She picked at the food for about fifteen minutes and then pushed it away. Brandon sat beside her silently as she finished the orange juice and sat the glass on the bedside table.

"We need to talk," she muttered.

Mia really didn't have too much to say to Brandon. She was not only mad at the fact that Chris had done this, but even more upset that this was Brandon's best friend. She couldn't tell him what happened because there was no telling what Chris might do to her if she talked. Mia figured there was only one way to move this cloud out of her life, and that was to break up with Brandon.

"I think we need some space," she said softly. "This whole thing is just too much for me to handle, and I just can't deal with this and our relationship right now."

Brandon put his head down. *Shit,* he thought. This was not a good sign. Every time someone said they needed space, that usually meant things were over. Brandon had to think of something quick so he could make sure that this whole thing didn't blow up in his face. He still needed Mia. He was two months behind on his mortgage, and with Lynn quitting her job, she had become a bill herself.

"Look, I understand you need space, but at least let me take care of you until you get better." He grabbed her hand. "Can we at least agree upon that?"

"Yes, we can do that," she said reluctantly, "but I want you to take home all of your things."

Mia didn't want him to think that he could use the whole taking care of her idea to stay in her company. She meant it when she said she needed her space. He would have to sleep in the guest room. She didn't want him in the same bed as her. It was his friend that had hurt her. She was suspicious of Brandon at this point. He must have known his own friend was such a fucked up person. Mia just wanted to be alone. Right now it didn't matter to her if they were together or not. She pulled her hand away from his.

"I'll move my stuff out now," he said and left the room.

He gathered his clothes from the hall closet and laid them out on the couch. He stuffed everything into the bottom of his bag and then went into the bathroom to claim the rest of his belongings from the medicine cabinet. As he reached toward the back to grab his razor and aftershave lotion he knocked several things over, including a bottle of pills. He didn't remember seeing these in the cabinet before. He read the contents of the bottle out loud.

"Prenatal vitamins, prenatal vitamins?" *Why the hell would she need these?* he wondered. "Oh shit!" he said loudly. He peeked outside the bathroom door to see if anyone had heard him. She was pregnant. Mia was pregnant. Brandon felt even worse than before. Someone had run up in his woman while she was pregnant with his baby. That was some low-ass shit. He wondered why she didn't tell him. He knew exactly what to do to get her back into his life.

He carefully placed the bottle of vitamins back in the cabinet. Walking back out to the living room, Brandon grabbed the rest of his things off the sofa, and shut the front door behind him. All he could think about as he walked to the elevator was that his woman was expecting. Mia was pregnant with his firstborn. He smiled happily until thoughts of another man inside her instantly brought him back to reality. He swore that he would kill the person who was responsible for Mia's rape. With Mia on his mind, Brandon almost forgot about Lynn until his cell rang. He answered quickly.

"Hey, sweetie," he said. "You all right?"

"Are you coming over tonight?" Her voice was sharp yet cool. He could tell she had a borderline attitude. She was starting to act like she ran shit. Brandon had spoiled her with all that one-on-one attention, so now she had gotten used to having him around. It was definitely the right time to break her out of it.

"I might not make it over tonight, baby. I'll call and let you know." And with that he hung up the phone.

"But—" was all that Lynn had a chance to say, because the phone went dead in her hand.

* * *

Lynn couldn't believe it. He had actually hung up on her. Lynn was pissed off at his rude, out of the blue behavior. Keith was just sweating her a couple hours ago, and now he was acting like a nut. Lynn knew she shouldn't have started to catch feelings for him. He was acting up already. How was she going to tell him that she missed her period this month with him treating her like some bitch off the streets? She quit her job to make him happy, and everything was going smoothly. He had told her he loved her two days ago.

Lynn could feel the sandwich she had just finished eating churning in her stomach. She had been queasy all week. She ran to the bathroom and leaned over the toilet.

She knew Keith would be happy about the baby, and besides, something was bound to happen. She couldn't remember the last time they had used a condom. He must have known that this was going to happen. Lynn dragged herself back to her room. She was just so tired. She had never felt so drained in her whole life. School started next week, and she needed to be on point to keep her scholarship. She had it all worked out in her head. She would go to school until she was about eight months, and then she would take off a semester, have the baby, and return to school. It would be a piece of cake. She decided to dial Keith back.

"Yes," he answered as if she was bothering him. He was parking the car in the garage of his building.

"I need to know whether you're coming over," she said. "Because if not, I am just going to go out with my roommate."

She knew that this would get him to act right. He hated her roommate. Every time Keith came over, Corinne had a new nigga there. They had even talked about Lynn getting her own apartment because he didn't like the constant flow of male traffic in and out of their place.

"Yeah." She heard him sigh and pause. He was becoming agitated. "I'll be there. I just have to take care of a couple of things first." He hung up the phone again.

Lynn smiled as she hung up the phone.

Brandon was in a tight position. Mia needed him more than ever. He walked up the hallway and proceeded to open the door to his apartment. He could hear a woman moaning on the other side of the door. He walked right in and Chris was sitting on the couch with Sam on top of him. He was bouncing her up and down on his dick. She jumped up when she saw Brandon. Chris sat there with his dick out while Brandon stood in the middle of the living room.

"Y'all can't be fucking like this in my living room!"

Sam ran into the bathroom and covered herself with a towel. She was so stunned that Brandon had come in on them fucking that she was too embarrassed to come out. Sam stood behind the closed door waiting for the right moment to make her move. Her clothes were still out there and she wanted to grab them without making a scene. Chris sat on the couch and looked at Brandon as he stroked his dick.

"Nigga, put your shit away and tell Sam she has to go. I need to holla at you about something."

Sam could hear Brandon from the bathroom and wanted to leave quietly. She opened the door and quickly gathered her clothes from behind the couch. She ran back into the bathroom, put on her skimpy black dress, and eased herself out of the bathroom. After kissing Chris on the cheek, she grabbed her purse from the coffee table. She looked Brandon in the eyes as if to say the she was not ashamed of her actions, and walked past him and out the door.

Brandon eyed her and then turned his gaze back to Chris, whose dick was still exposed. Brandon wondered why Chris was so free with showing people his dick. He had no problem walking around the apartment naked. They did grow up together, but there were some things that just needed to stay private, and *that* was one of them.

Chris finally stuffed his dick in his boxer shorts and pulled his pants up from around his ankles. He was starting to work on Brandon's nerves. He had been staying at Brandon's nearly the entire time Brandon was gone. He didn't replace any of the beer he drank, and his dirty clothes smelled up the place. Brandon's living room was starting to smell like the locker room for the Philadelphia Eagles. Chris was turning into a dirty dude. He had a faint odor about himself. Brandon had no idea what brought this change on, but he didn't like it at all.

Brandon sat on the edge of the couch across from Chris and clasped his hands together. Chris looked at Brandon and grinned.

"What's up, man? Why you looking at me like that?" Chris asked.

"You're slippin', Chris. It's like you don't even care about yourself anymore."

Chris's easy grin turned into a frown.

"What's that supposed to mean?" Chris asked defensively.

"Just look at yourself," Brandon said. "I have never seen you sit around the house all day. I could hardly find you before, and now all I have to do is come home and here you are."

Chris stood up from the couch.

"You want me to leave?" He folded his arms and waited for a reply.

Brandon couldn't kick him out. Chris had given him the money to get his condo when he graduated from college. He dropped fifty grand in Brandon's hand and told him to get out of the projects, that he was too good to hang with those types of niggas anymore. If it wasn't for Chris helping him pay for college, Brandon would probably have nothing. He would be another street nigga selling coke in front of the Dominican store.

"You can stay here as long as you like," Brandon said.

Chris quickly sat back down. Brandon knew he didn't have anywhere to go. Ms. Ruth had called Brandon and told him that Chris was staying at his house and that he could no longer live under her roof with his wicked lifestyles, whatever that was supposed to mean.

"I just want you to get yourself together. You're not the old Chris I used to know," he said. "You don't go out anymore and your lineup of bitches has gone from ten to like one. Just man up and get shit back the way it used to be."

"It will never be the way it used to be. Tracy is gone." Chris was finally ready to admit that she was not coming back.

Brandon smiled. "Since when did a nigga like you care if a chick left or not? She's left you before, and you just kept doing what you do."

"Yeah, but that was because I knew she would be back. This time she is gone for good."

"There is plenty of pussy out there," Brandon said. "Just go get yourself some ass, a couple of asses, so you can have a little variety in your life. Get your mind off Tracy and her bullshit."

Chris shook Brandon's hand. "I got you, man," he said. "I'm gonna get my shit right."

Brandon got up from the sofa and proceeded to the bedroom. He quickly turned around once he remembered to ask Chris about Mia.

"By the way, you know Mia got raped?"

Chris's face filled with terror. *She better not have told him what happened,* Chris thought. Chris looked up at Brandon and then back at the TV. He knew he had to be easy. As long as she kept quiet with it, Brandon would never catch on.

"No, I didn't know. Man, that's some shit. Did they find out who did it?" he asked calmly.

"No, she won't say, but I swear if I find the man who did it, I'll kill him myself."

Chris was amazed by the words coming out of Brandon's mouth. Brandon was far from a gangsta type of dude, but he wasn't a nut-ass dude either. He knew that if Brandon found out that he raped Mia, they were gonna go to war. Still, Chris wasn't worried. Mia knew better than to mention his name to anyone concerning what happened.

"Why did you tell me she was cool?" Brandon asked, interrupting his thoughts.

Chris paused to try to find the right words.

"Sam said she was cool and that she was taking her home," he answered.

"But you told me that you talked to Mia yourself. What the fuck is going on? You told me she had food poisoning."

"I could have sworn I told you I talked to Sam," he replied. "Sam ain't really mention what happened but she did say that they were out at a sushi restaurant the night before so I just figured that was the reason".

"I felt like a fool when I walked into her crib like nothing was wrong."

"My bad," Chris said. "Sam didn't tell me anything about no rape." Chris chose not to admit he knew about the rape, because admitting he knew but didn't tell Brandon would only make him look guilty.

"It's cool, man. I should have followed my first intuition and come home."

Brandon thought nothing else about it. He had other things to be concerned about. He went into his bedroom to repack his duffel bag. He threw a pair of jeans and his boots in his bag and grabbed his keys and cell phone off the dresser. That was when he noticed the picture of his mother was moved. Brandon always kept it on the wall in the living room. He couldn't understand why it would be hanging on the wall in his bedroom, but he had to get going if he was going to see Lynn and then go to Mia's. He didn't have time to fix it or ask Chris about it. As Brandon left, he mumbled a quick good-bye to Chris, who was on the couch staring into space.

Brandon pulled out of the garage and drove down Twentieth Street to Lynn's apartment. He let himself into her apartment and walked back to her room. Brandon had made sure that Lynn gave him a key to her apartment once she quit her job. There was no way he was paying rent for a place where he couldn't come and go as he pleased. Lynn was lying on her back listening to her iPod when he sat down on the bed. He kissed her on the lips and took off his shoes.

Brandon knew he couldn't stay long. He also knew that Lynn was going to have a fit if he didn't spend the night with her. That just couldn't be helped, though. He had shit to do. He was on the verge of losing Mia, and that meant a fast trip to bankruptcy. He lay down beside Lynn and looked into her eyes. She was such a fine-ass girl. Brandon's dick was getting hard just looking at her. He tried to think of something to make it go back down, because he knew for sure he would never get to Mia's house if he fucked Lynn. She jumped on top of him and started to kiss his neck. He grabbed her petite waist and gently pushed her back on the bed.

"Chill out," he said.

He wanted to fuck her badly, too. She had her hair

braided to the back, and he loved the way her face looked with her hair pulled back. She reminded him of this Hawaiian girl he had a crush on his freshman year in college. Lynn had the perfect complexion. She was golden bronze with the most exotic facial features. He wanted to grab her, turn her around, and fuck her from behind. She jumped on top of him again and tugged at his pants. He pushed her hands away.

"What's wrong with you!" she screamed. "Keith, why are you acting this way?!"

Brandon looked at her as if she was crazy. He almost forgot that she didn't know his real name. She grabbed him again and he pushed her away for the third time. Brandon got back up from the bed and put on his shoes. He didn't have time to play around with Lynn and her young girl games. He knew he was moving too fast with her, but her pussy was so good. Brandon could stick his dick in and her walls grasped him perfectly.

"Where are you going?" she asked.

He didn't answer. Brandon brushed off his clothes and grabbed his bag. Lynn stood in front of the door so he couldn't leave. He politely picked her up while she kicked and screamed, and placed her back on the bed. She threw the alarm clock from her bedside table at the door as it closed behind him.

Brandon walked down the hallway to the apartment door and ran right smack into Corinne. She squeezed past Brandon in the tight hallway and grabbed his dick in the process. Brandon knew she was a little white whore, but pussy was pussy all the same. He knew he was going to bust her ass. He was just waiting for the right time.

Brandon hurried over to Mia's. Mia was in the shower when he arrived. He sat patiently on the couch until she was done. He didn't want to go into her bedroom. He was worried about making her feel uncomfortable, so he played it cool and just waited until she was ready to acknowledge his presence. When he heard the water turn off he announced himself from the living room, so she wouldn't be startled. Once she dried off and put on her pajamas, she came out and sat on the couch beside Brandon.

He looked at her. She was so cute. Her little belly was starting to stick out. He brushed her hair back out of her face. She looked much better than before. She smiled as he ran his hands through her hair, and he kissed her on the forehead. She lay back in his arms. Mia knew that Brandon was a good person. She was just so mad at Chris. She kissed him softly on the lips.

"So how many months are you?" he asked. Brandon rubbed her belly.

"How did you know? Did Sam tell you, or did Chris?" She sat up from his embrace. Brandon looked confused.

"Chris knew?"

"Sam told him a while back," she said.

"That muthafucka," Brandon said. "No, he didn't tell me. No one told me. I kind of figured it out on my own."

Brandon realized that Chris had been acting a bit strange lately. It seemed like he was having trouble giving up information about Mia. First he messed up information about the rape, and now he just left out her pregnancy. Something was definitely out of place.

"Well, I'm four months."

"So why didn't you tell me?"

"I was going to tell you when you came back from your trip."

Brandon laid her body across his lap. He was fascinated with the thought of his child growing inside Mia's belly. He knew that Mia wouldn't want to have a baby out of wedlock, because it would crush her career. She was doing so well that she was in the process of auditioning for a movie. This whole rape incident was already making her life uncomfortable. It was hard for her to keep this away from the media. That was why she only stayed in the hospital for two days. She wanted to leave before she was made a spectacle by the media.

Brandon made up his mind. He had to marry Mia. This would work to both their benefits. Brandon would marry into money, and Mia would still have a reputable career once the baby was born. He needed to do it quickly, because she was starting to show, but Brandon didn't have any money. He also knew that if he was going to propose to her, he had to have some major bling. He was getting a headache now. He had to figure out how to get a top-of-the-line engagement ring—a Harry Winston. He wasn't worried about paying for the wedding because her family would pay for that, and they were loaded.

"And you still want your space?" he asked.

"I've just been having doubts about us. I needed you here with me, and you were somewhere else."

"I can't even begin to tell you how sorry I am," he said and kissed her again. He lay there with her and rubbed her belly until she fell asleep. He picked her up, carried her to the bedroom, and tucked her under the covers. Brandon decided that he was going to sleep on the couch. This situation with Mia was delicate, and he had to treat it that way.

The next morning Brandon knew that he had to make some moves. He was still playing with the idea of how he was going to pay for a wedding ring. The only thing he had that was worth money was his condo. His bank account only contained about four-hundred dollars. He had been living on credit cards since he met Mia almost a year ago.

After Brandon peeked in to check on Mia, and saw that she was still asleep, he closed the door and went into the bathroom to brush his teeth. He was gargling when he came up with the answer to his problem. He would take out a small business loan. If he took out a loan, he could pay for the engagement ring, the wedding band, and the honeymoon. He figured thirty thousand dollars should be enough.

Brandon pulled out his cell and called the Citizens Bank where the record label had an account, and made an appointment to meet with a loan officer. He needed to go home and put on his lucky Armani suit to close the deal. Brandon always thought that if a person wanted to be taken seriously, he had to dress the part. He thought seriously about his plan the whole way to his apartment.

When he walked into his living room, he was surprised to see that Chris was not there. His talk with Chris must have done some good. It still smelled like a gym locker room, but it was definitely a start. Brandon cleared Chris's clothes off the couch and out dropped a visitor's pass from the hospital. Brandon picked it up to see what it was. He looked at the date.

"January nineteenth, two thousand six," he said.

That was the same date he had called Chris to find out about Mia.

Why does Chris have a visitor's pass to the hospital? Shit wasn't adding up. He put the pass on the coffee table and went to get dressed. Brandon was confused. *Maybe it's Sam's pass. But what would it be doing in Chris's pocket?*

Brandon couldn't keep thinking about the pass. He had to hurry up and get to the bank before it closed. He would figure the pass shit out later. He straightened his tie and took a final look in the mirror.

"You look damn good," he said to himself. He grabbed his Kenneth Cole briefcase and headed for the car.

He was already fifteen minutes late when he arrived at the bank. He walked into the loan office and his briefcase flung open. Papers came flying out and scattered all over

the floor. The loan officer did exactly what Brandon
wanted him to do. He quickly picked up the papers, glancing at them in the process. Brandon had placed last year's
sales figures and clippings of different magazine articles
about the label's success in his briefcase. He spilled the
papers in his briefcase on purpose, so that the loan officer
knew he was dealing with a professional who had a lucrative business.

"So what can I do for you today?" the loan officer asked
as he took a seat behind his desk.

"I need to take out a small business loan," Brandon said
in his most professional voice.

"How much do you need?"

"Thirty thousand dollars."

"Well I have all of the papers you need to fill out right
here. Please have a seat and take your time completing
the paperwork."

Brandon did as instructed and made himself comfortable on the other side of the desk. He opened the thick
package of papers and began what would be at least an
hour worth of paperwork. He placed the deed to his
condo up as collateral. Once he and Mia married, he
would be able to pay off the loan and his condo. Brandon
finished up the paperwork and handed it to the loan officer.

"Mr. Brunson, I can begin processing the loan applica-
tion later today."

"How long will it take for the approval?"

"I can have an answer for you by tomorrow at the end of
the business day."

"Now, we have been loyal customers here for about two
years. All of our banking is done here. Is there any way we
can speed up that response?"

"Mr. Brunson, I can give you a call by the end of business today to let you know if you're approved." He got up

and shook Brandon's hand. "Thank you for you business," he said as he held the door open for Brandon to leave.

"No, thank you," Brandon said.

Brandon hurried to the car and loosened his tie. He was almost sure that he would get the loan, so he called the Harry Winston flagship store in New York while he was in the car. Brandon didn't plan on wasting any time. He put a three-carat baguette diamond ring with a platinum band on hold. The ring alone was going to cost him twelve thousand dollars. He wanted to propose to Mia over a candlelit dinner overlooking the river. He needed it to be as dreamy as possible, and as perfect as possible. It also had to be a quick affair. Mia was already four months pregnant, and the form of their child was starting to become very noticeable. Brandon knew he had to marry her before anyone realized that she was expecting. If the press got a whiff of her being pregnant, it could ruin everything.

There were three weeks left before Valentine's Day, and that was the day on which Brandon wanted to have the ceremony. He recalled that Mia had mentioned how romantic it was for people to be married on Valentine's Day.

Brandon felt like he was making progress. He had the ring on order, he had made reservations to the Chart House for two days from now, and he had already contacted one of the best wedding planners in the city. This would definitely be a last minute affair, but it would be an event to be remembered.

When he arrived back at Mia's condo, she was in the kitchen fixing herself a salad. He grabbed her from behind and kissed her neck. At first she tensed and he felt her entire body go stiff. But once she realized it was Brandon, she smiled as she continued to chop up her tomatoes. He gently took the knife out of her hand and led her to the couch.

"Here, let me take care of that for you." Brandon took

off his suit jacket and laid it on the couch as he always did. He continued to fix her salad as she flipped through channels.

Once the salad was made, Brandon set up a tray and placed it in front of Mia. He placed her salad and a bottle of spring water on the tray and watched as she dug right in. She was definitely starting to look better. Brandon was glad that everything was starting to go right again.

He sat there and waited for her to finish, then took the plate and washed up all the dishes. Mia went to lie down, and since he was exhausted too, he sunk into the couch and nodded off. He was awakened by the vibrations of his cell phone going off. It was the bank.

"Hello," he answered.

"Yes, Mr. Brunson. This is Citizens Bank. Sorry I took so long to get back to you. I had to work an extra hour tonight to get this approval for you."

Brandon looked at his watch. It was a few minutes past six.

"So I'm approved?" he asked.

"You most certainly are, Mr. Brunson. The funds will transfer to your account within the next twenty-four hours."

"Thank you. I appreciate all your hard work."

"Not a problem. Bye-bye now."

Brandon got up from the couch and peeked in the room at Mia. She was sound asleep.

Brandon knew that Lynn was probably fuming. He hadn't called her all day. He liked her, but he had to handle his business. Mia was even more important now. She was pregnant with his child, and would soon be his wife. He still wanted Lynn, but his relationship with her was built upon lies. She didn't even know his real name.

Quietly he eased out of the apartment's front door and

dialed Lynn's cell. He left a message, since his call went directly to voicemail. He found it kind of strange that her phone was off. She never turned it off. Brandon decided to go past her place to see what was going on. He got there in less than ten minutes. After entering the apartment, he walked back toward her room and opened the door. Lynn was lying on the bed with her head covered. He sat beside her and pulled back the sheet from over her head. She looked up at him and smiled.

"Hey, when did you get here?" she asked as she sat up and kissed him on the lips.

"Just a few minutes ago," he said. "I stopped past because your cell phone was off."

"Oh, I was tired and my father kept calling me, so I turned it off. Are you staying tonight?"

"I don't know." *Here she goes,* Brandon thought. He knew he should have just left the message and went home. Lynn laid back down and put the cover back over her.

"Well if you're not staying, then you need to leave now." She turned her back toward him. Brandon got up from the bed and walked out of the room. He didn't feel like playing with Lynn tonight. He just wanted to go back to Mia's and rub her little pregnant belly.

Lynn was getting on his nerves. She was too moody for his taste. At least Mia was moody for a reason. She was pregnant and had a right to be. Lynn was just being a plain old bitch.

Brandon went to use the bathroom before he left. Lynn's roommate was peeking through her bedroom door and she saw him close the bathroom door, so she followed him down the hall and walked in right behind him. Brandon was fixing his pants when he turned around and noticed her standing behind him. Brandon knew that Corinne was a little white girl who loved black dick. Every time he saw her with a man, he was black.

He looked her up and down. She didn't even make his dick hard. Brandon had fucked plenty of white girls before, and she just wasn't his type. She was too frumpy for his taste. Her clothes were loose and wrinkled. He liked his white girls well dressed with plenty of cash. He smiled and walked around her so he could leave the bathroom. She frowned and stormed back down the hall to her room. Brandon was in enough trouble. He definitely didn't need her to add to the equation.

It was ten at night by the time he returned to Mia's house. Mia was sitting up watching Dr. Phil and eating chocolate ice cream when he came in. She was adorable. She had the half-gallon of ice cream propped up on her little belly. He kissed her on the cheek.

"I'll be in the guestroom if you need me," Brandon said.

He walked down the small hallway and into the room. After undressing down to his boxers, he got in the bed, but couldn't fall asleep. All he could think about was the baby. He really wanted a little girl. Brandon had never had an interest in having children before. It was funny how things changed with the right person. He knew that he wouldn't have to struggle because Mia had enough money for all three of them. He could stay home and raise the baby while she was off continuing her career. This was perfect for him. He would be Mr. Mom.

Brandon finally fell asleep with thoughts of his happy future filling his mind. At about midnight, Mia tiptoed into the guestroom and got into the bed next to Brandon. She had missed his warm body next to hers. She loved Brandon, but she hated that Chris was his right-hand man.

Brandon and Mia spent the next day playing cards and watching television together. He'd called to check his account and the money was finally available so he called the jeweler back to have the ring delivered via courier service.

Things were going so well that he had forgotten about Lynn and was focusing his energy solely on Mia and his unborn child. He couldn't wait for the next day when he planned to ask for her hand in marriage. He was nervous, but he knew that things would turn out just as he had planned.

Brandon got up super early the next morning to prepare for that night. Everything had to be perfect. When Mia woke up there were two dozen yellow roses on the nightstand. She smiled as she took a whiff of the fresh flowers. There was also a card which read:

> MEET ME AT THE CHART HOUSE AT SIX PM,
> AND WEAR MY FAVORITE DRESS—B

Mia lay around the house for hours wondering what Brandon was up to. She waited until about four in the afternoon before getting dressed. She slipped on her little black Gucci dress, the one Brandon loved. He asked her to wear it on every big occasion. But wearing the dress at this point, with a growing belly, was not something with which Mia was particularly pleased. She tried to suck in her gut, but it was a lost cause. She swept her hair back into a soft bun and applied her makeup. She was determined that if she was going to be somebody's mommy, she was going to be a sexy one. She finished up by applying her mascara and slipping on her three-inch heels.

She looked at the clock. She had an hour to make it to the restaurant, so she grabbed her purse and headed for the lobby where the doorman greeted her.

"Good evening. Your limo awaits," he said. She walked outside and there was a stretch Navigator waiting for her.

The chauffeur quickly got out to help her into the car. When she got inside Brandon was there holding a bottle of sparkling cider. Mia laughed as he opened the bottle and poured her a glass.

"I thought you would enjoy this because I know you can't have the real thing."

She took a sip from her glass and kissed his cheek. "What's all of this about?" she asked as she looked around the plush, fully loaded limousine.

"Let's just say we are celebrating us," he said as he lifted his glass for a toast.

"OK, if you say so." She held up her glass for the toast.

"To us," Brandon said as they toasted.

Mia drank the rest of her apple cider and enjoyed the view as they drove down Chestnut Street to the waterfront. It was exactly five-thirty when they walked in the door to the restaurant.

"Reservations for Brunson," Brandon said to the hostess. She led them over to a table in the corner where fresh yellow roses sat in a vase on the table.

"You are just too much tonight," Mia said as he helped her to her seat.

"Only the best for my baby," he said.

Brandon ordered the lobster spring rolls and calamari as appetizers, and then he folded his hands in front of him and stared at Mia.

"You are a beautiful woman, you know that?" he asked. "I know you could have any man you want, and you chose me." He grabbed her hand and kissed it. She blushed, and Brandon took a deep breath.

"I love you," he blurted out. "I want us to be together."

"We are together," she said as she took a sip from her glass of water.

"I mean forever." He pulled out the little satin box from his jacket pocket. It was covered with a big, pink, satin bow. Mia's eyes widened. She fanned herself in excitement.

"Oh my God. Oh my God. Oh my God." She was flustered now, and it showed. Mia instantly became teary-eyed.

He opened the box and there was the most beautiful ring she had ever seen. He slipped the three carat Harry Winston on her finger as he held her hands in his.

"Mia, I love you, and I want you to be my wife. Will you marry me?" Mia smiled.

"Yes, yes, I will marry you." She got up from the table and kissed and hugged him tightly. Apparently there was a crowd of people watching, and they clapped as he kissed her over and over again.

Brandon was shocked. He never thought he would be getting married. He was a ladies' man, but he had put everyone on hold for Mia. Mia was the one he was going to spend the rest of his life with. He savored their warm embrace. He had never seen her so happy.

Then there was Lynn. *What am I going to do about Lynn?* Brandon had almost forgotten her. There was only one thing to do. It was time to let her go, and officially go full-time with Mia. He wanted to do right. After all, they had a baby coming.

Chapter 10

The Best Man

Mia and Brandon finished off the evening with a short walk down to Penn's Landing. Mia was too excited to finish dinner, so they left after the appetizers. They walked hand in hand slowly up the pier. She was bundled up in her black fur coat and matching hat. Brandon had on his gray mohair wool coat and a tan scarf. They stopped to admire the view of the river.

"The wedding is in three weeks," Brandon said. "We need to get this over and done with."

"Why so soon?" she asked.

"Because I don't want to wait until you are really showing. Right now, no one will notice."

"That is so true. Three weeks it is." She took off her glove to look at the ring again. Mia loved the way it sparkled under the moonlight.

"I can't wait to get home and call Mom and Dad. They are going to have a heart attack!" she said.

"Do they know you're pregnant?" he asked.

"No, and they won't know until the baby is born." With Mia's super slender model physique, she would be able to pull it off.

"Well, who all knows?" he asked.

"Just you, me, Sam, and Chris, and the only reason he knows is because Sam opened her big mouth." Mia had just reminded him that he wanted to talk to Chris about that, and the visitor's pass.

"So what will be the exact date?" she asked.

Brandon quickly refocused his attention on her.

"On Valentine's Day."

"That's so romantic!" she said. "I can't believe this is happening. It's like a dream." He grabbed her close to him and looked into her eyes, kissing her so gently that she almost melted right there in his arms.

"Baby, this is no dream. I want you to be my wife. Now come on, let's get you home. It's too cold out here." They walked back to the limo and he helped her inside.

Brandon had his cell phone on vibrate all night. Lynn must have called him about twenty times. He had made up his mind, though, that tomorrow he was going over there to break up with her. She was becoming a nuisance. He didn't want to change his cell phone number again. It would be too much work on his end. She had no idea where he lived, and she didn't even know his real name. This was going to be the sweetest breakup he ever had.

When they got back to Mia's crib she hurried to the phone and dialed her parents. She must have been talking to her mother for half the night, because when Brandon woke up to go to the bathroom sometimes after three AM, she was still running her mouth.

Mia woke up early the next day and fixed Brandon breakfast. She couldn't help to glance at the ring every chance she got. She was impressed by the quality. She knew that Brandon was a tasteful man, but she never thought he would spring for a Harry Winston diamond ring. These were one of a kind, handmade rings. She looked at it one more time as she placed his plate on the table. After waking him, she led him to the kitchen table where she had breakfast waiting.

Brandon looked at his plate. *Same old Mia,* he thought. The eggs were runny and the bacon was burnt. *Oh well, at least she tried.* The thought of eating burnt bacon and runny eggs for the rest of his life kind of scared him, but the size of her checkbook brought him right back to reality.

He sat at the table, and Mia watched as he gobbled down his food. She washed the dishes and sat down on the couch next to him.

"I'm meeting with my parents and the wedding planner at two," she said. "The planner found the perfect place for the ceremony."

"I'm going to catch up with Chris. I need to let him know about the wedding and get him fitted for his tux," Brandon said.

Suddenly Mia looked uncomfortable.

"What's wrong?" Brandon asked.

"Nothing," she said. The thought of Chris in her presence made her stomach sick. She hated him now even more than before.

Kissing Brandon on the lips, she jumped up to get dressed.

"I'll see you when you get in tonight," she said and disappeared into the bedroom.

Brandon went into the guest room and threw on a pair of Gap jeans and a hoodie. He had to find Chris, and that meant that there was a possibility he might have to go to the projects. Chris wasn't at Brandon's house, because he called there about three times before he left out around noon. He tried Chris's cell phone on his way to the parking garage.

"Yeah," Chris answered.

"Where you at?" Brandon asked.

Chris looked over at Kane beside him and fell short on words.

"Uhm, some broad's house. Why, what's up?"

Kane lay there as if he was asleep, but he was listening to every word.

"I need you to meet up with me so you can get fitted for the wedding."

"Wedding?" Chris jumped up and began pacing around the room. "What wedding?"

"We're getting married in three weeks," Brandon said.

"Who? You and Mia?" Chris asked.

"Nigga, who else? Look, put your shit on and meet me at the office in an hour."

"Aight, man." Chris hung up the phone. *Brandon must be crazy,* he thought. He shook his head and went into the bathroom to shower.

Kane couldn't believe what he had heard. Brandon was going to marry Mia, and she had been raped by Chris. Brandon needed to know that his best friend was a rapist. Chris was going too far with this secret.

Is he actually going to participate in this man's wedding when he raped the bride-to-be? Kane wondered. Truth be told, Kane was tired of being with Chris. He was a self-centered asshole who always got away with doing whatever he wanted. *Not this time,* Kane thought.

Chris walked back into the room and put on the same clothes he wore the night before. Kane lay still, showing no signs that he was awake as Chris quietly slipped out of the apartment.

Brandon decided that he was going to swing past Lynn's apartment and handle his business before he met with Chris. Lynn was in the living room walking on the treadmill when he arrived. She had on her iPod so loud that she didn't hear him come in. This was becoming a bad habit of hers. He stood in front of the machine and signaled for her to take off the earphones. She gave him the finger and continued to listen. Brandon had no time to play with her today. He had shit to do, so he snatched the ear buds right out of her head. Lynn turned off the machine and stood chest to chest with Brandon. Actually, she was so small it was more like chest to face.

"What is your problem?" Her tone was razor sharp.

"It's over. I can't keep playing your childish games," he said.

Brandon chucked the apartment keys on the counter and was walking toward the door when a plastic cup hit him in the back of the head. He was so shocked that he turned around and grabbed her off the ground. He picked her up to eye level and she scratched him in the face. He shook her until she managed to break loose and fall to the ground.

Brandon's face was bleeding. He ran to the mirror and saw two long scratches down the side of his left cheek.

"What the fuck is wrong with you?" he yelled from the bathroom. He grabbed some toilet tissue and wiped off the blood. "I knew I shouldn't have fucked with you. Shit."

Brandon opened the door cautiously. He didn't know what to expect from Lynn now that she had proven herself crazy. She was standing in front of the apartment door, blocking him from leaving.

"Move, Lynn," he said as he pushed her out of the way.

"So that's it, huh?" she asked. "You're just going to leave me while I'm pregnant, huh?" she asked. "Well, fuck you, too, Keith."

Brandon took a few steps back. This was bad. Lynn was pregnant. This was going to ruin him. If Mia found out . . . She couldn't find out. Besides, Lynn didn't even know his real name.

"How do you know you're pregnant?" he asked.

"I missed my period," she said. "Plus I took one of those home pregnancy tests." She ran to the bathroom and returned with the stick. "See."

Brandon grabbed it out of her hand. There were two pink lines. She was indeed pregnant.

"Look, I'll give you the money for the abortion," he said.

"Abortion? Abortion? How dare you say that to me! Get out! Fuck you and your abortion. I'm having this baby, whether you like it or not." She opened the door for him and motioned for him to leave.

"You can't have this baby," he said.

Lynn slammed the door in his face and didn't shed one tear. She was going to have this baby, and he was going to take care of it whether he liked it or not. She didn't need him, but she was going to make sure he handled his responsibilities.

Brandon drove to the office in a daze. Chris had already been there for twenty minutes. Brandon came rushing into the office and saw Chris sitting in a chair by the door.

"What happened to your face, man?" Chris asked.

"Some bitch scratched me. I'm cool, though."

"So when's the wedding?" Chris asked, quickly changing the subject.

"Valentine's Day."

Chris could tell that Brandon had something else on his mind, and that made Chris uncomfortable. He thought that Brandon might know what happened with him and Mia.

"So, I guess I'm the best man, huh?"

"Yeah, you know it."

With that response, Chris knew that Mia had kept her mouth shut.

"We're going to have the hottest bachelor party ever. It's gonna be bitches everywhere." Chris smiled at the thought of being surrounded by big asses.

The party idea wasn't lost on Brandon, but he was still caught up in his own thoughts. There was nothing he could do about this one. He couldn't make Lynn get an abortion. He felt bad now about mentioning it to her. How could he suggest that she kill off something he had helped to make? He tried to refocus on the task at hand.

"Come on, we got to be at the tailor by three," Brandon said.

They got in the car and headed to South Street. Brandon drove without saying a word. He knew there was something he wanted to ask Chris, but he couldn't think of what the hell it was. Brandon was going to have to start writing notes to himself if he kept this up.

After finding a parking spot on Eighth and South, they hurried over to Fabric Row on Fourth Street to meet with the tailor.

Chris was kind of happy for Brandon. He had never been in a wedding before, and he didn't know too many people in the hood who actually got married. This would be his first wedding, and he was the best man.

Brandon and Chris finished at the tailor and walked over to the bar to get a drink. It had been a long time since they had been out together. Mia took up a lot of Brandon's time, and Chris seemed to be in his own little world.

Chris ordered a bottle of Moet.

"I can't believe you're getting married. That's crazy!"

"Why is that?" Brandon asked.

"I don't know. It's just not something you see every day."

"You were going to marry Tracy, right?" Chris clenched his hand around his glass at the mention of his ex.

"Yeah, but that's dead now." He threw back his drink and poured himself another glass. Brandon sat at the bar reminiscing about the fun he and Chris used to have.

"I haven't even been with Mia for a year and she has already changed my life. Remember all those nights we spent partying, fucking this girl here and that girl there?"

"Chalk that shit up, man," Chris joked. "You're going to be a husband now."

"Now that shit is funny."

They finished the bottle of Moet and walked back to the car. Brandon dropped off Chris in the projects and then went over to Mia's. Her parents were sitting on the couch when he came through the door. Brandon had only met them once before, briefly at a fundraiser he and Mia attended last fall.

Mia got up from her chair and greeted Brandon with a peck on the cheek. She reached up to touch the scratches on his face, but he quickly pushed her hands away. Mia sat back down next to her mother.

"Hello, Mr. and Mrs. Woods," Brandon said. He shook Mia's father's hand and kissed her mother on the cheek.

"Hello, son" her father said. "So did you get fitted for your tux?"

"Yes, sir, everything went fine," Brandon said. "Is the hall confirmed?"

"Yes," Mia chimed in. "We decided to have a small, intimate wedding with only a hundred people. I picked the Bellevue Hotel. It's beautiful."

"That place is expensive, don't you think?" Brandon asked, looking at Mia.

"Nonsense. Nothing is too expensive for my little girl," Mr. Woods said. He leaned over and gave Mia a kiss on her forehead.

Brandon really didn't care. He just wanted to make sure that he wasn't the one footing the bill. Between the ring and the honeymoon trip to Saint Tropez, he only had about two thousand dollars left from the loan he took out against the label.

Brandon was happy that they were not going to have a long, drawn out ceremony. If it was up to him, they would go to the justice of the peace and call it a day. Mia's father could afford an extravagant affair, though. He was a big time real estate broker. He never sold a house under three hundred grand, and there was no way he was going to start now. That was how Mia landed a condo in Rittenhouse Square. There weren't many black folks who could afford those types of accommodations.

"Your mother and I need to get going. It's getting late, and there's no telling what will happen in the city at night. Honestly, honey, I don't know how you can live around here." Brandon fought to bite his tongue. Mia lived in Center City, not the hood. They said their good-byes and left.

"I guess anything in the city scares the uppity Negroes from the suburbs, huh?" Brandon asked sarcastically.

"Oh, give it a rest. You know how he is. He's just not used to the city, that's all."

"Well we'll see how they like their grandchild being raised in the city. That's going to be interesting."

Brandon took off his clothes and went to shower. Mia lay in the bed and waited for him to finish. She was happy. Her plan had worked. She was pregnant and engaged, and Brandon was hers to keep. Mia planned on having another baby before the one she was carrying reached two. That way they could play together. She had wanted to settle down since the first day she laid eyes on Brandon. He was just what she needed—an unknown face. That way she didn't have to worry about competition. People knew who he was, but they only knew him as her man.

Brandon returned from the shower and jumped in the bed naked. As soon as he hit the sheets, he realized his mistake and quickly got back up and put on a pair of sleep pants. He didn't want to offend Mia, since she was just getting over a serious tragedy. Mia lay on his chest and quickly fell asleep.

Brandon lay awake for a long time thinking about Lynn. He should have covered up, but the pussy was just so good that he had to feel it raw. And now Lynn had become a straight bitch. She wanted all or nothing. Brandon was about to get married, and he was really going to be pressed for time. He couldn't possibly give Lynn the time he gave her before, seeing her at night, and Mia the during the day. It was just too tiring. He finally fell asleep after countless hours of hard thinking.

The next two weeks were hectic for Brandon and Mia. With countless appointments and last minute changes, there was hardly time for anything else. The day before the wedding finally arrived, and Brandon was nervous. He had a lot on his mind. There were two babies on the way with two different women.

Brandon hadn't talked to Lynn for two weeks. He wanted to apologize to her, because the baby was his responsibility, too, but he didn't want a relationship with her. It just wouldn't work. Instead he wrote her a letter, telling her the truth about his name and current situation. She was going to have to be able to accept things this way in order for them to move forward and raise a baby together. In the letter he gave Lynn his address and all the other information she needed in order to stay in touch with him. He placed it in his jacket pocket and planned to mail before he and Mia left for their honeymoon.

He was supposed to meet up with Chris that night at ten. Chris had booked a room over at the Marriott Courtyard for the bachelor party. Brandon took his last look at Mia before they were to exchange vows the following day. Her friends from college had taken over her place, so he went home to get ready for his bachelor party. Chris had left a bag of condoms on the table labeled FOR TONIGHT. Brandon packed them in his overnight bag with the rest of his stuff.

Opening his closet door, he looked at his suit for the wedding. Tomorrow he was going to be a married man— a rich-ass married man. Brandon finished packing his bag and called Chris. There was no answer, so Brandon grabbed a beer and flicked on the TV. He surfed channels for about an hour. Chris finally showed up a little before midnight. Brandon was lying on the couch asleep, so Chris nudged his leg.

"Come on, man, let's go," he said. "It took me longer than I expected to get shit going." Chris went down the hall and held the elevator while Brandon locked up the apartment. They rode down to the garage together, and drove over to the hotel.

When Brandon opened the door to the hotel room, he was in awe. Luke was blaring from the radio and there was pussy everywhere. Chris had twelve of the baddest exotic dancers in the city at this party. He had spared no expense for his best friend. He wanted to give his man the best night of his life. A couple of Brandon's friends from college and a couple street niggas they grew up with were also there. The party was already live. It seemed like he was the last to arrive, because everyone else was already drunk. Chris led Brandon to a chair and put a bottle of Cristal in his hand.

"This is for you, baby!" Chris yelled. "I saved the best for last!"

Chris went over to the stereo and turned it down. He opened the door to the bathroom and out came one of the hottest bitches Brandon had ever seen. She had a body like Buffie, and a face like Trina. She wore only a G-string and a bra with a pair of four-inch stilettos.

She came over to Brandon and sat on his lap. His dick

was hard from the time she walked into the room. He undid her bra and smothered his face in her chest. The whole crowd started cheering. Chris took a bottle of champagne and poured it on Brandon, and everyone watched as the dancer on Brandon's lap threw her G-string to the floor and straddled him. Brandon stuck his finger in her ass and watched as she masturbated. At that moment another girl came over and kissed the Trina look-alike on the mouth. The girls looked at each other, and then at Brandon as they led him into the bedroom.

Chris was busy himself. He had this big tittie Puerto Rican girl on his heels. He took her into the bathroom and closed the door.

By the end of the night, Brandon was hammered. He had two bottles of champagne to himself, and two fine-ass women. He couldn't thank Chris enough for that threesome. Brandon was so drunk that he had pissed his pants. The fellas had left two hours ago, and it was just about sunrise. Chris went into the bedroom to check on Brandon. When he noticed Brandon's pants were soaking wet, he unbuttoned the pants and pulled them off. Brandon was completely drunk, so when he looked up and saw Chris, he just thought everything was OK.

Chris stood over Brandon after he passed out again. He always thought Brandon was sexy, and he always had a thing for him. Brandon's chocolate, toned body and long eyelashes made Chris's dick hard. And now that Brandon was drunk, and Chris was half drunk himself, this was the perfect time for Chris to get a taste.

Chris got in the bed next to Brandon and just watched Brandon for a minute. His lips were nice and full. Chris leaned in and kissed Brandon over and over again.

Suddenly Brandon opened his eyes and realized what was happening. He reached out and grabbed the closet thing within his reach—an empty champagne bottle. He tried to hit Chris over the head with it, but missed. Chris jumped up and stood by the door.

"What's wrong with you?!" Brandon yelled.

Chris could barely stand. The alcohol had his vision blurry and his balance off. As Chris quickly stumbled down the hall, Brandon scrambled to his feet and leaned against the wall. He was trying to get sober.

Brandon wiped his mouth over and over with the sleeve of his shirt. He looked around the room for his pants and spotted them on the other side of the bed. He stumbled over and picked them up. Brandon couldn't concentrate. *Chris is a faggot?* Maybe he was dreaming. He looked at the wet spot on his pants. He felt it, and it was wet and cold. Nope, he wasn't dreaming.

Brandon was so mad that he stumbled into the hallway wearing only his boxers. He rode the elevator down to the lobby and spotted Chris talking to the concierge at the front desk. Brandon ran up on him and tackled him to the ground. Chris tried to push Brandon off him, but he couldn't manage to get the upper hand. As Chris looked at Brandon he saw fire in his eyes. Brandon kept slapping Chris in the head over and over again.

"You fucking homo!" Brandon howled. "What the fuck is wrong with you?"

Hotel security tried to pry Brandon off Chris. Chris was surprised that Brandon was getting the best of him. He always acted like such a bitch, but tonight it took two men to hold back Brandon.

Brandon went back up to the room, took a quick shower, and put on the change of clothes he had in his duffel bag. The wedding started at two, and he had about six hours to get himself together. He was so disgusted with Chris. This nigga was a homo thug. He had kissed Brandon on the lips. Brandon felt like a teenage girl who had just lost her virginity. He was so confused.

How can Chris be a faggot? he wondered. Pussy was too fucking good to want to bump dicks with another nigga. *Why would he try me?* Chris knew he wasn't gay. He loved pussy.

Brandon massaged his temple while he tried to figure out how this whole mess started. Chris was always up in some pussy, and he had a baby with Tracy. He had even proposed to Tracy. Brandon felt like his manhood had been compromised. He wondered if this made him a faggot.

So maybe he was one of those down low dudes all along, Brandon thought. He just acted like he wanted to fuck females to keep his rep. If fucking dudes was what he wanted to do, then cool. But he was not going to drag Brandon into that gay shit. He was a man, and today was his wedding day.

Brandon didn't know what to think about Chris anymore. He had changed. He had tested their friendship and Brandon's manhood in one night.

After about two cups of coffee and a couple Tylenol, Brandon was finally sober enough to drive home. He had about two hours before the wedding started, and he needed to get dressed. He could tell that Chris had been to his apartment because there was an open bottle of beer on the counter, and his dirty underwear was on the bathroom floor. Chris was pressing Brandon's buttons. He should have gone somewhere else to take a shower. Brandon was praying to God that Chris didn't show up at the wedding. He didn't care how fucked up the procession looked without him. He was sure that Chris wasn't that crazy.

Brandon had to be at the hall twenty minutes before the wedding started. He peered in himself at the mirror as he straightened his bowtie and smiled widely, practicing for the photographer. He had to admit, he looked good.

His smooth, black skin glistened from moisturizer, and his teal cummerbund fit around him perfectly. He was ready to see his bride.

The doorman buzzed Brandon when the limo arrived at the building. Brandon got in the car and there was Chris sitting across from him. They didn't say a word to each other during the whole ride. They just stared each other down. Brandon knew Chris wasn't the brightest nigga on the block, but he should have known that after the stunt he pulled, he would not be wanted at the wedding.

Chris didn't know what to say. He had got caught up in the moment. His true feelings for Brandon had seeped out. But he didn't want to miss Brandon's wedding because of his mistake.

When the limo pulled up to the Bellevue there was a small crowd of guests swarming around. Chris got out of the limo and went straight into the hall. Brandon waited until the guests took their seats and then he walked slowly into the lobby. Tracy and Little Chris were waiting to be seated. Tracy actually looked happy for a change. She had gained a few pounds, and the extra weight had done her well. Her face was fuller and her eyes were bright. She nudged Brandon on the shoulder.

"Congratulations," she said. "I never thought you would be getting married." Brandon picked up Little Chris and kissed him on the cheek.

"You got jokes, huh?" Brandon asked. "Have you seen Chris?"

"No, I don't really talk to Chris if it isn't about the baby."

Although he never cared before, Brandon was suddenly eager to find out why Tracy had left Chris.

"So why did you two call it quits anyway?" Brandon asked casually.

Tracy looked around and then whispered in Brandon's ear.

"I found out that Chris was sleeping with a man. I knew that Chris cheated on me, but with a man? That was too much."

Brandon had his mouth open and couldn't close it. It was confirmed. This nigga was a stone cold fag. Brandon couldn't understand how he had missed all the signs.

The music was starting to play, so Brandon handed Little Chris to Tracy.

"I'll talk to you after the ceremony," he said.

Tracy and Little Chris took a seat in the back of the hall. Brandon watched as the procession started. Chris was partnered with Sam, and she couldn't help but look like she was the luckiest woman in world to be on his arm. After Brandon made his way up the aisle, the music changed to "Here Comes the Bride." As Mia started up the aisle, the room fell silent in awe. Brandon looked in Chris's direction, and Chris winked his eye and turned back to watch Mia.

Why did he wink his eye at me? Brandon wondered. Chris probably thought Brandon was cool with that shit he pulled. Brandon wanted to grab him and beat the shit out of him. If the press wasn't there, he would have tried to take off Chris's head.

Brandon's violent thoughts came to a halt when he saw how beautiful Mia looked in her wedding dress. She had scored a brand new Roberto Cavalli gown that her publicist provided. As Mia walked slowly down the aisle to let the press take photos of the beautiful gown, Brandon could only think of how absolutely stunning she looked. The empire waist of the gown hid every bit of her pregnant belly, and the train was so long that it wrapped around the alter. She truly looked like a princess with her jeweled headpiece and her hair pinned in the prettiest updo with big romance curls falling in her face.

After Mia's father left her side and found his seat, Brandon took his place next to his bride. The ceremony proceeded quickly and ended with the sweetest kiss. Brandon lifted her veil and fell in love with her all over again, but this time she was his wife. The crowd clapped as they proceeded down the aisle and out of the hall.

Everyone stood and watched as the photographers took pictures of the wedding party. When it came time for Chris and Brandon to take a picture together, Chris put his arm around Brandon's shoulder and smiled for the camera. Brandon pushed his arm away as soon as the camera flashed. He was sick of Chris. He thought this whole situation was a joke.

Brandon searched the crowd for Tracy, but couldn't find her. He was eager to find out more about Chris and his secret. He noticed Ms. Ruth walking toward him with a huge smile on her face. As she walked over to give him a kiss, Chris saw her and backed off quickly, disappearing into the crowd.

"Hey, Mom, I didn't see you come in." He gave her a hug. "Thank you for coming."

"No problem, baby. Wouldn't have missed it for the world. How have you been?" she asked. "I haven't seen you in a while."

"Fine. Have you seen Chris?" Brandon looked around. "He was standing right here a few minutes ago."

She shook her head in disgust. "That boy is in bad shape," she said. "Somebody needs to pray for his soul. He been running around with those men. He can't ever come back in my house for the rest of his days."

Brandon must have been living in his own little bubble. Apparently he was the only one who didn't know that Chris was messing with niggas. He was getting more and more uncomfortable by the second. His own best friend fucked with niggas on the low, and he had no idea. Brandon gave Ms. Ruth another hug.

"Thanks again, Mom. I'll see you later," he said, not letting on that the news she had shared with him was another shock.

Brandon wanted to get back to Mia. This was their special day, and he wasn't going to let Chris spoil it. He found her talking with the press, and pried her away for a quiet moment alone. Grabbing her hands, he looked into her eyes.

"You look beautiful, you know that?" he asked.

Mia smiled and kissed him.

"You didn't look half bad yourself, Mr. Brunson."

"Why thank you, Mrs. Brunson. I really appreciate it." She kissed him one last time before she was pulled away by Sam and two of her college girlfriends.

The reception was held in the same location as the ceremony. The hall was cleared and tables were set up to accommodate the party. Everyone was mingling, yet Brandon was looking only for Chris, who was nowhere to be found.

Maybe he left? Brandon hoped as he headed into the bathroom to take a leak. He walked in and heard moaning coming from the last stall. Walking closer, he bent down to see who was in there, and two pair of feet were visible. He noticed Chris's black snakeskin Ferragamo loafers; they were the only pair of fine shoes he owned. Brandon busted open the door, and there was Chris and Sam fucking in the stall. Sam was bent over the toilet, and Chris was fucking her from behind. Brandon just shook his head. This was it. Their friendship was over. Chris couldn't even suppress his own needs so that Brandon and Mia could enjoy their wedding day. He looked at Sam and laughed.

"Sam," he said with a chuckle as he leaned against the stall door.

"Yeah?" She was embarrassed. Her whole ass was out.

"Why you fucking a faggot?" Brandon asked.

"What?" Sam was confused.

Chris's face turned red, and he was getting ready to charge Brandon when Mia's father walked into the bathroom. Brandon quickly closed the door to the stall and went to join his bride.

The guests watched as Mia and Brandon cut the cake. They fed each other a piece, and Mia put frosting on Brandon's nose. Mia was so anxious to throw the bouquet that she lined up the girls before the cake was served. She stood on the grand staircase and turned around. A crowd of women scattered about all looking for the right angle to where they thought it may fall. Mia tossed the bouquet and turned around quickly to see whom the lucky lady was going to be. The flowers fell right into Tracy's hands in an almost effortless manner. She blushed as she stood by Mia to take a picture. Brandon thought that Tracy catching the bouquet was the funniest thing he had ever seen in his life. He knew who she wasn't going to marry, and that was Chris. He was too busy fucking niggas in the ass for that.

Brandon spent the rest of the reception dancing with Mia, and Chris sat in the corner with Sam, glaring at Mia and Brandon the whole night. He envied Brandon. He envied both of them. Brandon had a wife, and Chris didn't even have a steady relationship. Every time their eyes met, Brandon's faced scrunched up at the thought of Chris fucking a man and trying his manhood in the process. He hated Chris for being so fucked up.

Mia and Brandon snuck off from the reception and went back to her place. She tore off her dress as soon as she closed the door. Brandon's dick was hard as soon as she dropped the first strap from her shoulder. She was finally ready to make love to her man, but Brandon was a little unsure about her decision. He wanted her badly, but he didn't want to have sex until he knew that she was really ready.

She stepped out of the dress right in front of him and kissed him passionately. Unzipping his pants, she massaged his fully erect dick. Brandon had to be strong. He kissed her on the forehead and backed away.

"What's wrong?" Mia asked.

"Baby, we need to wait. I want us to take our time with this. I know you have just been through so much."

"But I want us to make love. It's our wedding night."

"Baby, please, we have the rest of our lives to make love to each other. I just want things to be right. It's too soon."

Mia frowned.

"I want you now." She pulled him closer.

"Let's at least wait until the honeymoon. We're leaving in two days, just you and me for a whole month."

"OK, OK, so we'll wait, but only until the honeymoon."

He caressed her back and kissed her on the neck.

"Now go put on some clothes before I change my mind. You're making my dick hard." He smacked her on the ass. Mia grabbed her gown from the floor and went to change.

Brandon took off his bowtie and dropped it on the couch beside him. He still had no idea what to do about Chris. He did know one thing, though. Their friendship was over. Chris was no friend of Brandon's anymore. A friend would not have tried to test his manhood.

Brandon decided that he was going to leave the label. He was going to the office tomorrow to clean out his office. Brandon would only deal with the office in New York, and if he had to do business with Chris, it would be done by telephone. He got so mad when he saw Chris in person at the wedding that he thought he just might try to kill him if he saw him again.

With that settled, Brandon got up from the couch and went into the bedroom. Mia was lying on the bed naked.

"Are you trying to tease me?" he asked as he positioned his body on top of hers. She laughed and bit her bottom lip.

"Call it what you want," she said seductively.

"Well two can play that game," he said as he kissed her stomach and opened her thighs. He licked between her legs and then kissed her on the mouth.

"Good night," he said with a grin on his face.

He could see that Mia was sexually frustrated. She turned her back toward him while he undressed and lay down in the bed. Brandon fell asleep quickly, but Mia lay awake for some time thinking about how everything was so perfect. She was somebody's wife. She looked at the diamond ring on her finger. Now it was accompanied by a platinum band. She turned off the lamp and made herself comfortable.

Brandon woke early the next morning. He didn't want to run into Chris while he was getting his stuff from the office, and he had some last minute running around to do before their flight the next morning. He threw on a pair of sweats and drove over to the office. It was a little before eight when he got there. Turning on the lights, he looked around and saw that the office was vacant. They had really just been holding on to the space in hopes that they would do more business, but things were so bad that they had to let go of the part-time secretary a few weeks before the wedding.

Brandon ran back downstairs and grabbed two big boxes out of his trunk so he could pack up his stuff. He took the drawers out of his desk and dumped everything into the boxes. He wanted to be done as fast as possible. As Brandon was clearing his desk he came across a folder containing documents from the lawyer. The folder contained the papers Chris signed several months ago when he was in trouble with the law.

Something clicked inside Brandon's mind. Chris didn't own half the business anymore. Brandon had full ownership. Chris had signed all of his rights over to Brandon. Brandon grabbed the folder, rolled it up, and stuffed it in the inside pocket of his jacket.

This could actually work to my advantage, he thought. *I don't need Chris to make any decisions from this point on.*

Brandon finished packing and brought the two boxes down to his jeep. He took one last look around the office and locked the door. Thinking back to the first day they opened, Brandon remembered how excited he and Chris were about owning their own business. They sat in the office every day for two weeks before they opened for business. Now things were so messed up that they hardly ever went past there. They called the office in New York twice a week to check in, but it was practically running itself.

Brandon needed to pack up the clothes in his apartment next. He was officially moving in with his wife. He still hadn't decided what he was going to do with his place, but he was moving as soon as possible. He packed as much as he could into three large suitcases, and figured he'd come back for the rest later. As he was leaving his condo, he noticed a small white envelope on the floor by the door. He picked it up and stuffed it into his bag to read later. Chris must have left it there.

Brandon arrived back at Mia's house around noon. She was just rolling out of bed. Brandon dumped his bags in the living room and went over to the fridge to grab a beer. Mia started to pack her bags for the honeymoon. She still had no idea where they were going. Brandon told her it was a surprise, and that she would have to wait to find out until they boarded the plane. Mia looked through her closet. There was nothing in there that would hide her gut. She needed to make an emergency trip to the mall.

"I need to go to the mall," she yelled from inside the closet. "I can't fit any of my regular clothes."

Brandon walked into the bedroom to see what she was hollering about. He stood by the door with the beer in his hand.

"What did you say?" he asked. "I couldn't hear a word you said."

"I said I can't fit anything in my closet. I need to go to the mall." Brandon rolled his eyes. Mia just wanted an excuse to buy a new wardrobe. She had a little tiny gut. All of her clothes usually clung to her body. The loose thing was new to her.

"Whatever you need to do," he said. She backed out of the closet with her Luis Vuitton suitcases and carry-on. He looked her over as she laid them out on the bed. Mia was indeed a fine catch. She was beautiful. Her hair had grown to her shoulders, and her breasts were bigger now too because of the pregnancy. Brandon could definitely get used to that. She grabbed her car keys off the table and her purse from the dresser.

"I'll see you later," she said and kissed him. "I'll be back in a few."

"Mia," Brandon said. She turned around. "Try to get back before the mall closes. We have an early flight."

"All right, all right," she said. "How can I possibly visit every store if I rush?"

As she left he shook his head. That girl sure could shop. She went into every single store in the mall just to make sure she didn't need anything. She didn't care what type of store it was. She always said that you never knew what you needed until you saw it.

While Mia had her mind on shopping, Brandon was thinking about other things. He was still thinking about those papers from the lawyer. He had full control of the business, and that meant he could do what he wanted, including selling to Epic. He decided to stretch out on the couch and sleep on his ideas.

Brandon was still asleep when Mia returned. She tiptoed around the house to make sure that she didn't wake him. He looked so peaceful and cute, except for the slobber coming out of the side of his mouth, that was.

Mia decided she was going to cook her first dinner as a married woman. She tried frying chicken until the smoke detector sounded from all the smoke. Brandon jumped up and looked around. He quickly opened the balcony door to air out the apartment, and they ended up ordering Chinese takeout.

After dinner Brandon sifted through the clothes he brought to Mia's and packed for the trip. He put the envelope from his condo in his briefcase so he could read it while they were in the air. After taking a shower he set the alarm for two AM. The flight was scheduled to leave at four, so he wanted to get there early enough to get settled in before they took off.

The alarm must not have gone off, because when Brandon glanced at the clock it was almost three-thirty. He leaped to his feet and hurried into the bathroom to brush his teeth. Mia could hear him stumbling around the apartment, so she jumped up and put on some jeans and a top. When he returned from the bathroom she was fully dressed with her pocketbook under her arm. Brandon grabbed his jacket and keys, and they lugged their bags to the elevator and down to the lobby. The car had already arrived to take them to the airport. Mia hurried out to the car and Brandon followed quickly behind her. He stopped dead in his tracks and patted his jacket pocket, then took out the letter he wrote to Lynn and stuffed it in the mailbox by the lobby door and continued over to the car. He smiled uneasily at Mia as the driver pulled off in the direction of the airport.

They got there fifteen minutes before the plane was scheduled to take off. They ran through the terminal and arrived at the gate just as the doors were closing. Brandon's heart was beating so fast that he needed a bottle of water to calm down.

"Are you all right?" he asked Mia as the plane took off. She looked beat herself. She was running hard right alongside him. She was panting a bit, but managed to catch her breath.

"I'm fine," she said. "Are you going to tell me where we're going now?" Brandon smiled.

"Saint Tropez."

Mia was so excited. They were going to spend the first month of their marriage together, alone—no Chris, no Sam—just the two of them. Brandon laughed at Mia's excitement.

Mia settled into her seat, put on her earphones, and leaned her seat back so she could rest. Brandon pulled out his laptop from his briefcase, and out fell the letter. He had almost forgotten that he had stashed it there. He opened it, and it was a one-page letter written in fancy cursive. He read it carefully:

Dear Brandon,

I know Chris, or Chief, very well. I have been dealing with him for over two years. I know who raped Mia, and I can't stand by and let him get away with it. Chris is the man who hurt her, and he told her that if she ever told anyone he would kill her. I am sorry that I didn't come forth sooner.

Kane

Brandon sat up in his seat. Who the fuck was this Kane person? He looked at Mia, who was staring at him. She knew something was wrong because he was shifting all over the place. He stood up from his chair and looked around. Brandon needed to get off the plane. He needed to go back home and get to Chris. He was going to kill him. Brandon threw the letter on the floor, got up from his seat, and walked to the bathroom. He let out a loud scream that the whole first class section could hear. Mia grabbed the letter from the floor and began to read. She started to shake and cry as soon as she read the line about her rape. Brandon came back to his seat and held her tightly.

"I'm so sorry, baby," he cried. "I'm so sorry he hurt you like this." Tears were streaming down Brandon's face. Chris was a dead man. He had not only hurt Brandon, but he hurt his wife and endangered the life of their baby. This was supposed to be his best friend. They grew up together, and Brandon was just finding out that Chris was a monster.

Brandon and Mia spent the whole flight consoling each other. When they finally landed, Brandon turned on his cell phone and waited for a signal. After several minutes, he noticed that his phone wasn't cooperating so he ran to the first phone he saw. He dialed Chris's cell phone.

"Yeah," Chris answered.

"You're a dead man!" Brandon yelled and banged the receiver down over and over. Chris didn't recognize the voice because the person had yelled. He looked at number on his ID to see if he knew the number, but it came up as unknown.

Chapter 11

Nothing to Lose

Chris pulled the car over and put his cell phone back in his pocket. He had no idea who would be calling to threaten him, but he knew that he needed to start carrying his gun on him more often. He had stopped carrying it the day it discharged in Brandon's crib, because he knew that if Mia started talking, his weapon would be hot. Chris was reluctant to carry the gun again, but a phone call like that could make any nigga nervous. He had been keeping his nose clean. Chris needed to be cautious now. He pulled out his gun from the glove compartment, laid it on the seat beside him, and pulled off.

Chris's cash was low, so he was on his way to the bank to pull out the last of his money. He only had about five grand, and he needed to grab an apartment. He was tired of staying between Kane's and Sam's apartments. They were both nagging-ass bitches. He couldn't relax without one of them on his back about something. Sam was hinting at marriage, and they hadn't even known each other that long. Chris was trying to leave her alone all together.

She was starting to want to fuck raw, and Chris definitely didn't want any more kids.

Kane was becoming moody. He had been acting like he didn't want Chris around anymore. Chris was going to drop both of them and start new. He needed some variety in his life. He was going to have to find a whole new lineup of bitches once he figured out where he was going to stay.

Chris pulled into the parking lot of the bank, tucked the gun into the back of his pants, and walked inside. He went over to the counter and wrote out a withdrawal slip for four grand. He was broke. All of his cash was gone, and he had no plan set in motion to make any. His car note was due, and he still had to make sure that he took care of his son. Tracy had called him a couple of hours ago asking him for three grand. He still loved Tracy, so he didn't care if it was his last dime, he was going to make sure she had any money she needed. The bank teller handed him the envelope and he moved to the side to count his money. It was all there. He had one grand left in the bank.

As Chris walked out of the bank he starting thinking seriously about finances and about Brandon. He was mad at himself for spending all that money on Brandon's bachelor party. Those stripper broads cost him a grip. He had used five grand from the label's petty cash to front the bill. All that money spent, and now they weren't even talking.

Chris didn't really regret what he did, though. He had always wanted to taste Brandon's full lips. He dreamed about it for years, and the alcohol just gave him the courage to finally do it. He touched his jaw. The whole left side of his face was swollen from the fight with Brandon in the hotel lobby. The swelling was beginning to decrease, but it was still quite noticeable. He wasn't mad that Brandon had freaked out. He was more disappointed that

Brandon wasn't curious about what could have happened between them.

Chris felt like Brandon owed him something. He had been taking care of Brandon for years. He bought him his first car—an Infiniti. When Brandon was in his first year of college he had a better car than his roommate's parents' car. Chris always made sure Brandon had the best, and when he graduated from college Chris gave Brandon the down payment for his condo. Brandon wouldn't have made it without him, and now Chris was growing resentful of Brandon. He was married to this beautiful and rich girl, but Brandon had never given Chris any cash. All he did was take whatever he could. Chris had never had it easy. He hugged the block for years and built his street credibility murkin' niggas who stepped out of line. They didn't call him Chief for nothing.

After contemplating his financial situation, Chris left the bank and headed toward the projects. He was on his way to meet Tank at the Dominican store. Tank had finally made bail, and Chris still needed to borrow that money from him. He pulled up in front of the store and hopped out. Tank was back to his usual, sitting on a milk crate and rolling a blunt. Tank lit the blunt, took a few tokes, and passed it to Chris.

"Chief, you still need that dough?" Tank asked.

"Yeah, man, I need that shit," Chris said and passed the blunt back to him.

Tank dipped in the alley behind the store, came back with a whack of cash, and passed it to Chris. Chris waited until he got back in the car to count the bills. There was five thousand dollars. He rolled down the window and smiled at Tank.

"I added a couple grand to that for you," Tank said. "I gotta look out for my old head."

"Thanks, man. I'll holla at you later," Chris said as he pulled off.

Tank had made sure that Chris had enough money to cop a crib and pay the rent up for a while. He could tell his old-head friend was fucked up, and he also knew that Potts had sold him out. The only reason why Potts didn't get fucked up for leaving the label was because he was respected in the hood. He had to do what he had to do in order to feed his family, and if that meant a better deal with another label, then that was what it had to be. This was his hustle, and all hustles were respected as long as they didn't fuck up somebody else's hustle in the process.

Chris made his way to Diamond Street. He had seen a room for rent last week over there, and he wanted to see if it was still available. He rolled up in front of the building on Twenty-second Street and parked the car. The FOR RENT sign was still there, so he rang the bell. After waiting fifteen minutes, an elderly man on a cane finally appeared in the doorway. Chris could smell the stench from inside the front steps. It smelled like old people and cigars. He backed down the steps without saying a word and got back into the car. Chris sat there and let the car run. His best bet was to stay with Sam until he found something. He dialed her cell phone.

"Hey, sweetie," Sam answered. The sound of her voice made his skin crawl.

"I'm coming over."

"Well, when, because I have to go out of town for the weekend, and I'm leaving in about forty-five minutes for the airport."

This is great, Chris thought. He could stay there and not have to look in her face for the next couple of days.

"I'm on my way there now." Chris drove quickly down Twentieth Street until he reached Center City. He parked his car in the garage under her building and rode the elevator to the eighth floor. By the time he arrived Sam was lugging her bags to the elevator. He rushed over and picked up her suitcase. They rode the elevator down to the lobby and she handed him the key to her apartment.

"Don't have any other women in my home while I'm gone," she said. Chris rolled his eyes and looked at her as if she was stupid.

"Why the hell would I do some shit like that?" Chris asked, even though the thought did cross his mind.

Chris walked Sam outside and loaded her bags into the back of the cab. She kissed him and got inside the car. As soon as the cab drove off Chris let out a huge sigh of relief. He went back up to the apartment and took off all his clothes. Sitting on the couch naked, he flipped on the TV. Chris was horny, but instead of calling Kane he decided that he was going to jerk off. He turned the channel to BET and watched as the chicks' assess from Fifty's "Candy Shop" bounced up and down on the screen. Chris massaged his dick faster and faster until he came on himself. When he was finished he went into the bathroom to clean up.

As he stepped out of the shower he could hear his cell beeping, indicating that someone had left a message. He quickly walked into the living room and dug into his pants pocket for his phone. Tracy had left a message for him to meet her at the spot around three. Something must be wrong, because they never met there unless he was in trouble. He and Tracy always had an emergency meet up spot just in case shit got hot and they needed a place to stay. No one else knew where it was, and it had always remained that way.

Chris scrambled through the bag of clothes he kept at Sam's place, looking for a clean pair of underwear. He finally found a pair at the bottom of the bag. He slipped them on, and then bent over to find a pair of socks. Just as he located one sock, he felt his boxers split right down the back.

"Fuck!" he yelled.

After finding the mate to his sock, he put on his socks and then his jeans. He didn't have any other clean under-wear, so he'd have to wear the ripped pair. Chris glanced at the clock on the kitchen wall. It was twenty to three. He grabbed his hat and tucked his gun into his pants. After leaving the apartment, Chris took the elevator down to the parking garage. As he exited the garage he noticed two police cars parked in front of the building. His eyes met with one officer as he drove past slowly. Turning the corner, he drove down Nineteenth Street, made a left on Girard, and took it down to Thirtieth Street. He could see Tracy standing in front of the old stables from a block away. He drove up, parked, and sat on the hood of the car.

"What's up?" he asked.

Chris stared at Tracy. She looked sexy as hell. Those Rock Republic jeans were grabbing her ass so tightly that his dick was getting hard. Her fur jacket hugged her waist, and she wore her hair just the way he liked it—feathered to the back in Farrah Fawcett flips. Tracy's face was filled with concern.

"Chris, what the fuck did you do? Did you rape Mia?"

Chris's face went blank. *How does she know?* Chris won-dered. No one knew except Kane, and Chris knew Kane wasn't stupid enough to run his mouth.

"I don't know what you're talking about," Chris said.

"Well you can act stupid if you want to, but the cops are looking for your ass. Your mother called me early this morning and said they broke down her door looking for you." Tracy's voice held a mixture of disgust and worry.

After hearing that bit of news, Chris went into panic mode. Kane must have snitched. Chris knew he had Mia so petrified that she couldn't bear to stare him in his face, let alone talk to the police. *No wonder Kane has been acting shady lately,* Chris thought.

"Look, I'm just trying to warn you," Tracy said. "I don't even want you to tell me what happened." Tracy pointed her finger at him. "You better get ya shit together, because if you get knocked, I ain't visiting your ass, and I ain't bringing my son to no fucking prison either."

As Tracy continued pointing at him, Chris noticed something shiny on her hand. He got up from the hood and grabbed her left hand to inspect it more closely. The shiny object was an engagement ring.

"What the fuck is this?!" he yelled, holding her hand up to get a better look at the ring. She yanked her hand back and put it in her jacket pocket. Chris waited for an answer as his face turned red with rage.

"I'm engaged," she said simply.

Chris's eyes darkened at her response.

"To who?" He looked away. "You know what, I don't even want to know who the nigga is."

Tracy tried to focus back on the situation at hand. She looked directly into Chris's eyes as she spoke.

"You need to be careful. You need to find somewhere to stay where nobody knows you."

Chris was still thinking about the ring. He was so upset. He loved Tracy, and she was supposed to be his wife. They were supposed to be a family. Chris's eyes were watering partly from the cold weather, but also from the news of his woman's engagement. He walked around to the driver's side of the car and took the money he had for Tracy out of the armrest. He put it in her hand.

"I'll be in touch," he said.

Tracy walked back to her car and drove off without another word.

Chris banged his fist on the hood of the car. He had lost it all. There was nothing left. He should have listened to

Brandon and sold the label. Now they were knee deep in debt.

Chris got back in the car and tried to dial Kane, but his number was disconnected. Now he knew for sure that it was Kane who snitched on him. After rummaging through the glove compartment and finding the spare key Kane had given him a month ago, he drove over to West Philly. He parked in front of Kane's building, but only after circling the block twice to make sure there wasn't any police around. He got out the car, walked over to Kane's window, and peeked inside. The place was cleaned out. Chris ran inside the building and opened the door to Kane's apartment. Kane had moved out without telling him. There was nothing but a bag of garbage sitting in the middle of the kitchen area. Chris hurried out before anyone saw him and drove off.

He couldn't think straight. He rushed back to Sam's apartment and gathered his things. The only place he could stay without the cops knowing his whereabouts was the projects. He drove as fast as he could across town, avoiding every main road until he reached North Philly. He parked his car in front of the Dominican store, got out, and handed his keys to Tank.

"What are these for?" Tank asked.

Chris took the blunt out of Tank's hand and took a long drag. "I need to stay at ya crib for a while. Use the car if you need to. I can't drive the shit anymore. Just pay the note off and it's yours."

Chris knew that if he kept using that car they would find his ass easily. He still needed to get around, so he was going to cop a hooptie to get him by until he figured out his next move.

Without asking Chris another question, Tank handed him the key to his spot. Chris grabbed his two duffel bags out of the trunk and took them up to the apartment.

When he opened the door Tank's mother was lying on the couch in her robe watching Jerry Springer. She looked up at Chris briefly, and then went back to watching TV. Chris shook his head and went back to Tank's room to drop off his bags.

Chris's next move was to find Kane. This nigga had disappeared out of the blue. Chris knew that Kane's best friend Donnie worked at this small bar on Thirteenth Street, so he was going to pay Donnie a visit. Donnie always had a crush on Chris, but he was too feminine for Chris's taste. Kane knew that Donnie liked Chris, so he tried his best to make sure they never ran into each other. Chris's plan was to wrap Donnie around his pinky finger and string him along for the ride until he led Chris straight to Kane.

Chris undressed and walked through the house naked to grab a beer out of the refrigerator. He walked right in front of Tank's mom, but she didn't even bother to look up from the TV screen. Chris had dusted that old pussy off for her more than enough times. She liked to fuck young dudes, and for a dime bag of weed and a forty of Budweiser, she gave the best blow jobs a nigga could ever ask for.

He grabbed a beer and headed for the shower. By the time he was finished getting dressed it was seven PM. He wanted to take care of his car situation before he left, so he ran up to his homie Black's apartment on the tenth floor to see what kinds of cars he had available. Chris used to buy cars from this nigga all the time when he was a young boy. He was the perfect connect. You could get tags, stickers, and registration for the right fee.

"What's up, Black?" Chris asked, shaking Black's hand once he answered the door.

"What up, Chief? Where you been?"

Chris looked both ways to see who was coming down the hall, and then he walked into Black's apartment.

Black closed and locked the door behind him and took a seat at the kitchen table.

"I've been chillin', man," Chris said after he sat down at the table and folded his hands. "But listen, yo, I need to cop a wheel."

"What you trying to spend?" he asked. Black was talking business, but his eyes never left the dice game he was playing at the table.

"What you got?" Chris asked.

"I only got one car right now, until next week. You should have caught me earlier. I just sold two."

"Nigga, what you got?" Chris asked again.

Black threw the dice again and rolled a seven this time. He snapped his fingers and rolled again.

"I got an Impala. It's a two thousand, fully loaded. I'll throw in the paperwork and the tags for thirty-five hundred."

The price was right up Chris's alley. He took the wad of money out of his pocket, counted it off, and dropped it on the table in front of Black. Black put the money in his sock and went into the bedroom. Chris waited patiently for him to return. Black came strolling back into the room forty-five minutes later with a license plate, registration, and insurance cards all in the name of a Jamal Brown. He handed it all to Chris.

"Oh, yeah, I almost forgot." Black reached into his back pocket and pulled out a driver's license with Chris's face on it under the same alias.

"I threw that one in for free." Black smiled.

"How you get my picture?" Chris asked.

"Nigga, please. I got ya picture and everybody else's in the city. I got access to the database." He smiled. "The car is parked up the street." Chris shook his hand.

"Thanks, man, good looking out."

Chris left the apartment and waited for the elevator.
When the doors of the elevator opened the nigga Mike
was there. Chris reached for his waist to grab his gun, but
it wasn't there. He had left it in the car. Mike smiled as
Chris got on the elevator. Chris hoped this nigga wasn't
going to try anything in the elevator. There were two young
girls and a baby on there with them, and Mike couldn't be
that stupid. Their beef was supposedly over. Chris had hit
him up, and Mike's homies burned down Chris's crib.
They were even.

Chris positioned himself on the other side of the elevator, placing the two young girls and the baby between him
and Mike. This way if Mike tried anything, the innocent
bystanders would probably get hit up first. The second the
elevator opened at the bottom floor Chris sprinted out
the door and over to the Dominican store.

Chris expected to see Tank, but he wasn't there. He had
to get to Tank. He needed the keys to his old car in order
to get his gun. Chris looked around and noticed that Mike
was quickly walking up on him. Mike continued to follow
Chris as Chris jogged up the alley. Chris heard Mike cock
the gun, and he dodged to the side as two shots rang out.
Jumping back up, he ran out of the alley and into the middle of the street.

Mike continued to chase Chris while panting heavily.
Mike let off another shot. Chris ran up the block as fast as
he could while looking over his shoulder to make sure
that he was not being followed. After finally stopping to
rest for a minute, Chris was about to get moving again
when he felt the cold metal of Mike's gun on the back of
his neck. The breath that Chris had caught left him.

"Yeah, nigga, you thought I was going to let ya nut ass
get away?" Mike asked. "Get down on the ground."

Mike looked around to make sure no one was watching.

The street was so dimly lit that no one could see them. Chris lay on his stomach and prayed to God. He prayed that Mike would kill him then and there, because if he didn't, he wouldn't get a second chance. Chris knew he should have laid out Mike when he had the chance months ago.

Mike patted down Chris's pockets until he came across the money Chris had stashed in the inside pocket of his jacket. Mike grabbed the money and the keys to the car that Chris had just bought from Black.

"Turn around," he said. Chris rolled off his stomach and onto his back. Mike spit in Chris's face and cocked the gun again.

"I can kill you right now nigga, you know that?" Mike yelled. He kicked Chris in the stomach, and Chris buckled over from the pain. "I know you thought you killed me. You a stupid muthafucka if you thought you was going to catch me without my vest on," Mike said, kicking him again.

Mike was a bitch at heart. He talked a good game, but when it was time for action, he never followed through.

"I'm gonna let ya nut ass live. You know why?" he asked, and waited for an answer from Chris, but none came. He kicked Chris in the mouth this time, leaving his face a bloody mess.

"Answer me, Chief!" Mike aimed the gun directly at Chris's forehead. Chris decided to go ahead and humor him.

"Why." Chris said the one word more as a statement than a question as he spit the blood out of his mouth and onto the concrete.

"Because, Chief, I can do that. You're nothing to me, nigga." Mike turned and walked away.

This was the very moment Chris had been waiting for. He jumped up and tackled Mike to the ground. Grabbing the gun out of Mike's hand, Chris let off two shots into his left shoulder. Mike stayed still in hopes of slowing the bleeding.

"You dumb-ass nigga. You should have killed me when you had the chance," Chris growled.

Chris rummaged around in Mike's pockets to find his money and the keys to his car. Then he pulled out his dick and peed in Mike's face. He zipped his pants and began backing up to walk off, but then stopped short. Cocking his head to the side, Chris smoothly raised his gun.

"Nigga, I'ma kill you right now. You know why?" Chris asked as he took a step closer. "Because, Mike, I can do THAT." Knowing now that Mike wore a bulletproof vest, Chris let off two shots into the top of Mike's head.

Chris knew he had to move quickly. He needed to get rid of the gun because he knew that he had just caught a homicide case. Searching his contact list in his cell, he found his nigga Rico's phone number. He only called this nigga when he needed to get rid of a piece. This dude melted down guns and recycled them. No gun, no trace.

Chris had done some work for Rico back in the day. Rico owned an iron business and melting down guns was his side job. Chris used to be his informant. He let Rico know who was pushing what and where, and Rico would take over nigga's blocks and send them running home to mommy. If anyone tried to be tough, he went home in a pine box. Rico never did his own dirty work, though. He hired Chris to do that, too. Chris had popped a couple of niggas for Rico, and was paid handsomely in return.

Unfortunately Rico didn't answer the phone, but Chris knew where he could find him. He headed to where all major business was handled—the barbershop on Fifth Street and Indiana.

Chris went back to the projects to grab the Impala he just bought from Black. He walked swiftly and tried to stay alert of his surroundings. He noticed that there was a cop standing at the corner right by the car. Chris walked up and stood close to the door so the cop couldn't see the blood on the front of his shirt. As he fumbled with the keys, he dropped them on the ground. The police officer walked over and leaned on the trunk of the car.

"Is everything all right?" the police officer asked.

Chris turned his back to the police officer and picked up the keys.

"Yes, sir, everything is fine," Chris replied. He unlocked the door and got inside. The police officer knocked on the window as Chris turned on the car and put it in drive. He rolled down the window to see what he wanted.

"Your back tire looks like it may have a slow leak."

"I'll go to the gas station right now and take a look at it. Thanks a lot," Chris said politely.

The officer walked back up the street and Chris pulled off. He pulled up in front of the barbershop on Fifth only a few moments later. Grabbing the gun, he wrapped it in a hoodie that was in the backseat, and casually walked to the front door. He could hear Rico's loud ass from outside. When Chris walked inside, Rico was sitting in the barber chair getting a cut. He got up to greet Chris.

"What's on and poppin', Chief?" Rico asked as they shook hands. He noticed Chris's blood-stained shirt instantly.

"I'm good, man," Chris said. He looked around the shop. Rico and the barber were the only two people there. Rico knew exactly what Chris needed, and he wasted no time in getting straight to the point. He led Chris to the back where the bathroom was. Grabbing a hand towel from under the sink, he held it out. Chris took the gun out of the hoodie, wrapped it up, and gave it back to Rico.

"I appreciate this, man," Chris said.

"Anything for you, Chief," Rico said. "I only see you

when you're in trouble. Next time you stop by make sure it's just to chill, aight?" Rico patted him on the back.

"Aight, man, I'll do that."

Chris shook his hand and walked back through the barbershop to the front door. He put on the hoodie and strolled back to the car. Chris had no idea where he was going now. He looked at the time on his cell phone. It was almost eleven PM. His plans were fucked. He was supposed to catch Kane's friend Donnie, but that wasn't going to happen at this point. Chris figured he might as well leave Kane alone. He had caused that man enough pain as it was.

Chris drove around for two hours trying to figure out where to go. He couldn't stay in the projects because that meant it was possible that Mike's homies might try to set him up. It finally hit him. He would stay at this hotel in West Philly. No one would find him there, because anyone who knew Chris knew that he didn't fuck with West Philly, or so they thought.

He drove over to Fifty-first and Westminster to the Blue Moon Hotel. He had been then once or twice with Kane when they first met, and he liked the place. They didn't ask for ID, and he could pay up front. He walked into the lobby of the hotel and took a seat while he waited for the front desk attendant to finish with the man in front of him. Leaning back in the chair, he took a look around. The burgundy wallpaper was chipping and the waiting area reeked of cheap vodka and cigarettes. Chris started to get up and leave. This was what it had all boiled down to. He was going to stay in a hotel that usually housed cheap tricks and fiends. He was going to have to get another gun to stay here, because someone was bound to try to rob him.

"Can I help you, sir?" the attendant asked, interrupting his daze.

"Yeah, I need a room," he answered.

"For how long?"

"Two months."

She wrote up his slip without saying another word and handed him the bill. Chris dug in his pocket and counted out five hundred dollars, some of which was stained with Mike's blood.

"Here," he said.

He laid the money on the counter and picked up the room key. Walking up the stairs to the second floor, he entered the hallway, which was dark and murky, and the carpet had a damp, musky odor. Chris hated that he was going to have to stay there. He opened the door to his room and took a quick look around before going inside. The bed was neatly made, but the pillows looked dingy. He closed the door behind him and threw the pillows on the floor. After flicking on the TV set, which looked older than he was, he sat on the bed. He didn't have anything but the clothes on his back. He had left his bags at Tank's crib.

Chris lay back on the bed and closed his eyes. He wished he could turn back time. He was in such a fucked up position that he knew eventually he was going to have to turn himself in. His cell phone went off, interrupting his depressing thoughts. He looked to see who it was, and it was Brandon.

"Yeah," Chris answered quietly.

"Listen carefully," Brandon began, "when I get back, you're a dead man. You hear me!" Brandon shouted into the phone.

Chris's eyebrows rose in disbelief.

"What, nigga? I know you not threatening me!" Chris yelled back.

"It's not a threat. It's a promise." Brandon hung up the phone.

Chris threw his cell phone against the door of the room.

He jumped up and started to pace. This shit was going to get crazy. Brandon must know about the rape, too. This was bad. Chris loved Brandon. He was family. Even though they weren't talking, that didn't mean that he didn't have Brandon's back. But now Brandon had let some bitch come between them. Everything was good with them until Chris set up that meeting with Mia. He knew he shouldn't have hooked them up. Now they weren't friends anymore, and Brandon was married to Mia.

Maybe we can work it out, Chris thought. They had been friends for too long to let something like this end it. He had made a mistake. Brandon should be able to understand that. Chris lay back on the bed and closed his eyes, resting until he finally fell asleep.

For the next month Chris kept a low profile. He didn't want anyone to know where he was staying, so he hardly ever went outside. He ordered out all the time, and only left the building to grab a six-pack of beer and some weed. He spent the majority of his days high and drunk, and his nights jerking off while craving pussy and the occasional touch of a man. He hadn't washed his ass in over three weeks, and he was growing more depressed every day.

Chris had about a thousand dollars left, so he decided that he was going to sell the label. He figured he could sell the label and use that money to hire a good defense attorney to represent him. He just needed Brandon to sign the papers with him, and that was going to be the hard part. Brandon didn't need the money now that he was with Mia, but Chris did. Brandon owed him at least that much.

Chris looked at the date on his phone. He hadn't been keeping track of time because he had no schedule and nowhere to go. His heart skipped a beat when he saw how much time had passed. Brandon was due back in town in two days.

Chapter 12

Unfaithful

Brandon gritted his teeth as the plane landed in Philly. Their whole trip had been a nightmare. All Brandon could think about was getting home to take care of business. This was supposed to have been his honeymoon, and he was supposed to be enjoying his wife. Instead, Mia was so embarrassed that she couldn't even stand to look at Brandon. He wasn't taking it well either. He couldn't believe Chris would stoop this low.

Brandon and Mia's relationship had been rocky ever since the plane ride. Brandon was scared to touch her. The thought of Chris fucking his woman made him want to vomit, and Mia felt like a dirty whore. She felt like she had cheated on Brandon, and she could feel them growing apart. They didn't make love the entire trip. All Brandon did was sit on the beach and stare out at the ocean. Mia spent the majority of her days walking the beach and sleeping. They didn't go out to dinner once. Mia could tell that Brandon was hurt. The only brother he knew had betrayed him.

Brandon held Mia's hand as they stepped off the plane.

He inhaled and looked around. It was definitely game time.

Brandon and Mia hailed a cab back to her condo. Brandon held the bags while Mia unlocked the door to her apartment. After lugging Mia's two Louis Vuitton suitcases back to the bedroom, Brandon grabbed some papers out of his briefcase and kissed Mia on the lips.

"I'll be back," he said and left. Mia just nodded and continued to unpack her things.

Lynn had been calling him almost every day since the start of the honeymoon. She had left messages telling him that she was going to be evicted at the end of March, which was about two weeks away.

Brandon had a lot to do in a short amount of time. He had been planning all of this since about day three of his honeymoon. If he had anything during that vacation, it was a lot of time to think. Jumping in the car, he quickly drove over to Lynn's apartment. He rang the doorbell and she came to the door. She looked a little chubbier than before, but she was still beautiful. She stood there in the doorway wearing an oversized T-shirt and a pair of sweatpants. Her face was glowing. She had her hair braided back just the way Brandon liked it.

"Can I come in?" Brandon asked, shivering. "It's kind of cold out here."

"No. This is as far as you come, BRANDON!" she yelled. After reading the letter Brandon had mailed to Lynn, she knew that Keith had never existed. He stood on the second step from the bottom and looked up at her in the doorway.

"Look, I just want to apologize for everything again," he began. "I was wrong, dead wrong. I should have told you my real name. I know it was a fucked up thing to do, and I'm sorry."

"And what about your wife?" Lynn asked. She was disgusted at the fact that she was a mistress. Her child was going to be a bastard, and his wife's child was going to have a full-time father.

Brandon looked away and then back at Lynn.

"I'm sorry I lied about that, too. I want you to have our baby, and I promise I will be there to help you."

"Did you get my messages?"

"Yeah. Just pack your stuff. I'm going to make sure that you have somewhere to stay." Brandon looked down at his watch. It was three PM. "Well, I gotta go handle some business. I'll give you a call later."

"Wait a minute," Lynn said. She pulled a folded piece of paper out of her pocket and handed it to him.

He opened it and stared at it.

"It's an ultrasound of the baby," she said. "I had it done last week when I went to the doctors."

"Thank you for sharing this with me," he said as he folded it back up and put it in his jacket pocket. Lynn closed the door and Brandon got back in his car.

Brandon's mind was still on Chris. It all made perfectly good sense now that he thought about it—all the lying about talking to Mia and the visitor's pass to the hospital. Chris had seemed a little nervous, now that Brandon looked back on it. Mia had told Brandon everything while they were on vacation. She even told him about the gun discharging in his room, which explained why the picture of his mom had been moved.

He rode to his condo to grab his mail. He opened the door cautiously, since he didn't know where Chris was, and he hadn't had a chance to change the locks yet. Flinging open the door, he stood back and carefully walked inside. No one was there. He closed the door and locked it behind him. All of his furniture was still there. As he sifted through his mail, he saw a foreclosure letter from the bank. They were going to take his condo if he didn't pay his mortgage. He was going to take care of all of his business first, and then he was going after Chris.

Brandon meant every word he had said to Chris. He was going to lay that nigga down for raping his wife. He stopped at the bedroom door and peeped inside. Brandon looked around and focused all of his attention on the picture of his mother hanging on the wall. He went over to the picture, took it down, and placed it on the bed. That picture had always been in his living room, so obviously Chris had put it in the bedroom to hide the hole from the bullet.

Brandon looked at his watch. He had a meeting with the record label's lawyer and Epic in ten minutes. Brandon had made a lot of phone calls while he was away, and one of those calls was to Epic to renegotiate the selling of Indigo Records. Now that he didn't need Chris to make the decision, he was going to go ahead and sell the label to pay off his bills. Brandon locked the door and stopped at the front desk to leave a message for maintenance to change the locks.

By the time he made it to the lawyer's office, he was already five minutes late. Brandon didn't live too far from the office, but traffic in Center City was a son of a bitch, so he ended up walking in right after the meeting had started. Brandon took a seat next to the label's legal counsel, Attorney John Richardson. On the other side of the table sat three lawyers from Epic, and the vice president of the company.

Brandon sat quietly next to his lawyer for over two hours while both sides negotiated. He started to become restless, so he excused himself and went to the restroom to splash some water on his face. Brandon looked in the mirror, rubbed his hand through his curly hair, licked his lips, and smiled.

"Let's get back out there, Mr. Brunson," he said. When

he got back to the table everyone was shaking hands. Epic's lawyers were packing their briefcases and were getting ready to leave. The vice president came over to Brandon and shook his hand.

"It was nice doing business with you, Mr. Brunson," he said, and they all left. Brandon hadn't approved any deal. He turned to his attorney with a stern face.

"Why didn't you include me in this? I didn't approve a deal," he said.

"I got you the best deal I could. The label was in debt and on the verge of bankruptcy. I think 2.5 million is more than a satisfactory price, don't you?" Richardson asked.

Brandon's eyes brightened. With no partner to share it with, the money was all his. Brandon shook his lawyer's hand.

"How long until the funds are available?" Brandon asked.

"Forty-eight hours," he replied. "Mr. Brunson, Epic assumed all the responsibility for your debt with the label. I will cut my 10 percent fee once the money is available, and then cut you a check for the remainder," he said.

"I'll see you in two days," Brandon said and left.

All he had to do now was chill until the money came through, so he drove back to Mia's. Brandon also decided to keep the fact that he sold the label to himself. He figured Mia had already been through so much, and telling her would only create more problems.

Mia was lying in the bed when Brandon came into the bedroom. He sat on the edge of the bed and started peeling off his clothes so he could get in the shower. She rolled over to his side of the bed and sat beside him. He grabbed her face and kissed her so softly that she began to tear up. He rubbed her now rounded little belly. Mia continued to help him get undressed. She unbuttoned his shirt slowly and he took it off. Mia lay back on the bed. She was already naked, and Brandon's dick was getting hard just looking at his beautiful wife. Mia smiled as his boxers hit the floor. Brandon crawled in bed next to her and kissed her again.

"Are you sure you want to do this?" he whispered.

"Yes, yes, I'm sure," she whispered back.

Brandon opened her legs gently and entered her. Mia's body tingled all over from the first stroke. He kissed her neck and gyrated slowly, paying full attention to her body's needs. Mia felt like the most beautiful woman alive. He caressed her nipples so tenderly that she could feel his love in every touch.

"I love you so much," she repeated several times. Mia scratched Brandon's back and caressed his face. Brandon's smooth, chocolate skin glistened from perspiration. After her third orgasm she lost track. Mia was enjoying what she had waited so long to have—her husband.

Brandon enjoyed every moment of their newlywed sex. He rocked up and down until he exploded, and then he held her in his arms and rubbed her belly. Mia was satisfied. She finally had a clear conscience, and her man still loved her. She fell asleep cradled in his muscular arms, and Brandon followed shortly thereafter.

Mia awoke in the middle of the night with a craving for cookies and cream ice-cream. She nudged Brandon several times in hopes that he would wake up but he wouldn't budge. Mia put on her Coach slippers and made her way to the kitchen looking for just about anything she could find to fill her ice-cream void. She opened the freezer and to her delight, a half a gallon of vanilla ice cream was hidden way in the back. It wasn't cookies and cream, but it would do the job. She opened it up, grabbed a spoon from the kitchen drawer and plopped down on the sofa.

Mia reached for the remote, which was sitting on the couch beside her. She flipped on the TV and threw the remote on the other side of the couch.

Mia began devouring the ice-cream almost instantly, making sure only to stop in order to breathe. Her stomach felt like it was about to bust, so she placed the empty container on the coffee table and stretched out on the couch. She noticed Brandon's jacket lying on the back of the couch. She pulled it down and placed it over her body. She closed her eyes and allowed her nose to take in the alluring scent of his Issey Miyake cologne. She smiled at the thought his muscular arms surrounding her body. Mia noticed a folded piece of paper had dropped from his pocket when she pulled it down from the back of the couch; it was lying at the other end of the sofa. She sat up from the couch and grabbed it. She opened it and looked it over thoroughly. The ultrasound picture had six weeks printed at the top along with the name Lynn Whitmore. Mia didn't want to jump to conclusions; it couldn't be Brandon's it just couldn't. She heard Brandon moving around in the bedroom so she jumped up from the couch and placed the ultrasound picture behind her back.

"Baby, you okay?" Brandon asked as he fumbled out into the living room.

"I'm fine." Mia hesitated. She wanted to confront him about her new discovery, but decided against it.

"Come on back to bed," Brandon said, looking at Mia through sleepy eyes.

"I'll be there in a minute, baby, let me finish up my ice cream," she said, still hiding the paper behind her back.

"Aight, baby, but don't be too long," Brandon wandered back into the bedroom and closed the door.

Mia sighed with relief and placed the picture in her purse for safekeeping. She was still trying to convince herself that Brandon had nothing to do with this Lynn Whitmore and her baby. Mia forced herself to go back into the bedroom and lie down in the bed. She never expected her craving for ice-cream would lead to this.

Brandon woke early the next morning and cooked Mia breakfast. He felt so good that he was singing in the kitchen. He finished cooking Mia's vegetable omelet and served her breakfast in bed. She was still asleep when he came into the room. He set up the tray beside the bed and nudged her until she opened her eyes. She rolled her eyes at him and yawned.

"Hey there," he said. "I made you breakfast."

She could smell the freshly toasted bread and vegetable omelet instantly. Mia sat up and took a sip of orange juice.

Brandon sat on the other side of the bed, working hard to keep thoughts of Chris in the back of his mind, but without much success. Brandon wasn't going to offer Chris even a cent of the label's money, not after what he had done. Chris was now a stranger to Brandon. He didn't deserve any of that money. Brandon had busted his ass to make that business work, and Chris had spent more time in the streets than he ever did in the office. Brandon was going to enjoy his money, and he didn't care if Chris was living in a cardboard box. He hadn't told Chris that he sold the label, and he didn't feel the need to. Chris lost that privilege when he decided to rape Mia. Brandon was going to make his life a living hell.

Brandon cleared the tray after Mia finished eating, and then he cleaned the kitchen. When he returned Mia was lying her clothes out on the bed. He wondered where she was going.

"Are you going to get dressed?" she asked as she stood on her toes and tried to grab her scarf from the top shelf of the closet. Brandon stood behind her, grabbed it from the shelf, and sat back down.

"Where are we going?" he asked.

Mia placed her hand on her hip in frustration. "Today is the day we find out what we're having. I thought I told you."

"No, you didn't," Brandon said sarcastically.

"Well maybe it slipped my mind, but the appointment is at two-thirty PM." She grabbed a towel and stomped toward the bathroom. Mia was still hot under the collar about finding that picture, and even though she told herself she was going to wait to confront him about it, her temper was beginning to show through.

Brandon sat there on the bed and said a silent prayer.

Lord, please let it be a little girl. I promise I will be the best daddy any baby girl could ask for.

He got up and pulled on a pair of jeans. Brandon hadn't been his usual self lately. He didn't care about fancy suits anymore. All he wanted was for his children to be healthy and for him to be the best father he could possibly be.

When Mia returned from the bathroom, Brandon was fully dressed and waiting to leave. He was eager to find out if his prayer would be answered.

Mia finished getting dressed and grabbed her purse from the kitchen counter. Brandon took her hand but she snatched it away. They walked silently to the elevator. Brandon couldn't understand for the life of him why she had an attitude. They had the perfect night of lovemaking and everything had been perfect between them.

Mia waited in front of the building while he pulled the car out front. Opening the car door, he helped her inside. The drive to the hospital was silent as Brandon continued to recite his prayer in his head.

He dropped Mia in front of the doctor's office while he found a parking space. Mia signed in at the waiting area and took a seat. There were two other women waiting to see the doctor, so she picked up a magazine and began flipping through it. Brandon came in and took a seat next to her. He put his arm around her shoulder while she read.

"Mrs. Mia Brunson," the nurse called. Mia sprang to her feet. She loved the way her name sounded with Brandon's last name behind it. She was still in awe about being married. Brandon held her hand as they walked down the hallway and entered the examination room. Mia lay down on the examination table and the doctor applied a clear jelly on her stomach. Brandon crossed his fingers as the doctor began. They all watched the screen expectantly as the doctor pointed out the different body parts of the baby. Finally the doctor got to the sex of their baby, and Brandon squeezed Mia's hand.

"Well, it looks like we have a little girl," the doctor said.

"Thank you, Jesus," Brandon blurted out.

Mia clasped his hand tightly. She was crying. Partly because she knew that Brandon wanted a little girl and also because she knew in her heart that Brandon had something to do with that ultrasound she found in his jacket pocket. They left the office soon after and drove to the King of Prussia Mall. He tried to talk Mia out of it, but now that she knew that the baby was a girl, she was ready to shop, and he couldn't stop her. Brandon held the packages as Mia explored every store. While Mia was inside the Children's Place, Brandon's cell phone rang. The number was listed as private.

"Hello," he answered.

"Nigga, I thought you were coming for me," Chris said. "I knew you were a bitch." He laughed in Brandon's ear.

Brandon was so angry that he forgot he was in the mall and began yelling.

"You wait. I'm coming for you. You best believe I'm coming for that ass." Brandon hung up the phone. He looked around and people were staring at him. He went into the store and grabbed Mia from the checkout line.

"What's wrong?" she asked as Brandon took the baby clothes from her hands and laid them on the counter.

"I'm sorry, but we won't be taking these," he said to the cashier. Mia frowned.

"What is going on?" she asked again. Brandon ignored her until they approached the exit to the mall.

"Chris just called me. I need to get you home. I don't trust him, and I don't know what he is capable of."

Brandon was walking so fast that he practically dragged Mia to the car. She was out of breath by the time they got settled in and pulled off. They made it back to the condo safely, and Mia put the packages that she did buy for the baby in the hall closet and continued on to the bedroom.

Brandon checked the door and followed Mia back to the bedroom. She was already undressed and under the covers. He slipped off his clothes and got in beside her. It was too early to be in bed, but he just wanted to lie for a minute and hold his wife. When he tried to embrace her, she turned her back to him. Brandon just figured her hormones was getting the best of her. Brandon placed his arms behind his head and watched *Flavor of Love.* It was mind boggling to him that these pretty women would actually like Flavor Flav. He was ugly as hell. *People will do anything to be on TV,* Brandon thought.

Around nine PM Brandon got out of bed and ordered Chinese takeout for dinner. Mia was still asleep, so he left her plate in the microwave. She had a thing for eating after midnight now that she was pregnant.

Brandon ate two plates and laid back down. He was still thinking about Chris. This nigga thought he was a joke. Brandon was going to make sure that Chris knew he wasn't a nut. He couldn't wait for him to find out that he sold the label. Chris should have made sure that he was reinstated as partner once his issues with the law were resolved. He probably forgot all about those papers.

Brandon realized that he was thinking too hard about Chris. He needed to focus on what mattered—his children and his wife. He was going to get up first thing tomorrow morning to get to the bank when it opened. He wanted to pay off the mortgage to his condo, and all of his credit card bills. He figured that would total about five hundred grand or so. Then he was going to set up a trust account for Lynn. He wanted to make sure that she was able to take care of the baby and finish school. He owed her that much.

Brandon didn't get to bed until around three AM. He was thinking hard and time passed so quickly that he didn't even notice how late it was. Mia had gotten up around twelve-thirty AM to eat and then lay back down. Brandon was careful not to move an inch as he lay in bed next to her. He didn't want her to know he was awake, because he wasn't in the mood to talk.

Brandon woke up around eight AM. He showered, dressed, and made his way to Attorney Richardson's office, and then to the bank. He had the bank make out a cashier's check in the amount of three hundred thousand dollars to cover his mortgage, and created a trust fund account for Lynn in the amount of five hundrd thousand. He wrote personal checks to all of the credit card companies, and mailed them off. Brandon had one more thing he had to do. He drove up Walnut Street until he reached Center City Toyota. Lynn needed a car. She was going to be a single mother and Brandon wanted to make her as comfortable as possible. He bought her a brand new 2006 Camry to be delivered to her house, and then he called Lynn on his cell phone.

"Yes," she said. Lynn was irritated. She was still getting morning sickness, and she had been up all night going back and forth to the bathroom.

"I'm on my way over there," he said. "I need to talk to you."

"Whatever," she said and hung up the phone. Brandon caught her at a bad time. She was in the middle of losing her breakfast in the toilet.

He arrived at her house an hour later. He rang the doorbell, and it took Lynn ten minutes to make it down the steps. She opened the door and Brandon jumped back. She looked horrible. Her lips were dry and her hair was all over the place. She had big yellow stains all over her shirt and bags under her eyes. Brandon came up the front steps, picked her up, and carried her to her room. He could smell the vomit on her. He placed her in the bed and went into the kitchen to make her some tea. He returned from the kitchen and placed the tea on her nightstand. She sat up and took a sip.

"Thank you," she said and smiled faintly.

"No problem." He brushed her hair back out of her face. Pulling a set of keys out of his pocket, he dropped them in her lap.

"What are these?" she asked.

"These are the keys to your new apartment."

"What?"

"I paid my condo off, so you and the baby will now have a permanent place to live. You can stay there for as long as you like." He pulled a second set of keys out of his pocket and dropped those on her lap, too.

"And what are these to? Let me guess, my brand new car?" she asked sarcastically.

"Yes, they are." Brandon said.

Lynn couldn't believe it. *He's got to be joking,* she thought.

"The dealership is going to deliver it tomorrow," he

said. "Oh, and one more thing." He ran down to the car and returned with a big, brown envelope. "I created a trust fund account for you and the baby." She opened the package and her eyes instantly grew to the size of saucers.

"It's five hundred grand. I want you to be comfortable and finish school," Brandon explained.

Lynn gave him a hug, and Brandon rubbed her back as they embraced.

"Well I have to go now. You can move in whenever you're ready. Call me if you need anything."

Brandon was supposed to be home by five, but he was running late. He and Mia had plans on having a romantic dinner at home and he didn't want to upset her in any way, so he called to alert her that he was on his way home. When he got to the condo Mia was sitting at the counter in front of a full plate of food. She must have ordered out, because there was no way she could cook fried chicken and mashed potatoes that looked like that.

Brandon threw his coat on the couch and washed his hands in the kitchen sink. Then he turned around and froze. He thought his eyes were playing tricks on him. The sonogram of Lynn's baby was on the counter beside his plate.

It can't be, Brandon said to himself.

He picked the picture up from the counter as if he had never seen it before. He glanced up at Mia's facial expression. She continued to stare down at her plate, swirling the mashed potatoes around with her fork.

How the hell did this happen? Brandon wondered. It then came to him: She must have found it in his jacket pocket. *How could I be so stupid?* Brandon thought.

Brandon's heart plunged.

"Baby, I-I-I . . ." Brandon tried to find the right words but couldn't.

Mia threw the fork at him and ran into the bedroom and shut the door. Brandon froze in his tracks still stunned at what was happening. He finally snapped out of his daze and ran after her.

He tried the doorknob to the bedroom, but it was locked.

"Mia, baby, let me in," he said.

"No! I can't believe you!" she yelled. Mia was crying hysterically. "How could you do this?!"

Brandon kicked in the door and grabbed Mia close to him. She hit him as he cradled her in his arms.

"Get off me!" she yelled as tears flowed freely down her face. He held her until she settled down.

"Please just let me explain," he said.

"No!" she said and started hitting him again.

An hour later when she was finally calm, Brandon tried talking to her again.

"Can we talk now?" he asked.

Mia lay lifelessly on the bed. She was so hurt that her body was stiff.

"Mia, I'm sorry. I was wrong. I cheated on you before we got married. She got pregnant, and there's nothing I can do about it but take care of my responsibilities. I married you because I love you and I wanted to do right by you and our baby girl. That's why I'm with you and not her."

"Were you that unhappy with us that you had to cheat?" she asked.

"I was a dickhead. It was before I knew you were pregnant. I knew I had to tell you sooner or later, but not like this. I want to be your husband, and I want you to be my wife. I still want to be with you, but if you feel that you can't forgive me, then I'll have to accept it and move on."

There was no way Mia was going to let her man go and be with another woman. She was hurt, but she was willing to work through it. She needed to be alone to think.

"Can I have some time alone to think about things?" she asked.

"Sure, whatever you need. I'll be back later," he said.

Brandon left without a place to go. He drove around for an hour and found himself at the same bar where he met Lynn. He took a seat in the corner of the bar and ordered a glass of gin. The bartender placed the glass in front of him on a coaster. He took a sip and looked around. It was dead in there as usual. There was an old white man sitting in a booth eating peanuts and drinking beer, and a young black guy sitting opposite Brandon at the other end of the bar. The young black guy whispered something to the bartender, and the bartender returned to Brandon with another drink.

"From the gentleman over there," the bartender said as she placed another glass of Seagrams in front of him.

Brandon raised his drink to show his gratitude. The guy got up and started to walk toward Brandon. He looked a little fruity as he got closer. Brandon hoped he hadn't given this guy the wrong impression.

"Hi, my name is Kane." When the guy introduced himself, Brandon almost choked on his drink. Could this be who he thought it was? He played it cool to see where the conversation might lead.

"Nice to meet you," Brandon said. "My name's Keith." Kane smiled and took a seat next to Brandon. Brandon looked Kane up and down. It was obvious he was a fag. He didn't dress like it—he had on a leather jacket and a black Polo sweater—but Brandon could tell by his demeanor. Kane seemed to be intrigued by Brandon's good looks.

"So do you come here often?" Brandon asked.

"No, I'm just passing through," Kane responded. "I'm on my way out of town."

Brandon took another sip of his gin.

"So where you headed?" he asked casually.

"Atlanta. Got family out there," Kane said. "I need to get away for a while."

"So where are you from?" Brandon asked.

"West Philly," he said, "but I'm staying with a friend near South Street until I leave."

Brandon finished off his drink and left the bartender a tip on the bar.

"Well I'm about to get out of here. Would you like to come with me?" Kane smiled.

"Why not? I'm not leaving for another four days."

Brandon got up from the stool and Kane followed. Brandon turned to look at Kane once they were outside.

"My car is parked at the other end of this alley. Let's cut through here so we won't have to walk far." Kane followed closely behind Brandon. When they got to the middle of the alley Brandon turned around and threw Kane against the wall.

"Tell me everything you know about Mia," Brandon said as he punched Kane in the face. "I got your little letter."

Kane tried to break free from Brandon's hold.

"I thought your name was Keith?" he asked.

Brandon punched him in the face again.

"Nigga, answer the question. Tell me everything you know about Mia, and I'm not going to repeat myself again."

"Chris raped her. I put everything in the letter," Kane said. "What do you want from me? I already told you everything I know!"

"So how do you know Chris?" Brandon asked.

Kane remained silent. Brandon pushed him on the ground.

"Answer me!" Brandon said.

Kane was petrified. Chris was a crazy son of bitch, so he had no idea what to think about Brandon.

"I told you it was in the letter. We were seeing each other for about two years."

"So you're the fag he's been creepin' with?" Brandon asked. "So tell me, how does it feel to get fucked in the ass?"

Kane scrambled to his feet and tried to take a swing at Brandon, but missed.

"Fuck you!" Kane said. "I risked my life for you and your wife. Chris would try to kill me if he knew what I did."

Brandon pushed Kane against the wall again.

"Get the fuck out of here, man, before I kill you!"

Kane took one last look at Brandon under the dimmed light and took off.

Brandon walked to his car at the other end of the alley and drove off. When he got back home it was a little after midnight. He closed the front door quietly, trying his hardest not to wake Mia. He tiptoed around the bedroom and undressed. When he got in bed he felt Mia's hand touch his bare shoulder.

"I love you, Brandon, but to make this work we're going to have to go to counseling. That's the only way I can be with you. I need you to promise me that you'll try your damnedest to make things work."

"I promise," Brandon said. "Thank you for giving me another chance." Brandon got under the covers and held Mia tightly. He kissed her on the forehead and lay silently next to her until he fell asleep.

Brandon's cell phone woke him the next morning. He looked at the clock on the bedside table. It was only seven AM. *Who the hell would call me this early?* Brandon wondered. He picked up the phone without looking to see who was calling.

"You fuckin' sold me out! You sold the label, you unfaithful bitch!"

News about the sale of Indigo Records had been on the front page of the newspaper that morning. Chris read the paper every day. He always wanted to be alert of what was going on in his city. As soon as he read the headline about the label's sale, he called Brandon.

Hoping not to wake Mia, Brandon jumped up from the bed and hurried into the living room to continue the call.

Brandon laughed wickedly into the phone.

"How does it feel, Chris? Huh?" he asked. "How does it feel to be broke and not have a single friend in the world?"

"I am making YOU a promise," Chris said. "The next time we meet up, I'm going to be spitting on your grave."

"We'll see, nigga, we'll see," Brandon said and hung up the phone. Brandon looked over at Mia, who was sound asleep. It was time for Brandon to get a gun. He had never used one before, but that wasn't going to stop him from using one now, if necessary.

Chapter 13

Friend or Foe

Chris flipped through the paper and there was a picture of himself and Brandon together from the label's launch party over a year ago. *He couldn't have sold that label without me,* Chris thought. *We had equal ownership rights.* Chris wanted to call their lawyer, but it was too early. He sat and watched the clock for almost two hours until it reached nine AM. These were the longest two hours of his life. He picked up his cell phone and dialed the lawyer as soon as the secondhand on the clock reached the twelve.

"Good morning. Richardson Entertainment Law Group," the receptionist answered.

"Let me speak to Attorney Richardson," Chris said.

"I'm sorry, but he's just getting in. May I take a message?" she asked.

"Bitch, just put him on the phone!" Chris yelled. She covered the phone to speak to someone, and Attorney Richardson picked up the line.

"Yes, this is Attorney Richardson. Can I help you?" he asked.

"How did Brandon sell the label without me?" Chris asked.

Attorney Richardson took a deep breath and then began to speak.

"You signed over your rights, Chris. You don't remember?"

Chris became quiet. The lawyer must be talking about those papers he signed a few months back when the law was on his heels. Chris hung up the phone and sat down on the bed.

Brandon must have planned this all along, Chris thought. He pressured Chris to sign those papers, and Chris was too busy to read them through. He figured he didn't have to because he and Brandon were like brothers, and Brandon would always have his best interests at heart.

Chris wanted his half of the money. Brandon had him hot under the collar, talking to Chris like he was some big shot nigga. He didn't run shit. Chris was the one who put Brandon on. When Brandon's mother died, it was Chris and his mother who accepted Brandon into their family.

Ungrateful bastard, Chris thought. Brandon was getting way out of line, and Chris was ready to put him back in check.

It was time for Chris to show his face around the projects again. He'd been in hiding for a month. Chris knew the cops were probably still searching for him, but he had to make some serious moves. He had never gotten another gun, and he needed one now more than ever. He had a hunch that things were going to get ugly between him and Brandon. Chris wanted his share, and he was going to come for it full force. As far as Chris was concerned, Brandon was just another nigga from off the street that needed to get dealt with.

Besides, Chris thought, *it ain't like I don't deserve my cut.*

Chris had worked hard finding artists and putting all his money into Brandon's dream. Plus, if he was going to do some time, he needed to hire an expensive lawyer who knew his shit, and for that he needed money.

Chris put his hood on his head as he left the hotel. He got in his car and drove to North Philly. As soon as he crossed the Philadelphia Zoo bridge, his blood started to rush. He was home and ready to get shit poppin'. It was still early when he got to the projects, so not many people were out. Still, he circled the block three times before he parked, and then he got out of the car and went straight into the building. The guard was too busy running his mouth on the phone to even see Chris pass by. Chris got on the elevator and made his way up to Tank's crib. He was going to get the rest of his clothes while he was there.

When Chris opened the door to Tank's bedroom he walked in on some fine-ass red bone giving Tank some head. Chris walked right past the bed and grabbed his bags from the closet. Tank was too tied up to say a word, so Chris opened up every one of Tank's drawers until he found a gun. Ever since he had known Tank he always kept his money and drugs in one drawer, and guns in another. Chris quickly stuffed the gun in his bag and rolled out.

As Chris approached his car he noticed a piece of pipe lying in the grass. He grabbed it and put it in the backseat with the rest of his things, figuring it couldn't hurt to have an extra weapon.

Next Chris drove over to the parking lot of Mia's building to shake Brandon up a little bit, and cause a little confusion in the process. He rode up beside Brandon's jeep and got out the car. Grabbing the pipe from the backseat, he used it to bust Brandon's front windshield, and then he took his keys and keyed the side of Brandon's car. The car alarm was going off, but Chris needed to add a finishing touch, so he quickly ran over to the passenger's side of his own car. He pulled out a switchblade from the glove compartment and used it to flatten every tire on the jeep. Once Brandon's car was totally vandalized, Chris got back in his own car and pulled off.

Chris smiled to himself. Not only did he just fuck up Brandon's main mode of transportation, but he made it look like a bitch did it to stir up trouble on the home front. Chris wanted to hang around in the cut to see the expression on Brandon's and Mia's faces when they saw the jeep, so he parked two rows over and waited.

The alarm sounded for a good twenty minutes before the building personnel notified Brandon. As the phone rang inside the apartment, Mia looked over at Brandon, hoping he would answer, but he was sound asleep. She reached over Brandon and grabbed the phone off the receiver.

"Hello."

"Mrs. Brunson, the alarm on your husband's jeep is going off. It seems that someone has vandalized it," the front desk agent reported. "Please report to the parking lot. The authorities are on their way."

Mia threw the receiver on the floor and scrambled to her feet.

"Wake up! Wake up!" she shouted at Brandon.

Brandon sat up, looked around, and wiped the slobber off the side of his mouth.

"What's wrong?" he asked.

"Someone broke into your car," she said as she slipped on her slippers and tied her robe.

Brandon put on his slippers, grabbed his keys, and headed to the elevators. Mia locked the door behind them. A police officer was already on the scene by the

time they got down to the parking garage. Brandon's face
wrinkled up as soon as he saw the car. Chris watched as
Brandon threw his hands up in the air.

This is only the beginning, Chris thought.

"What the fuck?!" Brandon blurted out as he observed
the damage.

The car was so fucked up that Brandon wanted to trade
it in as soon as he saw the smashed front windshield. Brandon turned and looked at Mia. She was standing there
tapping her foot as if she was about to have a fit. He knew
that she probably thought Lynn had done this, but Brandon didn't think so. Brandon finished making the report
with the police officer, and then walked back over to Mia.

As the officer pulled off, Chris could tell that Brandon
and Mia were arguing. She was pointing her finger in
Brandon's face. Chris was making Brandon's life miser-
able, and enjoying it. Yet it wasn't enough. Chris wanted
Brandon to know that it was him. He turned the car on as
Mia and Brandon walked back to the elevators.

"I know it was her," Mia said. "I knew she was going to
do something like this."

Mia has it all wrong, Brandon thought. This wasn't even
Lynn's style. He knew that Mia was never going to forgive
him.

"It wasn't her," Brandon said.

"So who was it?" she asked. "Some other bitch that you
forgot to tell me about?"

Chris rode past slowly, rolled down the window, and
smiled. Mia was too busy chewing out Brandon's ass to notice the car slowly riding by. Brandon grew angry as soon
as he realized it was Chris.

"Did you see that!?" Brandon yelled to Mia.

"See what?" she asked.

He grabbed her hand and hurried to the elevators.
When they got back to the apartment Brandon put on a

pair of sweatpants and a gray thermal shirt. He slipped on a fresh pair of Timberlands went into the bathroom to brush his teeth. Mia stood in the doorway of the bathroom and watched while he gargled.

"Where are you going?" she asked.

He finished up and wiped his mouth with a hand towel.

"I gotta go out for a few. I'll be back a little later," he said.

By now Mia had grown suspicious. He could be going to see another woman.

"Why can't you tell me where you're going?"

He grabbed her shoulders, turned her around, and led her to the bedroom.

"Look, I have to go handle something with Chris," he said. Mia's stomach instantly dropped. "Do me a favor and stay in the house, OK? At least until I get back home. If anything strange happens, call the police."

After Mia agreed to stay inside, Brandon grabbed his Sean John coat and left. He had no means of transportation, so he dialed Lynn's cell phone.

"Hello." She sounded as if the phone had interrupted her sleep.

"Hey, it's me. I need you to pick me up," he said.

"When?"

"Right now. My car is fucked up and I need to use yours."

"Where are you?" she asked.

While Brandon walked and talked, he kept glancing over his shoulder to make sure he wasn't being followed.

"Meet me on the corner of Nineteenth and Market, in front of the bank."

"OK, OK, I'll be there," Lynn said as she dragged herself out of bed.

Brandon waited by the entrance to the bank. He watched everyone who passed him, making sure that Chris didn't walk up on him. Lynn honked the horn and Brandon got in the car. She drove back to her apartment, got out of the car, and left the keys with Brandon.

Brandon knew that Chris was a dirty-ass nigga, but he never thought he would stoop that low. Leave it to Chris to do some fag shit and key his car. Only bitches did shit like that. Brandon knew he needed to buy a gun, because he knew Chris wouldn't let up until he got what he wanted. When Chris and Brandon were little, Chris had to win at everything or he started a fight. Brandon remembered the time when Chris lost a basketball game in summer camp when they were about sixteen-years-old. Chris missed the last shot and was so mad that he punched the ref in the mouth. He was a hot-headed nigga, and Brandon was going to have to cool him off.

The only person Brandon knew in the hood who sold guns was Tank. He knew that Tank was Chris's man, but he also knew that Tank was about his business. If you needed it, he had it, and he didn't care what you did with it as long as you didn't mention his name when you got caught. Brandon was sure that he would find Tank in front of the Dominican store. He always saw him there when he used to drop off Chris at the projects.

Brandon pulled around the side of the store and parked. Peeping around the corner, he waved for Tank to come over. Tank looked around and then pointed to himself.

"Who, me?" Tank asked.

"Yeah, you," Brandon said.

Tank pulled up his pants as he walked around to the side of the store. Once he got closer he started to smile when he figured out who Brandon was.

"Oh, shit, it's the uppity nigga who thinks he's from the suburbs," Tank said. He looked Brandon up and down. "What you need?" Tank already had an idea about what was going on. In fact, the whole hood knew that Brandon had sold out Chris. Brandon looked Tank in the eyes.

"I need gun."

Tank laughed. He pulled out a dime bag of weed and a blunt.

"So what kind you looking for?" He continued to roll up while he waited for Brandon to answer.

"I don't know. Nigga, just give me what you got," Brandon said. He looked around to see who was watching. There was no one around, but Brandon was a bit paranoid. He had never purchased a gun before, and he had no clue what kind of gun he needed. He just wanted to make sure he could protect himself and his wife if Chris came after them.

Tank shook his head. *This nigga is about to go to war with a veteran in the game and he don't even know what kind of gun he needs,* Tank thought.

Brandon leaned on the car while Tank disappeared into the alley a little farther down the street. He returned with a brown paper bag.

"How much you tryin' to spend?" Tank asked.

"Whatever," Brandon said

"Give me five hundred," Tank said. "I charge extra for uppity niggas."

Brandon got back in the car and counted his money. He had taken a grand out of the bank while he was waiting for Lynn to pick him up.

"It's all there," Brandon said as he watched Tank count out the money. When Tank finished, he handed Brandon the brown paper bag and walked off.

Brandon got back in the car, drove up a block, and parked. The bag felt kind of light, so he wanted to make sure Tank ain't gagged him. He opened the bag and took out the gun. It was a baby .22 with a pearl handle.

This is a bitch's gun, Brandon thought. It was so small that a chick could put it in her purse and no one would ever know. But it would have to do for now.

Brandon drove back to the apartment. When he got there Mia was in the kitchen cooking. There was smoke in the hallway, so she must have burned something, as usual.

Brandon came in and grabbed a beer from the fridge. He could tell by the look on Mia's face that she was annoyed. She looked at him and continued flouring chicken. Brandon got a glimpse of the meal and lost his appetite. He could tell that Mia had never fried chicken before, because she didn't clean off the feathers. He had suffered through some meals, but he was not eating that shit today. He sat down on the couch and tried to relax, but he couldn't shake this eerie feeling that someone was watching him.

In fact, Chris had followed Brandon all day. He knew that Chris bought a gun from Tank. He had watched Brandon's every move, and he knew Brandon was scared. This was a battle that Brandon couldn't win. Chris ran the streets, and nothing got past him.

Chris dialed Brandon's cell phone. It was time for negotiations.

"Yeah," Brandon answered.

"Nigga, you ready to talk business?" Chris asked. "I want my half."

"I ain't giving you shit! Especially after you pulled that shit this morning! Fuck you!"

"I swear on your dead mother's grave, if you don't give me my half, you're going to be buried right next to her." And with that, Chris hung up the phone.

Chris handed the blunt back to Tank and got back in his car. Chris had wanted Brandon to be strapped. If Brandon wanted to be a big man, it was time for him to see how big men played. He told Tank to sell Brandon the smallest gun he could. Deep down inside Chris didn't want to hurt Brandon. He just wanted to scare him.

"Who are you talking to like that?" Mia asked as she fixed him a plate. She brought it around to the couch and handed it to him. He took one look at it and passed it back.

"No, thank you, sweetie. I already ate."

Mia took the plate and threw it in the trash.

"You ate over her house, didn't you?" She began to cry. "I knew that's where you went."

"What the hell are you talking about?" Brandon's faced scrunched up. "I was out taking care of business. I wasn't with another woman."

She ran into the bedroom and shut the door. Brandon waited a half hour before going after her. He figured she should have cooled off by then. He went into the bedroom and found her sitting on the side of the bed whispering on the phone. She hung up as soon as she noticed Brandon standing there. He took a seat and put his arm around her. Chris had got him good. Mia didn't trust him. His marriage was already on the rocks, and his beef with Chris was just making things worse.

"Baby, I wasn't with another woman. I promise you that," he said and kissed her on the cheek.

"My mother gave me the name of a marriage counselor. I think we should make an appointment," she said.

"Do you really think that we need a counselor?" he asked as he kissed her on the neck.

"After what happened this morning, we need a miracle."

She excused herself and went back into the kitchen.

Mia looked at the food she had prepared. Who was she kidding? It looked awful, and she wouldn't have eaten it either. She threw it all away.

As Mia cleaned up the kitchen, Brandon took a shower and got into bed. He might as well just give Chris what he wanted. The only thing was that he only had about a million left, after paying all of his bills. Brandon was going to call Chris in the morning and put an end to this silly shit.

Mia came back into the room, dripping wet from taking her own shower. Times like these made Brandon feel like he had made the right choice by marrying Mia.

He pulled her wet, naked body on top of him. Kissing her, he then positioned her pussy on his face. He licked her pussy as she gyrated all over his face. He could tell that she was about to cum because her body stiffened. He quickly got up and began fucking her from behind. She came as soon as he stuck his dick inside her. He didn't care, as long as she was satisfied.

Brandon got up and lay beside her. Mia disappeared under the covers and began sucking his dick. It was so good that Brandon had to hold on to the bedpost. He ran his fingers through her hair as she bobbed up and down. Brandon began to moan when she started to lick his balls.

"Oh, baby." He bit his bottom lip. "Damn."

Mia came from under the covers and started to ride him. Brandon bounced her up and down on his dick until he came. He cuddled Mia in his arms. He was just going to give Chris the money. He didn't want to fuck up what he already had at home.

Brandon slept until noon the next day. Mia was already up and dressed when he rolled over.

"Where are you going?" he asked.

Mia was applying her makeup. "We have a marriage counseling session at two," she said. Brandon grabbed his cell phone off the night table and dialed Chris.

"Meet me at the office in a half hour," Brandon said. "Come alone, and no weapons." He hung up the phone. Brandon dressed quickly and was almost out the door before Mia caught him.

"Where are you going?" she asked.

"I'll be right back," he said.

"You know we have that meeting," she said.

"I'll be back way before then," he said and closed the door behind him. He was just going to write a check to Chris for the money he owed him.

Brandon drove to the old office and let himself in. Epic had given him forty-five days to move out his shit. Brandon had taken all of his stuff before he left for the honeymoon, so there was nothing there but a couple pictures and some office furniture. Brandon sat quietly and waited for Chris to show.

Mia watched from the parking as Brandon pulled off in this gold Toyota Camry. Her suspicion was again getting the best of her so she hailed a cab and instructed the driver to follow closely behind him. She overheard him saying he was going to meet someone, and she was damn if another bitch was going to have her man. She instructed the driver to park right in front of the building. Mia paid the driver two hundred dollars to stay put. As she waited, she saw Chris walking up and slouched down in her seat.

Brandon heard the keys jingling in the lock. He checked for his gun, and made sure it was tucked securely in his boot. Chris came through the door nice and calm. He looked at Brandon.

"So where's my money?" he asked.

Brandon took the check out of the back pocket of his jeans and flicked it at him.

"Here," he said. The check fell on the floor. Chris bent down to pick it up, and when he got back up Brandon was aiming the gun at him. Chris didn't think Brandon had the balls. He knew he should have carried his piece.

"Go ahead and shoot me, nigga, if you so tough," Chris said.

"I should fuckin' kill you," Brandon said.

Brandon looked at the gun and finally figured out how to cock it. Chris took a step toward Brandon. He hated to be threatened. Chris rushed Brandon and tried to take the gun. They tussled back and forth until the gun finally discharged. Brandon opened his mouth, but before he could say anything, he fell to the floor. Chris looked down. Brandon was hit in the stomach.

"Oh shit!" Chris said. "What did I do?"

Chris ran down the steps of the building and out onto the street. Mia was on the sidewalk in front of the building by now. He took one look at her and took off in the other direction. Brandon stumbled down the steps behind Chris, falling down the last flight. His clothes were stained with blood. Mia started panting heavily.

"Oh my God, somebody help me. Please!" She was screaming at the top of her lungs. "Call the police!"

Mia grabbed Brandon's heavy body and put his head in her lap. Blood was seeping out of his mouth as she rocked him back and forth until the ambulance arrived. Brandon's vision was blurry. He looked up at Mia. He could feel every one of her tears hitting his face. The thought of Brandon not being by her side made her crazy.

"Baby, please don't die," she said. "I love you. You can't leave me like this."

Chris ran for five blocks straight. His thoughts were so scrambled that when he looked up he was surprised to realize he was standing in front of the police station.

The gray stone walls gave him the chills. He pulled out a cigarette from his pocket and lit it. Chris took two long drags and exhaled.

What the hell just happened? Chris wondered. He rambled through his back pocket and pulled out the blood-stained check. He shook his head.

"One million dollars," he said out loud. He folded it back up and put it away. He took one last drag from the cigarette and put it out on the bottom of his shoe. Chris walked into the police station and waited at the front desk.

"Can I help you?" the police officer asked.

"Y-Y-Yes," Chris stuttered. "I'm here to turn myself in."

To Be Continued . . .

Judgment Day

By

Anya Nicole

"Every idle word that men shall speak, they shall give account thereof in the day of judgment."
—*Matthew 12:36*

Chapter 3

Rehab

Brandon

Brandon sat up in his hospital bed and watched the early morning news. It had been three weeks since he awoke from his coma, and due to the fact that Brandon was in great physical shape, he was coming along very well. His speech had already returned in full swing, and he'd been working hard with the physical therapist to fine tune his mobile skills. Brandon was able to walk with the help of a cane but that was more than enough for him. As each day passed, he felt more confident about his recovery.

Brandon listened closely as the news began to report a robbery at the Crazy Market, a local store across the street from the projects where he grew up. He grabbed the remote control and turned the sound up as high as it would go. He'd missed most of the important part of the report, but what he did recognize was the face in the surveillance video, and it was none other than Chris. He could tell by the long braids that extended to the middle of his back. Brandon had begged him to cut that shit time and time again, but Chris refused. Brandon told him that hair was going to get him in trouble and this was a prime example. Chris was the only nigga in the hood who had reddish-brown hair. Brandon smirked as he reached over to the table beside him and picked up the phone. He dialed 9-1-1 and waited for an operator to answer the line.

"Hello, 9-1-1," an operator answered after the second ring.

"Yes, I want to call in a tip," Brandon said with a wicked smile on his face.

"Go ahead." The operator assured him she was listening.

"The guy who robbed the Crazy Market name is Chris Black. He's known around the way as Chief," he blurted out, giving his whole government to the law.

Brandon hung up the phone, making sure not to give the operator the time to ask him any other questions. He placed the phone back on the hook and moved his bed back to its regular position. He was amused with himself; even from the hospital bed, Brandon was a threat. *Chris must be real desperate anytime he was sticking up corner store markets,* Brandon thought. Chris had money; a million dollars to be exact. The problem was that as soon as he cashed the check the cops would scoop his ass up. Brandon had been checking his account on the daily basis just to make sure it was still there. He knew Chris would rather chalk that mil up as a loss and make his money back on the street. Brandon was already one step ahead of him. He'd called ahead to Tank and offered him a million dollars to take Chris out. If things went the way they were supposed to, he'd be gone by the end of next week. Chris was living on borrowed time, and Brandon loved every minute of it.

He looked over at the clock on his bedside table; it was almost time for his workout with the physical therapist. Brandon closed his eyes and tried to relax. Just as he was nodding off, Amy, his physical therapist appeared in the doorway. She knocked lightly before entering the room; Brandon opened his eyes and waved for her to come in. She closed the door behind her and leaned against it in a seductive manner. She smiled deviously as she pulled her lab coat open and revealed her tanned naked body. Her plump size C breasts stood at attention and her phat pussy was neatly trimmed like a landing strip. Brandon's dick hardened as he thought of landing his plane right in between her thighs.

"Are you ready for your workout?" she said, dropping her coat to the floor.

Brandon looked at her well sculpted body and licked his lips; he was definitely ready to get worked over. He enjoyed his sessions with Amy. They'd been going at it strong for the past two weeks. He knew it was only a matter of time before he got the ass. Amy had been flirting with Brandon since he started his rehabilitation plan. She would bend over from time to time during the sessions and to his delight, she wouldn't have any panties on. Brandon would look up and her big phat white pussy would be planted dead in his face. One day they were doing exercises on the floor with the cardio ball and Brandon decided to try his luck. He was sitting on the floor and she in front of him on the ball with her legs wide open. Brandon lifted her jacket up just enough to slide his tongue between the lips of her pussy. She moaned and groaned as Brandon wiggled his tongue around in a circular motion. He didn't demand anything from her that day; he just wanted to make sure she was game to try it again. The next day Amy showed at his room, on her day off, in a pair of black crotchless panties and fire engine red stilettos. They went at is so hard that Brandon had a red lipstick stain around his dick for three days.

"Bring that ass over here to daddy," Brandon demanded in an alluring tone.

She obeyed his orders and sauntered over to the hospital bed. She climbed on top of him and planted a long, inviting kiss on his lips. She swirled her tongue in and out of his mouth and began biting his bottom lip. Brandon had something else in mind for her to bite on; he pushed her down to his throbbing hard-on and waited for her to accept him in her mouth. She licked up and down his erect penis as if it was a Popsicle and massaged his balls at the same time. Brandon couldn't stand teases; he grabbed Amy's head and forced her mouth around his hardened member, causing her to gag. His eyes rolled in the back of his head as she slobbered up and down on him. Brandon watched as she spit on his erection and sucked him off like a vacuum cleaner. He just couldn't help himself; Amy had the best head game Brandon had ever experienced. He released himself on her lips and watched as she licked it off. Brandon reached in the bedside table drawer and pulled out a rubber. He opened it up and placed it on Amy's lips. He watched as she carefully applied the condom to his swollen member with her mouth. She then positioned herself over top of him and pushed his hard-on deep inside her. She moaned heavily as he filled her walls.

Brandon grabbed her tiny waist and guided her up and down in several hurried thrusts, causing her to moan heavily. He then grabbed her long beach-blond hair and began pulling it tightly.

"Tell daddy how good this dick is," he said, putting a firmer hold on her hair.

"Oh, daddy your dick is so good." She tried to kiss him on the lips and he moved his face, allowing it to land on his cheek.

He liked Amy in all, but he wasn't into kissing her. He'd allowed her to kiss him today and a couple of times before, but he was really trying to break her out of it. She was a smut jawn and he knew that she probably fucked other dudes; besides, kissing was for people in love, and Brandon was far from in love with her. She'd been begging him to eat her out again, but he refused each time. Yes, he did it once before but that was just to get that ass. He regretted doing it then because there was a not so-nice-odor he encountered while doing it. He continued guiding Amy up and down on his dick and suddenly he was bored; she just wasn't throwing it the way he wanted it. Brandon wanted the animal fuck she gave him when they first started messing around, and she was stroking him like she was starting to catch feelings. He knew that this was going to have to be the last time they fucked. If he wanted to make love he would be fucking his wife instead of her. He took his hands off of Amy's waist and placed them behind his head in a restless manner. He already knew that he wasn't going to cum; his fascination with her was over. He closed his eyes and allowed her to continue to get her shit off.

Brandon knew that Amy was just a snack to quench his thirsty appetite for women. He'd come to a conclusion about his relationship with Mia also. It wasn't that he didn't love her; it was just that he was a man who liked to be loved by a lot of women. And being with one was just not enough for him. He would always be a ladies man; he loved pussy and it was that simple. So, Mia had to either get in line or roll out. He knew she would never leave him; she was too loyal.

Mia walked slowly down to Brandon's room which was stationed at the end of the hallway. She had great news to share; the doctors finally agreed to induce her labor and she was scheduled to have the baby tomorrow morning. Mia was thrilled because Brandon would be able to witness the birth of his first child and she would have him there to support her. She stopped midway down the hall to catch her breath; there were strange panting noises coming from the direction in which she was headed. As she continued down the empty corridor the sounds were clearer than before.

"Fuck me, baby!" Amy screamed and began to pinch her swollen nipples.

Brandon decided to give it back to her so she could cum faster. He pounded her small frame against his body; pushing himself deeper into her sweetness.

Mia placed her ear against the door; the moans were even louder than before. She cracked the door enough for her to peep in the room; Mia's eyes glazed over in fury as she witnessed Brandon's physical therapist pouncing up and down on her man like a jack rabbit in heat. Mia quietly closed the door and slid down to the floor. Tears started flowing freely down her face, only these were not tears of sorrow, but instead tears of rage. After all she had done for him, Brandon still had to go and fuck another woman. Mia was going to fix Brandon; if she couldn't have him, then no one else would either. She carefully got up from the floor and made her way back in the opposite direction. Brandon was a dog, and in Mia's mind every dog has his day. She was going to make sure Brandon got his; she just didn't know how just yet. For the time being, she was going to act as if nothing happened. It would be better this way. Plus when she did get him, he wouldn't suspect it was coming.

About the Author

Anya Nicole was born and raised in Philadelphia. Realizing as a child that both her household and neighborhood was plagued with drugs and crime, Anya strived to break the mold and became the first person in her family to graduate from college. As an adult, Anya became driven to help the same community she could have easily become a product of. She currently counsels young adults at an alternative program who have dropped out of high school and are seeking a GED. Anya believes that it is her responsibility to help young people realize their full potential.

Writing has always been Anya's way of relieving the pain she has seen around her. As early as the age of fourteen, she has always kept a journal of poetry and short stories by her side. Her debut novel, *Corporate Corner Boyz,* is Anya's way of showing the world that not all hustling is illegal. When you're educated and from the streets, you have the best of both worlds. Anya thanks Mark Anthony and the Q-Boro staff for blessing her with the opportunity to share her talents with the world. Anya continues to live in Philadelphia and is currently working on her next novel *Judgment Day*, the sequel to *Corporate Corner Boyz.*

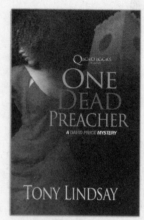

MORE TITLES FROM

Q-BORO BOOKS

JANUARY 2008
1-933967-34-X

FEBRUARY 2008
1-933967-36-6

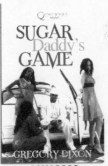

MAY 2008
1-933967-41-2

ANNA J. BRINGS BACK THE HEAT WITH...

SEPTEMBER 2008
1-933967-56-0